w9

That's Another Story

A Novel

G.T. London

MAVITAE
Publishing

Dedicated to my husband, Jason—my partner-in-adventure, always my first reader, as well as my inspiration and guide.

Contents

A few words sprinkled across the pages

Basilica Cistern – An ancient underground water storage system in Istanbul, known for its columns and eerie, beautiful atmosphere.

Blue Mosque – A famous mosque in Istanbul, known for its stunning blue tiles and impressive architecture.

Bosphorus Strait – The narrow waterway that separates the European and Asian sides of Istanbul, connecting the Black Sea to the Sea of Marmara.

Çay – Turkish tea, traditionally served in small tulip-shaped glasses.

Galata Tower – A medieval stone tower in Istanbul offering panoramic views of the city.

Galataport – A newly redeveloped waterfront area in Istanbul, featuring shops, restaurants, and cruise ship docking.

Hagia Sophia – A historic landmark in Istanbul, originally a cathedral, then a mosque. It's known for its massive dome and stunning interior.

Kazandibi – A traditional Turkish dessert made from caramelized milk pudding, known for its slightly burnt bottom layer.

Kedi – The Turkish word for "cat," a beloved animal often seen throughout the streets of Istanbul.

Merhaba – The Turkish word for "hello."

Midye dolma – Stuffed mussels, a popular street food in Turkey, filled with spiced rice and mussel meat.

Mosaic cake – A no-bake Turkish dessert made with broken biscuits and chocolate, often shaped into a log.

Sahaflar Çarşısı – The secondhand and antique book bazaar in Istanbul, a treasure trove for book lovers.

Simit – A circular Turkish bread encrusted with sesame seeds, often compared to a bagel.

Taksim Square – A major public square in Istanbul, known for its cultural, political, and social significance.

Tavuk göğsü – A Turkish dessert made with milk and shredded chicken breast, known for its unique texture and sweet flavor.

Teşekkürler – The Turkish word for "thank you."

Topkapı Palace – A grand palace in Istanbul that once served as the primary residence of Ottoman sultans, now a museum.

Chapter 1

Ava

I stare at the chandelier. It's been a constant source of light in my life for almost twenty years. Tightening my grip on the golf club, I swing with all my might. Delicate crystals rain to the hallway floor. A few shards graze my skin, and my arm instinctively shoots up to protect my face.

Several pieces shimmer and sparkle on the ground while others cling to the structure. I swing the club once more, striking the chandelier harder. "All alone again," I say, watching it sway like my emotions, exposed and bare.

I lower my ex-husband's precious golf club. I had a thing about chandeliers when John proposed to me twenty years ago. I was eighteen and pregnant. He was twenty-six and ambitious. I carried only two important things from those years into the next chapter of my life: the wooden box and the chandelier.

I gingerly step over the sharp pieces scattered across

the floor and wince as a few prick at my bare feet. Then I run upstairs to the guest room, slide open the wardrobe door, and retrieve the box hidden within the drawer of a tall dresser. The aroma of aged wood and cedar fills my nostrils. The wood has lightened over time, but my memory recalls a deep-brown color. With careful fingers, I lift the gold clasp in the center to unlock it—for the first time since I locked it, at fifteen—but then my hands start to tremble.

I snap the clasp shut, slip the box back into the drawer, and rush out into the hallway. "One step at a time," I say with a grimace. I'll pencil in my wooden-box breakdown for after my upcoming trip to Hawai'i. Tears stream down my face as I slowly lower myself to sit against the wall.

Two days ago, my lawyer called to inform me that my divorce was finalized. John had casually asked for a divorce one morning over a year ago, just before a business trip. He wore an indifferent expression, as though telling me he'd be late for dinner.

Meanwhile, this chandelier kept shimmering away as if nothing had happened. Now it hangs lopsided, the metal centerpiece stripped bare. Like a naked truth. Like me, standing alone in this empty house.

On the same day my lawyer called, my son, Zack, left for his second year of studies at San Jose State University. He's working toward a bachelor of science in aviation. He's still in California, but a five-hour drive up. I'm so proud of him.

I pick up a matchbox-sized shard from the floor. It still

lets the light through. Why is the light even brighter through a broken piece?

Shard in hand, I head back upstairs. My suitcase, half packed and open on my bed, awaits my attention. I just booked the trip to Hawai'i, and I'm departing in two days. This will be my first time traveling and vacationing alone, and I want everything to go smoothly, so I went through a travel agency. I also purchased travel and medical insurance. I've been reading all about the different islands and already feel like an expert on them. Each day of island-hopping is carefully planned out.

I gently place the crystal into a zippered compartment of my checked luggage. It's a broken but familiar piece of me.

Chapter 2

Ava

As I sweep all the broken glass into a dustpan, the doorbell rings. I pause. It's late Sunday afternoon and I'm not expecting anyone. I fling open the door to see my neighbor and friend Elaine. Her forehead creases and her lips form a tight line. I glance behind her, but there's no one else in sight.

"Elaine! Hi. How did you get here?"

"I live on the same street, you know. I walked over."

Elaine recently had a fall and is now quite fragile on her feet. She has a caretaker during the day, but she doesn't work on Sundays.

"You shouldn't have walked alone."

"Well, you should have returned a ninety-year-old woman's phone calls," she replies indignantly, before noticing the shattered crystal on the floor. "Oh dear. What happened here?"

"I'm so sorry. I returned your call and left you a voicemail. Please come in."

Elaine walks inside. Her silver hair is neatly pinned up, and her pearl necklace matches her drop earrings, which sway with each step. I met her over ten years ago, when John and I bought this house—our second home, in my dream neighborhood in LA. The chandelier and the wooden box arrived first. Soon after we moved in, Elaine introduced me to Starlight Scholars, a nonprofit organization. She was one of the founders and now a regular donor, actively supporting the education of girls from disadvantaged backgrounds. I now volunteer as a board member.

I never told her that I gave up my dream of going to college to marry John, especially once I found out I was pregnant.

"I'll get the dry martinis ready," I say, while we walk into the living room. "We're celebrating."

"Celebrating? What are we celebrating?"

"Martinis coming right away, and then I'll tell you," I say, as Elaine sinks into the sofa.

I fetch two long-stemmed glasses from the corner cabinet and place them on the island. The kitchen area seamlessly blends into the living room.

"What happened to the chandelier?" Elaine asks, her eyes narrowing.

"Not all celebrations are filled with joy and laughter. Some involve destruction and chaos." I remove the bottle of chilled vermouth from the fridge and then open the cabinet above the counter and grab the gin bottle. Carefully measuring the liquids, I pour them into a mixing glass and stir the mixture. Elaine's eyes follow my every move, her gaze intense. I pour the drink into the glasses and drop in green olives, watching them sink.

"Here you go." I pull the small coffee table closer to Elaine and set her martini down in front of her, then sit on the sofa beside her, gripping my own glass a little tighter than necessary. "We're celebrating because I'm no longer married to that man. What's his name again?"

"Don't remember," she says, laughing.

We each take a large sip before I announce, "And we're also celebrating because I booked a vacation in Hawai'i."

"That's fantastic, Ava. You deserve some time off after everything you went through. And you work so hard."

"I know. The separation, the divorce proceedings, adjusting to living on my own here—it's been a lot to handle."

Plus, my business is booming and busy. I run a small business that specializes in designing user-experience maps and creating flowcharts and instructions for gadgets. I've been working with a major global client for several years now, and I've just started working with a new client as well.

"You'll be fine," says Elaine.

I nod hopefully, but deep down, a fear has been nagging at me for months now. What if my client decides to leave? What if John doesn't contribute his share of the college fees? What if my savings run out completely?

I take another large sip, and my swallow is audible in the quiet room. Glancing at Elaine, I notice that the lines on her face seem deeper.

I frown. "Are you all right?" I ask, leaning forward to place my martini glass on the coffee table in front of Elaine before settling back on the sofa as I move closer to her.

"Yes," she says, avoiding my eyes.

My head tilts as I observe her. "You have a crack on your pinky fingernail," I say. I reach out to gently push a lock of hair away from her face. "And your hair—there's a tiny twist here, like you've been running your hands through it."

Her collar is also crinkled, which is unusual, but I keep that to myself.

"Okay, detective." Her eyes well up with tears behind her thin-framed glasses. "I lost my most precious gift from Harold."

Harold is her late husband. Elaine has been without him for almost two years, and I can't remember a day that she hasn't mentioned him in our conversations. Her eyes glisten and she blinks faster.

She sighs. "You know the book *Pride and Prejudice*, the Peacock edition?"

"The one that Harold proposed to you with?"

"Yes." Elaine nods.

I look at my fantastic, loving, caring neighbor who became family. She moved here from the UK in her twenties with Harold, and I never tire of listening to their story. They met in London, but Harold's family rejected Elaine, who wasn't part of their society, so the couple ran away to Los Angeles together. He became a successful movie producer.

"You know your love story is still my favorite."

A smile spreads across her face. "I still remember the day he proposed. His hands shook when he went down on his knee and handed a large box to me. You can imagine my thoughts. I stared at the box." Laughter escapes her, and I join in.

She sips her drink. "I thought I'd never forgive him for getting cold feet."

"What happened?" I ask, even though I know.

"I wasn't good enough for his mother, so under her pressure, he broke up with me. Soon after, he begged me to take him back. But I wasn't having any of it. I was so heartbroken. Then, a few days later, he turned up with the book, proposed, and asked for forgiveness. He knew it was my favorite book."

"And then?" I prompt.

"We tied the knot. Seventy years of marriage, a son, and lovely grandchildren." Her eyes glisten beneath paper-thin eyelids. "And now, I can't find the book." She laces her fingers, her thumbs making circles. "It's just disappeared. Harold would be so upset to know I lost it." Her lips quiver.

"Oh dear, Elaine." I shuffle closer and place my palm over her arm. "Maybe you misplaced it."

"No, I only remove it from its protective glass on our anniversary and Harold's birthday. You know that."

The book has a dedicated area in the middle of her bookshelf. The centerpiece, it stands alone amid the surrounding books.

I nod. "When did you see it last? Did you ask Maria?" I ask, hoping her caretaker has seen it.

"I asked. She thinks it was there a week ago, but we don't go into the library often. Do you think someone might have entered my house?"

"Hmm . . . Is anything else missing?"

"I don't think so."

"You still have security cameras running, right?" I say. John and I used the same security company to set up our system a few years back.

"Yes. I was actually hoping you could help me look at the footage."

"Of course."

"But there's a lot to go through," she adds grimly.

"I don't mind!" I exclaim. "I'll help as long as needed. Let's get back to your place."

The cul-de-sac in our Beverly Hills neighborhood isn't the celebrity-mansion-filled Beverly Hills that we see in the movies, but it's still my dream street. As part of the divorce agreement, I'm now the sole owner of the house, though most of our savings have gone to John.

Elaine on my arm, we stroll. It really is the most

beautiful street, and I was filled with pride living here with my family, the three of us. My eyes drift to the far end. The memory is still vivid: Zack's bike wobbled before tipping over, sending him tumbling to the ground. A kind neighbor rushed over and quickly helped us into their car to get Zack to the hospital. The memory fills me with warmth but also sadness—a reminder of how quickly everything can change.

We approach Elaine's house, the most impressive on the block due to its grand size. It's spread onto two lots at the end of the cul-de-sac. It's also grand in its design, its white exterior and elegant architecture exuding an air of class and charm.

But this house also symbolizes my husband's betrayal. It's where he first met *her*, at a barbecue Elaine hosted three years ago. His affair with Elaine's grandniece, almost two decades younger than him, was not only shocking for me but also devastating for Elaine when it was revealed a year ago.

I push that memory away as Elaine leans on me a bit more, her steps unsteady. I tighten my grip on her arm, saying, "I've got you."

Chapter 3

Lev

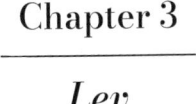

"Calls at six thirty in the morning should be banned in the business world," I grumble to myself. I'm in my home office in London wearing track pants and a T-shirt. The computer screen casts a glow on my stubbled face. I'm about to video-chat with my head of security in Istanbul. After fifteen years of working together, I know that when her name pops up on my personal phone on a Monday morning—or any day of the week—I need to brace myself.

"Do you want to brew a cup of coffee first?" Frederica asks, appearing on my screen.

I sigh and scratch my face. "Yeah, it's brewing. Hit me with it. What's the emergency?"

"We just received an envelope from a courier. It's addressed to SkyBridge Global Security."

The envelope was delivered to our temporary operation

hub at a convention center in Istanbul, where our next high-profile event will take place.

Frederica holds up the envelope to the camera, making sure it's clearly visible on the screen.

ATTN: Pretty Boy
SkyBridge Global Security

I cringe. "Yuri," I say, through gritted teeth.

Frederica raises an eyebrow. "Anyone else addressing you as 'pretty boy'?"

I shake my head. My shoulders are tight, and the muscles at the back of my neck are as tense as a bowstring.

Yuri is a notorious art thief in Europe. He's fond of rare books and I own a top-tier security company that specializes in protecting such treasures. My elite team of security experts and I are trained in state-of-the-art technology and meticulous protocols. We've earned a sterling reputation for our discretion and effectiveness and are trusted by affluent collectors, renowned institutions, and auction houses worldwide.

"Do we have intel that he's currently in Istanbul?" I ask. Our upcoming event is an antiquarian book fair.

"Yes, unfortunately. I've already increased our security level to red alert and called in extra personnel, including plainclothes teams."

A year ago, Yuri and I ran into each other at a rare-book auction in Paris, one of the largest in the world. He was attempting to steal a page encased in a glass frame. I chased him, but he managed to escape—without the page, thankfully. It all happened in a matter of minutes. His cocky grin still haunts me. He'd taunted me, saying, "Calm down, pretty boy," as he freed his arm, slipping off his jacket while running away.

"I've already done all the usual checks on the envelope," Frederica reports. "Nothing seems suspicious."

"Let's see what's inside," I say. What kind of thief in their right mind would contact the security director of a rare-book event?

I watch as Frederica puts on a pair of gloves and carefully makes an incision along the sealed edge of the envelope. She peers inside and pulls out a folded piece of paper. After reading it, she turns it toward the screen.

I know exactly who you are, pretty boy! It shall be kept under the seal of my lips . . . or perhaps not!

My eyes are glued to the words on the screen, but my mind races with the ferocity of a thousand distressed bees.

"Boss," Frederica says hesitantly. "May I ask what this means?"

I rub the back of my neck. "It doesn't matter," I murmur. It's a secret that's better left buried.

I could continue my day as if nothing happened, stay in London, and watch my daughter's show. But Yuri is something else. I've studied him closely, combed through the public court records from his previous convictions—he doesn't even see art theft as a crime. He takes risks, constantly pushing the limits, and more than once, he's come dangerously close to getting caught. I get the sense it's all just a game to him, a thrill he craves. In the end, Yuri's a real maniac.

Frederica adds, "We also have intel that he might be interfering and creating a security weakness as we prepare for the event."

"Bloody hell," I blurt.

"I increased the background checks on all security personnel."

"Great, now every security guard will need a PhD in not-being-shady. Can't he just turn up and try to steal something rather than send a note? That way, I can finally catch him in the act, the slippery eel!" I hiss.

"I'll take charge of perimeter security myself," Frederica says. "We'll be fully prepared, inside and out."

I nod in agreement. The team and I have spent months preparing for this event, but this week is crucial, especially the few days leading up to the event, when we gain full access to the convention center. We conduct thorough inspections, secure the site, hold final briefings, and strategically deploy personnel. We also test all communication systems and finalize emergency-response plans, which includes conducting drills for different scenarios.

"I'll fly to Istanbul tomorrow," I say.

I was scheduled to go on Friday. I have a lot of

confidence in my skilled team in Istanbul, but the possibility of Yuri being there changes everything.

My blood pounds at the thought of breaking the news to my fourteen-year-old daughter, though. I won't be able to attend her show on Thursday. Pera has been diligently practicing her dance routine since returning from summer dance camp, and her school is hosting the show. She'll be disappointed.

After ending the call, I stand by the office window overlooking our expansive garden in Hampstead, the northern part of London. A lump forms in my throat. I sense something big and unexpected looming on the horizon.

Chapter 4

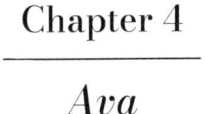

Ava

I sit in Elaine's cozy living room, eyes fixated on her laptop screen as I meticulously comb through hours of security footage. It's well into the evening now. I steal a glance at Elaine, who's in her favorite armchair watching me.

I tilt my head slightly. "I'll watch as long as it takes."

"Thank you, dear," she responds.

My eyes flick back to the screen, and I stifle a gasp. The screen has lit up with surveillance footage from five days ago. It was Tuesday evening, the night Elaine always goes to her bridge club. In the footage, someone is walking away from the camera in front of Elaine's home. A hoodie obscures any trace of hair, and there's a bag dangling at the person's side.

It looks like a man.

I glance at Elaine again. She's doing a crossword puzzle in the newspaper, her reading glasses on her nose.

How could anyone do this to her? I hit the rewind button and watch the footage again. And again. My eyes bulge in terror. I see him entering, but the face isn't clear. His walk is familiar, though. A knot appears in my gut. That walk. That small waddle.

A bitter taste floods my mouth, sharp and metallic, as though I'm sucking on a rusty nail.

My sweet son? Zack? I shake my head. It can't be. The mouse feels as if it's burning. My hands tremble. After rewinding and replaying a few more times, I'm almost positive that it's Zack's walk I'm seeing on the screen. Maybe he was visiting Elaine, as he does sometimes? Why would he cover his head like that, though? My breathing gets heavier. I look at Elaine, but she's lost in the crossword.

I watch it again, hoping that there might be a direct correlation between the amount of time I watch it and the possibility of the footage changing.

Nope.

The truth sinks in. It's him. I close my eyes and let my fingers brush the edge of the laptop. Memories come alive. I can almost feel the tiny grip of his baby hand as he took his first wobbly steps on the living room floor. I remember the smooth fabric of his graduation gown, the slight tremor in his step as he walked across the stage. I'd know that gait anywhere. Even in the dim light of a computer screen.

My throat constricts, my chest heaves with each ragged breath I take, and my ribs seem to crack and splinter. I sense Elaine's gaze and force a smile.

In the footage, he walks out of the house at a quick pace, looks down, and disappears into the dark street.

What are you doing, Zack?

My brows are tight-knit, hurting my forehead. My mind screams, but my voice remains trapped in my body. What do I do now?

"I'm going to take a short break, go out into the backyard for a while," I say, trying to control my shaking voice, unable to look at Elaine.

"Sure. Your eyes have been glued to that screen for hours."

I wish I could simply erase what I've witnessed. But maybe there's an explanation. I need to speak with him before jumping to a conclusion. The backyard feels as large as a football field as I rush to the other end of it, away from the small pond where the water trickles with an unsettling intensity. I dial Zack, and my heart races with fear and dread. "Pick up, pick up, pick up!" I urge silently.

He doesn't answer. Panic claws at my chest. I redial, my heartbeat pounding in my ears. I redial, the silence on the other end growing louder and more painful. I redial. Why isn't he picking up?

Finally, his face appears on the screen.

"Hi, Mom." He sits at his small desk in his dorm room.

"Zack, what did you do?" I hiss.

"What's up?" he asks, eyes darting around.

"I saw you leaving Elaine's house when she wasn't home. In the dark, on Tuesday evening. She has security cameras."

"What?" he cries. "What are you talking about?"

"Zack, don't! Just don't. I saw you."

Color leaks from his face. He looks like a deer caught in headlights. "I don't know what you're talking about," he blurts. "I have an early class tomorrow morning, so I have to go."

"You stay there and answer me. What were you doing at Elaine's on Tuesday evening? You entered the house at eight fifteen precisely and left at eight twenty-three."

"Oh, that. I-I went to see her, but she wasn't there. Is that the night you're talking about?"

"In a hoodie that hides your face?" I try to keep my voice low, but my words come out loud. "Stop this nonsense and tell me what's going on. Why were you at Elaine's?"

I pace, clutching the phone, its bright light stark against the surrounding darkness. My breath quickens, and the rising panic feels as relentless as the night.

Zack wipes his forehead swiftly. "I visit Elaine all the time. You know that."

"Did you take the book?" I press. I feel my face going crimson, a burning flush spreading just beneath my skin.

He pauses. "Um, um . . . What book?" He brushes the top of his swooped hair with his hand as his blinking increases.

"Oh, dear god, you did." I wince.

"I-I . . ." His voice cracks. "Mom."

I cup my temple, trying to push back the pressure in my forehead. "I'm losing my mind. Why, Zack?"

He dips his head and whispers, "She has so many books. I didn't think she'd notice."

"She wouldn't notice the book that's most important to her? Are you for real? And how is that a good enough reason to steal?"

I blink a few times, hard, trying to clear my vision. Tears well up in my eyes as the realization that he committed the crime truly hits me.

Zack's jaw tightens as he swallows. A nervous twitch plays at the corner of his mouth. He shifts uncomfortably, beads of sweat forming on his forehead.

"Sorry, Mom. I'm in trouble. I need money."

"What kind of trouble?" I demand. It hurts that he didn't come to me for help.

"I'm in debt," he confesses.

"What do you mean? What kind of debt?"

"I got into an online game," he explains miserably. "It got out of hand. You hate debt, so I called Dad. He told me to grow up and sort out my own mess. So I borrowed money from some loan people."

"Loan people? Is that what they're called now? The loan sharks? Zack, what are you doing? Stealing a rare book? From Elaine? This is a nightmare. Can. I. Wake. Up?"

My anger is boiling, and I want to scream at the top of my lungs. Instead, I clench my teeth. My nails dig into my left collarbone. "Okay, where is the book?" I say, forcing out the words in a whisper. "Bring it back. Immediately. I'll give you the money. I'll lend it to you."

His head slowly tilts down until I can see only the top of it.

"Zack?"

"I gave it to a friend, who has a contact in the rare-book world. He's apparently taking the book out of the country."

"What? What friend? How do you guys even have a contact like that?" My voice rises. "Where is he taking it?"

"Istanbul," he whispers.

I lower my voice again. "Are you telling me that the book is on its way to the Middle East right now?"

The corners of his mouth droop. "Mom, Istanbul isn't in the Middle East."

"Really, Zack? Time for geography lessons?"

"Just saying." He looks sheepish.

"Well, I don't care where it is. The book isn't on Elaine's shelf."

"Sorry, Mom. Listen, I gave the book to a friend here in San Jose when I arrived on Friday. He gave it to that contact yesterday." Zack is still interested in the floor.

"Zack, look at me right now. Are you saying the book might still be in San Jose?" It was only Sunday evening. Maybe there was a chance we could get it back.

"He said his contact would be already on his way to Istanbul. Sorry, Mom."

"Stop saying sorry and do something about it," I snap. "You already caused Elaine pain. Do you realize how sad she is and how hurt she'll be when she finds out it was you? I thought you loved Elaine."

I try to breathe. It feels as though a vacuum is sucking the air out of my lungs. "And do you realize what kind of trouble you're in? You could go to jail. Aviation isn't a place for convicts."

"No, no, no, Mom," he pleads. "Please don't tell her. She'll be upset. And please don't send me to jail."

My heart breaks into pieces. The severity of the situation is just unreal.

"It's only been a day," I say. "I'll pay. I'll loan you the money to buy it back. Or give me his phone number and I'll handle it. Have you met this person? And who's this friend of yours? From college? Do I know him?" I bombard him with so many questions that Zack looks lost.

"Give me his phone number," I repeat.

"Let me phone him, Mom. He's from the gaming world, but we also met in person. I doubt that he'll talk to you."

My mouth falls open before I speak again. "Okay, where does he live?"

"I don't know, but I'll call him right now." Zack grimaces. "I'll see where the book is, and if we can stop it from going to Istanbul."

"You do that." I hang up, unable to look at my son's distraught face any longer.

As I return inside, a tingle spreads across my chest. Elaine is slumped in her armchair, her head lolling to the side. I sob silently, standing still, not wanting to wake her from her peaceful slumber.

Chapter 5

Lev

I have to tell my daughter. It's already late afternoon and I'm flying tomorrow. When Pera arrived home from school, she went straight to our home gym, which we've turned into a dance studio. I walk down the long hallway to the thud of bass-heavy beats pounding from the gym. "Pera," I yell, cracking open the door a little. "Sweetheart, can we talk for a minute?"

She turns down the music. Her hair is pulled back into a high ponytail, and she's wearing big hoop earrings. Her cheeks are flushed. Her body remains mostly hidden behind the door.

"I'm a very busy dancer, Dad." She grins mischievously.

"I know, I know. Uhm, okay, I need to tell you something," I say with a heavy sigh. "Something urgent came up. I have to travel to Istanbul earlier than I intended."

Pera's eyes narrow. "Earlier?" Her mouth purses.

"Yes. Tomorrow."

"But tomorrow is Tuesday, Dad." She releases the door handle and storms off.

She's wearing a crop top with blue and purple abstract graphics paired with high-waisted white joggers.

Pera stops the music abruptly and crosses her arms. She leans against the wall as I enter the room. She starts shaking her head, her chest heaving. The searing look in her hazel eyes could probably slice an apple in half.

I regularly handle tense situations and know how to stay calm. Just a few months ago, a suspicious package was left in a museum lobby during a special exhibit. At a more recent event, a guest, after too many drinks, insisted on touching a painting and became disruptive and aggressive.

However, in this moment, I am anything but calm. My fourteen-year-old daughter is erupting, her cheeks a bright shade of red, her eyes wide. "You promised!"

Despite my training in martial arts and years of experience in intelligence and security, I feel helpless. Everything flies out the window when I face my daughter.

"Peanut, I'm sorry. It's something I can't avoid. Your grandma will be there. And I'll watch the livestream."

"But you said you'd be there, Dad. I told everyone that you were coming." Tears glisten in her eyes. I expected her to be disappointed, but I'm surprised by how badly she's handling it. Lately, she's been more interested in spending time with her friends and her dance routine than with me.

"Hon, I didn't know until this morning. I planned to be here until Friday, but in my line of work, emergencies happen that I can't avoid. You know that."

She takes a deep breath and exhales slowly, and her face relaxes slightly. Could I possibly be winning her over with my explanation? But then she blurts, "Can I go to the Taylor Swift concert with my friends, then?"

"We talked about this before," I reply firmly. "That's not possible."

"Ugh, it's like your business needs are the only ones that matter," she huffs. "Can I please be alone?" Her arms are still crossed, but her voice trembles and her chin quivers.

Returning to my office, I sink into my chair and take a deep breath. It's hard to believe how quickly she's grown up; it seems like just yesterday she was my little girl chasing butterflies and hosting tea parties in the tree house out back.

Pera handled the divorce remarkably well. Her mother and I split up six years ago, and when Isobel moved abroad a couple of years later, Pera remained strong and resilient. My lovely daughter, no matter what. But we've been arguing a lot in the last couple of years.

Is there any way I could stay for her show? I wonder.

Yuri pops into my head, and my stomach twists. I need to be in Istanbul. It's black-and-white. I have to be there not only for the security operation, but also to reassure my client in Istanbul, who has organized this book fair for many years. I've provided security services for the event

year after year, always with success, and I'm directly
involved in the process, hands on, every time.

This year shouldn't be any different.

I press play on the footage of me chasing Yuri through
the crowd in Paris. I've watched this video thousands of
times. It still pains me that he got away.

Minimizing the video, I text Pera and ask if she wants
a pizza evening at her favorite place. Three dots blink a
few times, but she doesn't respond.

A knock sounds at my door. "Come in," I say happily,
but it's not Pera. It's my mother, Denise.

"Hello," she chirps. Her silver hair is short and stylish,
with side bangs resting on her forehead.

"Hi, Mom, I didn't realize you were back," I say, rising
to kiss her cheek. "How was your day?"

"It's always great to catch up with my gals," she says.
She meets two of her friends every week for afternoon tea.

We head to the kitchen to get dinner ready. After my
stepfather's passing and my divorce, my mother came to
live with Pera and me. It was initially supposed to be a
temporary arrangement—extra support for all of us for a
few months—but it worked out so well that months turned
into years. The three of us live comfortably in our spacious
house and had help from a couple of live-in au pairs until a
few years ago.

"But then Pera called," my mom says.

"Was she complaining about me?" I ask, bothered.

"No, but she's heartbroken."

"Heartbroken? Seriously?" I snap, shaking my head as

I begin cutting greens for a salad, the sizzle of salmon grilling on the skillet beside me filling the kitchen.

My mom sets the table. Each plate and utensil creates a clinking or clattering sound. When dinner is ready, she tells me she'll go get Pera. I take a seat at the dinner table. Minutes pass, and then my mom comes back with a sigh and takes a spot next to me.

"She says she's not hungry," she murmurs.

I rise, but my mother stops me with a hand on my arm. "Let her be. She's upset. I'll take some food up to her room later."

"There's a difference between being upset and being rude," I say.

"And there's a vast ocean between your father watching your performance in person and half paying attention on a livestream," she counters.

"I won't bother responding to that," I mutter. Lately, my mother and I haven't been seeing eye to eye either. The more Pera and I argue, the more strained my relationship with my mother becomes.

I cut a piece of my fish and shove it in my mouth; it feels as if I'm trying to swallow shards of glass. Sipping my water offers only slight relief.

My mom continues. "Pera is growing up. Her mother isn't around. She needs more of her father's presence in her life."

"Yeah," I say, after a loud swallow. "The divorce wasn't my choice, and neither was the affair."

My mom stabs through the leafy greens in her salad

bowl. "I thought you'd have someone stable in your life by now."

I glare at her. I don't like this subject, this meddling. It's my life.

She puts down her fork. "Okay, sorry, not my place. But for Pera's sake, I'm asking you to consider making some changes in your life. This business of yours is taking up more and more of your time. Can you be proud of what you've achieved so far and maybe slow down, travel less, spend more time with us?"

"I hear you."

After dinner I sip a gin and tonic, but it does diddly-squat to help my mood. I can't help but brush my fingers against Pera's bedroom door as I walk past, hoping she knows how much I love her.

"Goodnight, sweetheart," I whisper, pressing my index and middle fingers into a V shape against her door. It's our secret code, a silent "I see you."

Hopefully she'll be in a better mood tomorrow morning and I can steal a hug from her before leaving.

Chapter 6

Ava

I t's seven thirty in the morning and my eyes feel heavy and swollen from staring at my laptop all night. I barely slept. I'm still in shock. My sweet boy stole Elaine's book. When I woke Elaine last night to help her get ready for bed, she looked so fragile. I couldn't bring myself to tell her about Zack and her book. Instead, I promised I'd stop by in the morning.

As I'm preparing to leave, Elaine's caretaker calls me. "Elaine isn't feeling well and needs more rest. Can you come by at nine thirty instead?"

"Of course," I reply. Elaine's health is the top priority.

Sitting down at the desk in my home office, I call John and leave him another message. How could he not tell me our son was in trouble? How could he prioritize his new life over helping his only child? I'm freaking out about Zack not being able to get the book back. Elaine is already devastated. And Zack could go to jail.

My heart clenches. I open a drawer and take out a framed photo, one of the few I have of my family. It's a snapshot of my mother, Corinne, my sister, Grace, and me outside a movie theater in Phoenix. We're all smiles, filled with joy. We'd just watched *Notting Hill* and were dreaming of one day visiting that neighborhood in London.

I set down the photo on my desk and continue my online quest for rare books and auction houses. I'm organizing all my findings into a spreadsheet. I take breaks to read up on Istanbul—a city of 15 million people—and contact private investigators, leaving voicemails for some and connecting with others. It's fascinating how quickly one can gather information when time is of the essence.

When nine thirty comes around, I head to Elaine's hugging my laptop. The sharp scent of freshly cut grass invades my nose, and the sound of gravel crunching under a neighbor's car tires jolts me, making another crack in my fragile shell of normalcy.

Maria opens the door. "She's on the back patio."

Lush greenery and vibrant flowers surround Elaine, who's sitting on the cozy outdoor sofa. I take a seat across from her. A small table covered in a tropical-print tablecloth sits between us. The gentle trickle of water from her small pond fills the air. Despite the peaceful setting, fear clings to my throat, cold and suffocating. My head tilts involuntarily, burdened by unbearable heaviness.

"Did you find anything?" asks Elaine.

Yeah, I found out that I'm a terrible mother, I think. "Um . . . okay. It was Zack."

Elaine's sharp eyes land on me. "I'm sorry, what?"

The guilt in my mouth tastes like bile. "Zack took the book."

"I'm not following. Zack took the book?" Elaine shifts slightly. Then her tense expression softens, and she releases her grip on the arm of the sofa. "Oh, does he want to read it? That's a relief. It's very old, though—he needs to be careful with it."

"No," I choke out. "He's not borrowing it. He stole it." I want the ground to swallow me. It pains me to witness her bright-blue eyes cloud over. "I'll do anything to try to get it back."

"Get it back? What do you mean? He doesn't have it?"

I shake my head. "He doesn't."

Elaine looks at her backyard. "Please give me a moment," she says, almost inaudibly.

"Should I leave?"

"No, I just need a minute."

My phone rings; it's Zack. "Let me take this call and give you some time," I say, and she nods.

I quickly walk home while answering his call. "Do you know how utterly heartbroken Elaine is? It's unbearable, Zack. She's shattered. I can't fathom how you could do this. I'm still in shock. I don't know if I'll ever be able to forgive you."

Zack's voice is thick with sobs. "Mom, I'm sorry." His breathing is ragged. "I contacted the guy who took the book. It's already on its way to Istanbul." His voice cracks.

"He was furious that I asked for it back. He told me not to reach out to him anymore—or else."

I stand firm. "Zack, you need to find out who the contact in Istanbul is. Tell him we just want the book back. If we return the book to Elaine, we might avoid involving the police. But if we can't, he's in trouble too. Both of you, no doubt about it."

As soon as the call ends, I panic at the thought of Zack being arrested. An image of his wrists in cold metal handcuffs flashes through my mind. I leave John another message asking him to return my call right away. First he had another home for two years before walking out on me, and now he won't help Zack?

When he finally gets back to me, he tells me Zack is an adult and should sort out his own shit. I hang up, not even wanting to argue with him.

Never mind. Zack has a mother. He has me.

Elaine reaches for the glass of water on the small table beside her armchair in the living room. Despite the warmth of the September morning, she has a shawl around her shoulders.

"Are you all right?" I ask.

She nods, but deep creases line her pursed mouth, and her eyes are cloudy with unshed tears.

I hesitate for a moment before saying, "The book is possibly on its way to Istanbul."

Her eyelids, thin as silk, flutter open. "Istanbul?" she asks softly.

"I'm afraid so. But, I looked into the top private investigators. One specializes in finding lost treasures and has an 80 percent success rate." I pull the ottoman over and sit close to Elaine, then open my laptop and turn the screen toward her. "I contacted five of them. This one is really promising." I point. "I maintained confidentiality but informed them that the book was going to Istanbul." I swallow. "This is a big ask, but could you give me a chance to get the book back before you report the theft to the police?"

Elaine shifts again. "If it was up to me . . . But I told Rayner after you left. He said he'll deal with reporting it to the police. He may have already contacted them."

"Rayner, yeah." I try to sound strong, but my voice cracks. Rayner is Elaine's son who lives in San Diego.

"Private investigators?" Elaine asks.

"Yes, I'll take care of everything. I have savings, and I'll put the house on the line to retrieve the book if necessary."

"So the book is in Istanbul?" she asks. Sadness dampens her voice.

I'm almost tongue-tied with guilt. "Yes, I'm afraid so."

"To be sold?" Elaine's disbelief is palpable. "How ironic. Istanbul was one of Harold's and my favorite cities."

"I'm really sorry," I whisper. "But the private investigator said that once I give the green light, they'll move forward with the pursuit. I've done extensive research on Istanbul and discovered there's an antiquarian book fair starting in a few days. The investigators believe it could be an important lead. I'll do whatever it takes to get it back."

"Any lengths?"

"Yes, absolutely. Without hesitation. I just need time to try."

"I might be able to persuade Rayner not to report it, but . . . only if you go to Istanbul to get the book back."

"Me?" I shriek. "I'd have no idea what to do. I wouldn't know where to start."

"I trust you more than anyone."

"Me?" I repeat. "I've never even been outside the country."

"Yes, you. You'll do anything for your son and me. You still have your passport, right?" Elaine's words hit me like a shower of hope. Could I really get it back?

"I do," I reply, thinking about the family vacation we never took.

Istanbul—until now, my knowledge of that part of the world pretty much starts and ends with the Turkish marble we had installed during our home remodel.

Elaine looks directly at me. "And after everything you had to go through because of that grandniece of mine, my family owes you some slack. I'll ask Rayner to give you time."

"Oh Elaine, that had nothing to do with you," I say, my voice tender.

But she continues, her tone steely. "Shall I call Rayner and tell him to hold off on the police because you're going to Istanbul?"

I chew my lip. "But what happens if I can't get it?"

She shrugs. "We'll cross that bridge if or when we come to it."

Fear grips me. Spontaneity has never been my forte, and the thought of facing a foreign city sends shards of ice through my veins. Still, I manage to nod and say "Call him. I'll go." I close my laptop.

She dials her son's number.

I hold my breath. This phone call could mean the difference between Zack being charged and Zack remaining free.

"Ray, have you made the theft report yet?" She pauses then looks at me and shakes her head. Elaine fills Rayner in on the details, and I listen to his angry voice coming through the phone until I can't sit quietly any longer. I head to the back patio, still able to hear Elaine's conversation. My nerves on edge, I pace, anxiously awaiting the outcome of their heated discussion, and begin browsing flights to Istanbul on my phone.

After what feels like an eternity, Elaine hangs up and I return.

"Ray agreed," she says tensely. "But you have two weeks."

"Two weeks?" I repeat, my voice rising in pitch.

"Yes."

My stomach tightens and my hands go cold. A sharp

itch burns across my collarbone, and my hand flies to it. I process what's happening. I'm going to Istanbul with a ticking timeline.

I take a deep breath and straighten my posture, trying to focus on what comes next. Every minute counts; I need to get there before the book changes hands.

"Well then, I guess I need to book my flight and repack," I whisper, my voice shaking.

"Repack?"

"Yes, the vacation I mentioned. I was supposed to go to Hawai'i tomorrow. I saw flights to Istanbul departing this afternoon. Apparently it's not in the Middle East."

Elaine nods. "While the Middle East is a mosaic of traditions, languages, and landscapes, that is correct. Istanbul isn't in the Middle East. A portion of it spans into Europe."

"Even in these circumstances, you are such a graceful and compassionate human being. Thank you."

Elaine stands, and I stumble toward her. We fall into an embrace.

My heart aches for Elaine, and for Zack's loss of innocence, as well as my own all these years ago. When I was seventeen years old, my life changed with the sound of a loud knock on our apartment door. It had been two years since my sister and I lost our mother and were left orphaned. Grace and I were struggling to make ends meet and pay rent, but we were staying afloat. It was tough, but we leaned on each other for support. Grace was only twenty but she was my constant, my anchor.

When I opened the door, I was met with two officers. They arrested Grace for possession of illegal drugs, shattering our world. She was escorted out in handcuffs.

"Don't worry," Grace said. "Everything will be okay. I'll be back."

Her words still haunt me.

She never did come back. She returned home briefly for her court date but was ultimately sentenced to three years in prison. And just like that, I was utterly alone until I met John a year later.

I can't bear the thought of Zack facing jail. I have to find a way to avoid seeing him in handcuffs, no matter the cost or actions needed.

Chapter 7

Lev

As I settle into my seat, a flight attendant in a crisp uniform approaches with a warm expression. "May I offer you a preflight beverage, sir?"

Politely, I decline. The only thing I want is that hug from Pera. She didn't come out of her room before I left for the airport. That was a first.

My first task when I arrive in Istanbul is to meet with Serra, the event director and curator of the antiquarian book fair. I'm feeling uneasy about this conversation because I need to inform her about the increased risk at this year's event—and I hate seeing clients unhappy. Serra is a major figure in the rare-book world in Istanbul and internationally. She comes from a family of art collectors, and my company has provided security at many of the events she's led. Our paths cross at least once a year, sometimes more frequently.

She's not only a good friend but also a casual date. Sometimes we wake up together in her room—never mine. That's how she prefers it, and it suits me just fine as well.

The drive from the Istanbul airport is slow due to evening traffic building up. In the distance, her hotel looms, tall and sleek. When I arrive, I leave my luggage with the concierge and take the elevator to the two-level rooftop restaurant and bar on the nineteenth floor.

I climb the stairs to the second level of the restaurant, where the bar area offers a stunning view of the bridge between Europe and Asia. I've always been drawn to bridges. The sun descends toward the horizon, making the vast waters of the Bosphorus Strait shimmer. This city excites me. Its vibrancy is a stark contrast to my quiet, suburban life in North London; it's also distinct from my Central London headquarters, with its own liveliness and chaos.

While I'm lost in the view, I hear Serra's voice. "Hello, hello. I knew you'd be up here."

She's wearing beige trousers, a three-button waistcoat, and a stylish blazer. Her straight blonde hair is shoulder length, and a few strands elegantly frame her face. Despite my being over six feet tall, her heels bring her eyes level with mine.

"Hello, gorgeous," I say, as I hug her. We walk back

and sit at the table by the edge on the lower level, watching the city lights sparkle. The last time Serra and I saw each other was in Dubai, nine months ago, at another high-profile event. Serra lives in Dubai, though she's originally from Istanbul, where most of her family lives.

"It's good to be back," she says. "I should come here when I'm not on a business trip."

I do that. I fly to Istanbul every other month for a few days to visit someone dear to me. I have for years now. Serra doesn't know. "Yeah, something about this city."

"I thought you weren't joining us until Friday."

"Thought I'd come early to oversee last-minute preparations."

"Or you just can't let go of control," she says, a laugh escaping her.

"Well, that too. But there's something else," I say, biting the bullet. "I wanted to tell you in person that we'll be running the operation on high alert. We'll brief you and your team in detail at the meetings tomorrow, but I wanted to give you a heads-up."

Serra's expression sinks, and her large glass of water makes a slight clink as she sets it down. "High alert?" she asks, her voice tight, as if she's about to take a sip of the most repulsive drink imaginable. "Why?"

"We believe Yuri is in Istanbul," I say, agitation crawling under my skin.

"Yuri?" Serra exclaims. "The Yuri? The bibliomaniac?"

"I'm afraid so."

"Oh," she says, exhaling.

I nod.

Serra leans back and crosses her arms for a beat. Then she asks, "What happened in Paris? Can you tell me now?"

I shift in my seat. I hadn't wanted to talk about it last time I saw Serra.

"It's not a memory I'm fond of, but yes."

"Thank you," she says, resting her hand on the tablecloth.

"But first let me reassure you that we operate well under pressure. When there's a heightened risk, we simply increase our resources and personnel accordingly. We adapt our operation fast. Our technology is top-notch."

"I have no doubt in your ability or your team's," she replies smoothly.

I clear my throat. "Here's what happened. We were at a rare-book auction in Paris. One of the items was an invaluable page from an early draft of *Hamlet*, in a protective glass cover. The page dates back to the seventeenth century and contains Shakespeare's handwritten annotations. I think you know what I'm talking about." I swallow.

Serra leans in, her chin resting in the palm of her hand, staring wide-eyed at me. "Wait, are you saying it's the same page we'll have on display here?"

I give a small nod. "Another collector acquired it. It will be at your book fair," I say, before continuing my story. "As I surveyed the auction hall, two women speaking to a dealer caught my attention. One of them was standing too close to the dealer. The other was just behind them. As I approached them, I noticed a small man at the back of the stand, his head down and facing away from me, wearing an oversized jacket. He shifted his stance and placed his hands at his sides. I had a feeling something wasn't right. Then he casually slipped something into his pocket."

"What gave you the feeling he was up to something?" Serra asks.

"I've learned to trust my instincts. My gut never fails me, so when it speaks, I listen. I also have an understanding of a thief's body language—I've studied it thoroughly. The moment I saw the way his arm moved, I knew he wasn't just putting his cell phone in his pocket. So I sprang into action."

"Unbelievable."

"Yeah. I quickened my pace, and when he noticed me, he started hurrying away. The dealer then noticed the missing page. Everything happened so fast. I ran after him, but one of the women threw herself in front of me. I'd never encountered Yuri before, but I knew his face pretty well. I recognized it despite the prosthetics he wore. I also knew he was short, only five-foot-four. We study them, the potential predators of the rare-treasure world."

My eyes dart toward the bustling city in the distance and linger there for a few beats. "I caught him by the arm despite the interference. At the same time, other security members ran toward us. Some dealt with the women. But he broke free. I managed to grab his jacket, but he slipped out of it and continued running." I take a big inhale, but the air gets stuck in my throat.

We sit in silence for a while. That moment—those piercing light-blue eyes and his voice—is often part of my nightmares. *Calm down, pretty boy.* I spare Serra that detail.

"This must be hard for you," Serra says. "I know your standards. Protecting is in your DNA."

"Extremely painfully," I huff.

"So you saved the page?"

"Yes, it was in his jacket, but he got away. Both of his companions were apprehended. They denied knowing him, but authorities recognized one as his girlfriend."

Serra exhales and moves a strand of hair that fell onto her face.

"Serra, we're prepared. We're on red-alert protocol. The page is in the high-security room with sensors."

"I know. It's the world of sick-minded thieves that gets me. Thanks for the heads-up."

I nod. "I'm informing you so that we'll all be more vigilant. In some ways, it's good that we know." I'm still perplexed about why he sent me a note, though.

"Thank you for stepping in," she says. "I feel much better knowing you're here to oversee the preparations. I have a few other things to catch you up on, but I really need a good rest for now."

"Sure, we have the whole week," I reply.

We finish our meal around 10:30 p.m. and say our goodnights. My hotel is only fifteen minutes away in the light traffic. In Istanbul, travel time is measured by traffic rather than distance.

As I walk into my hotel, I'm relieved to see a familiar face. "Hello, Melisa," I say to the hotel manager.

She appears as if she's just strolled in after a restful night's sleep. Her hair is pulled back in a half-ponytail, and waves and curls fall over her shoulders and back. A pang rushes through me. Pera adores curly hair. She's always got a curler in hand to shape her light-brown locks.

"Hello, Mr. Bowman. Welcome back. Let me check you in. I have great news," she says, smiling mischievously. "I managed to get your room for you."

"Thank you, you're the best." I prefer staying in the corner suite on the fourth floor.

"Just shuffled a few bookings around." She's an exceptional manager. Her ability to meet and exceed guests' expectations is truly remarkable.

She hands me a dark-brown key. The worn metalwork is cool and heavy in my fingers.

"Thank you," I say, glad this hotel hasn't replaced room keys with those modern cards.

As I press the elevator button, I hear a woman with an American accent speaking to Melisa at the reception desk.

"I was wondering if there's a store nearby. Is anything open at this hour?"

The question makes me smile. She should be asking if anything is closed at this hour in this part of Istanbul.

The elevator arrives. Entering, I cast a brief look at the woman. Her hair cascades down her back in waves, striking against her blue outfit.

As the elevator lifts with a hum, I check my phone, but there are no messages from Pera.

Chapter 8

Ava

I t's my first time traveling to a foreign city, and of course I've landed in one of the most chaotic places in the world. *Go me! Go life!* My nerves are already on edge. The taxi ride from the airport feels like a rally race, my palm turning red as I grip the door handle tightly.

Horns blare and traffic weaves around us as my taxi screeches to a halt. It's just after 3:00 p.m. I step onto the noisy street, happy to be that much closer to a quiet hotel room and a long shower. A friendly concierge takes my suitcase, and I enter the expansive lobby through sleek glass doors.

One of the five receptionists in gray suits, a young man with glasses, welcomes me politely. "Are you checking in, ma'am?"

I hand over my passport, trying not to let my anxiety show.

"I see a booking for October 9," he says.

My heart drops. "What?"

"Today is September 10."

I stare at him in disbelief before panic takes hold. I'm known for my attention to detail. I always check things twice or three times. This can't be happening.

"It's an easy mistake," the receptionist says calmly. "In Europe, the day appears before the month in a date."

I ask desperately if we can change the dates of my reservation.

"I'm afraid we're fully booked," he says apologetically, crushing my hope.

I never used to be one to shed tears easily, but since this weekend, it seems as if I'm on the verge of crying every other minute. I force the emotion back. My plan to check in and quickly freshen up before heading to a famous book market is now out the window.

My list of bookstores and collectors is extensive, and I originally planned to head into the city after a shower to start my search at the book market. But I'll need to adjust my plans. Today, I'll focus on nearby bookstores. I'll save the book market for tomorrow. Yeah, that's the plan.

"Is there a nearby hotel you'd recommend?" I ask the receptionist.

He unfolds a map. "We're here," he says, pointing, "and there are several other hotels within a ten-minute walk. A few even closer. See here." He quickly draws three circles on the map. "These are the closest options."

I take the map gratefully. I like maps—the ones on paper even more so. "Thank you. There are lots of hotels here. Right, so, can I leave my luggage here for a while?"

He checks with his manager and then turns back to me. "You're already in our system, so we'll hold onto your luggage."

Stepping out of the lobby, I'm instantly enveloped in sensory overload. Turning left, I begin navigating a cobblestone street that slopes downhill, then I stop for a moment to listen to the sounds filling my ears. The chatter of locals mingles with the rumble of yellow taxis and the screeching of seagulls. A small table outside a gift shop is crammed with all sorts of knickknacks and trinkets, from handcrafted jewelry to souvenirs. A plump cat is draped across some colorful pieces, completely oblivious to the world. I can't help but chuckle.

On the other side of the street, the Seven Hills Bosphorus Hotel is circled on my map. There are arched windows, and its facade is full of geometric patterns, almost lace-like. It has an elegant stone archway and a grand lobby with shiny marble floors.

"Please have a room," I whisper to myself. At the entrance, I pause. There's a seven-layer chandelier—yes, a chandelier. My heart skips a beat as I take in the lights and the glimmering crystals.

As I step into the lobby, my feet sink into the plush red carpet, which contrasts with the polished marble floor. Two grand marble columns flank the staircase, which leads to another level after the wide steps. A domed ceiling painted with intricate artwork looms overhead. It's both intimidating and intriguing, but I remind myself that this is no time to be an awestruck tourist.

I try not to stumble over the Turkish word I've carefully rehearsed as I approach the front desk. "Mehr-hah-bah." I give myself a mental high five for not butchering it completely.

The receptionist beams. "Merhaba!" She's dressed in a crisp white shirt and a tailored navy skirt.

"Sorry, that's the extent of my Turkish," I say, feeling silly.

"No problem, and welcome. Are you checking in with us?"

"I hope to," I say. "Do you have availability?"

"Let me check."

Time crawls as I wait. I note her skillfully applied black eyeliner. Its subtle flicks are complemented by well-defined eyebrows.

"You're fortunate indeed. We received a last-minute cancellation, and I have the Golden Horn Room."

"That's great."

"For how many nights?"

"Hmm. Seven days. Might have to stay longer." I'm hoping to find the book as soon as possible so as to put less strain on my budget.

"Yes, it's available for seven nights," she says, and then tells me the cost, which is significantly more than I would have paid at my initial hotel. She mentions that there's more availability next week, so extending my stay wouldn't be a problem if I wanted to.

"I might have to check elsewhere," I say, wincing.

"Certainly, but I should inform you that this week is particularly busy; most local hotels are fully booked. As I mentioned, we just had a cancellation. This is the last room available here."

My mouth feels drier than a desert. The possibility of not finding a hotel increases my pulse. "Okay," I say, exhaling slowly. "Golden Horn Room, please." I hand over my card, and she checks me in.

"It's on the third floor," she says. "Do you need assistance with your luggage?"

"Oh, my luggage. It's at a hotel up on the hill."

She gives me a curious look.

I think of explaining before deciding it's a long story. "I'll go and get it."

I drag my luggage back down the road, and it occasionally rattles as the wheels bounce over cracks and bumps in the pavement. When I pause momentarily, I taste sweat on my upper lip.

As I walk into the quiet room, I pause, noticing there's no immediate hint of a golden horn theme. My room is spacious and elegantly decorated. "Atta girl," I murmur.

Through the door, the balcony comes into view, with a petite table featuring a circular white marble top, supported by a sleek black base. On either side of the table, two black chairs with lattice patterns.

I grasp the smooth handle and step outside. Istanbul

comes alive again. This city talks. And every sound from the buzzing streets only adds to my already mounting nerves.

It's after 4:00 p.m. I've lost an hour. I need to get to work.

Chapter 9

Ava

My eyes snap open. I'm not in LA but Istanbul. I glance around the room, dimly lit by the lights outside. How long was I asleep? I push off the covers and feel the chill of the air on my skin. My arm stretches in a wide arc, releasing tension in my shoulder. I turn on the lamp and flex my toes against the crisp sheets. It feels as though a large plane has parked on my chest, engines roaring.

"Shoot!" I say, catching sight of the bedside clock. It's 11:00 p.m. I slept for hours. The plan was to briefly close my eyes after my shower, but my body transitioned into a deep sleep before I had a chance to take off the towel. It's the afternoon back home.

So much for checking out nearby stores. I haven't eaten much since I left home—Monday evening in LA. With tomorrow being a busy day . . . or wait, will it already be Wednesday here in Istanbul? Oh, right—it's still

Tuesday night. I really need to get some food in me before I lose track of more than just time. Is there even a room service at this hour?

I quickly grab a pair of jeans and a white T-shirt from my suitcase then slip on my long light-blue bamboo cardigan. I dash down to the lobby, rolling my tight shoulders with each step. Soft light fills the lobby as I walk in. A guest stands by the elevator, and the same receptionist who checked me in greets me.

"Hello again," she says. "How do you like your room?"

"It's wonderful, thank you. I was wondering if there's a store nearby. Is anything open at this hour? I'm just looking for something to eat."

"Lots of places are open at this hour. Let's grab a map."

"Thanks, I appreciate it."

"You're in for a treat." She spreads open a map. "See, Galata Tower is here, about a fifteen-minute walk. It's a historical tower, a landmark. You'll see it from many angles of the city. And here on this street, between the hotel and the tower, there are many places to eat. Also, we are only a few minutes' walk to İstiklal Caddesi, a busy road with restaurants, through this little street here."

Galata Tower

"You circled so many places," I say, my eyes moving from one circle to another.

"Yes, lots of choices. Our bar also offers snacks, but the kitchen closes at 10 p.m. There's also a restaurant just around the corner from us."

She looks at me. "I was about to grab food there before heading home. I can show you where it is."

"Yes, that would be great. Thank you."

"You are welcome. I'm Melisa, the hotel manager," she says. "Nice to meet you."

As Melisa said, just a short distance away is a large restaurant. In the front window is a colorful display of premade dishes: stuffed peppers, chicken with potatoes, meatballs, and so much more. I wish I were in the mood to feast, but my heart isn't in it.

"Is this place okay?" asks Melisa.

"Sure," I respond. "Lots of food."

We walk in, and I'm surprised by how busy it is. At the back, clean white tables are neatly arranged, and the air is alive with the hum of lively conversations.

"Do these people realize it's after 11 p.m.?" I say jokingly.

"Yes, the night is young in Istanbul," Melisa says. "We order first. There's no set menu—the chef chooses the dishes each day. Just point out what you want and they will serve it up. Then we pay and take our plates to the table. The trays are here." She points.

We line up in front of the glass panels, and my attention is drawn to a hearty stew. At the center of the pot, chunks of succulent meat are nestled among an array of vegetables—carrots, potatoes, onions, tomatoes, and fragrant herbs. But I end up ordering only lentil soup, a small bowl of yogurt with cucumber, and some type of creamy milk-based dessert in the shape of a rectangle with a golden-brown caramelized crust on top.

After paying, we carry our trays toward the back of the restaurant.

"Enjoy your meal," Melisa says, before sitting at one of the vacant tables.

I pause for a second. "Is it all right if I join you?" I gesture to the empty seat across from her.

"Please do," she replies. "I wasn't sure if you preferred to eat alone, so I didn't offer."

"I also don't want to disrupt you after a long workday."

"Please join me." She beckons to the empty chair.

I gingerly place my tray on the table. They say traveling changes a person, and boy, are they right. I'm someone who loves home and finds comfort in the familiar. Yet here I am, dining in a foreign city after 11 p.m. with a hotel manager I just met. Clinging to my fork, I scan the food on my tray. On Melisa's is a small salad and a vegetarian dish. "Your tray looks very healthy," I say.

"It's a late dinner for me. When I eat here after a night shift, I try to eat light."

My phone pings—a notification from my bank informing me of the amount charged to my card. "This can't be correct," I say. "They only charged me seven dollars. I have three dishes here."

"That's about right," she says with a laugh. "You can easily pay seven or seven hundred dollars for dinner in Istanbul."

A man approaches our table, and Melisa rises and hugs him. He nods at me, and I nod back with a smile. Melisa introduces us, but I don't catch his name. As they chat in Turkish, I look at the map to get my bearings and then add a few markings of my own.

Before he leaves, Melisa's friend smiles again and nods at me. Melisa looks at my map. "You added triangles."

"Yeah, I like creating my own areas. This way, a large, unfamiliar map becomes a few key triangles. I turn it into something that becomes familiar. I like studying maps." Then I pause and apologize for rambling on about maps especially at the end of her workday. I'm not usually a chatterbox, but when I get nervous or tired, I tend to go on. And I've been full-on nervous since the moment I saw Zack's face on the screen.

"No worries," she says. "You're not eating much."

"Must be the jetlag. I don't feel like eating, but I'm kinda forcing myself." I push the soup to the side and pull the dessert closer. "I'm sure I'll enjoy this though."

I grab my small square spoon to cut a piece.

"Sprinkle on some cinnamon," says Melisa, pushing a small metal container toward me.

"Thanks," I say. As the warm, familiar scent hits my nose, I'm transported back to my kitchen. I always add just a touch of cinnamon to my morning coffee.

I cut off a piece of the wobbly and delicate dessert then quickly shove the spoon into my mouth. The texture is a surprising mix of silky and firm, and the rich flavor takes me aback. "Wow, what's this? It's delicious."

Melisa's smile widens. "Chicken breast."

My throat tightens and I stop midbite, caught off guard. Chicken in a dessert? "You're kidding, right?" I say, before swallowing.

She shakes her head, still grinning. "Just a touch. Along with rice flour, milk, starch, vanilla, and rose water. It's a cultural delicacy."

"What's it called?"

"Tavuk göğsü, which means 'chicken breast.' This caramelized version is called kazandibi, or 'bottom of the pan.'"

I find myself enjoying the dessert. I'm pleased that I didn't ask what it was beforehand—if I had, I might not have tried it. *Look at me, leaping into another unknown, one wobbly spoonful at a time.*

I scoop up another creamy, thick piece. "It's unique, for sure."

Memories of my beloved dad surface. He used to tell me I was unique, one of a kind. It's hard to remember him now. He suffered a fatal heart attack when I was only six years old. I dreamed of becoming a math teacher, like him. At the time, I despised being called unique because I stood out. I had olive-toned skin and wavy chestnut hair while my mother, dad, and Grace all had blond hair and blue eyes. My dad wasn't my biological father. I know nothing about the sperm donor. My mother once mentioned "a mistake."

I snap back to the table. "Thank you. Umm, te-shek-kewr-lehr," I say, carefully enunciating *teşekkürler*, the Turkish word for thanks. "Did I say it right?"

"Yes, you did. And you are very welcome. I was on my way here anyway. So, what brings you to Istanbul?"

"A book," I say. "And to see Istanbul," I add, as if trying to justify my presence in the city. *Desperation to save my son's future.*

"A book?" Melisa pulls back her long wavy hair and uses a pencil to make an updo.

"Yes. A specific book. I'm trying to get tickets for the antiquarian book fair, but they're all sold out."

"I heard. Those tickets sell out months prior. It's a big event here."

"I might try my luck at the convention center in the morning, in case they release more tickets."

"That could work," Melisa says. "What book you are after?"

"*Pride and Prejudice*, a specific edition."

"So, it's a rare book?"

I nod.

"Ah, that makes sense."

Nothing makes sense lately, I think, while forcing a smile at Melisa.

Chapter 10

Lev

The city is awakening. It's just before 7:00 a.m., and I have an hour before I'm scheduled to join my team at the convention center. I wander down a narrow cobblestone street toward Galata Tower and am greeted by several gift shops and stores, a solitary barber with just one chair, and cozy cafés—all beneath Istanbul's old buildings. Most of the stores are closed, but a few of the cafés are open. I head for one with small tables outside. The morning sun is warming my skin, and I want to continue enjoying it.

Two men are chatting over small glasses of traditional Turkish tea, *çay*. Their camaraderie is visible in their relaxed postures and animated gestures.

Two teenage girls huddle together, the glowing screens of their smartphones capturing their attention. One is wearing a graphic tee just like Pera's. My daughter is still upset with me. Last night, she replied to my usual goodnight message with a curt "night" instead of her usual cheery tone. It's hard not to feel like I'm failing somehow.

I spot an empty wrought iron table. "Perfect," I whisper to myself, making my way toward it, already craving a Turkish bagel, *simit*. I love my coffee-and-simit mornings in Istanbul.

A woman is sitting next to the teens, one hand delicately wrapped around a steaming cup while the other turns the pages of a book lying open on the table. The English cover is visible.

A solitary strand dances away from her pinned-up chestnut hair. Her head turns toward me, and our eyes briefly meet before she quickly averts her gaze. Her long neck, sun-kissed cheeks, and deep-brown eyes are dazzling.

Then joyful children's voices catch my attention. Down the street, two kids, barely old enough to tie their shoes, are engrossed in a game of soccer. Their laughter echoes off the buildings around us.

Suddenly, the ball comes flying toward me. I instinctively kick it back to them, but my aim is a little off —the ball veers to the left and crashes into the woman's table. Her mug shatters, sending light-brown liquid in all directions. Startled, she jumps up.

Everyone in the area looks to see what caused the disturbance.

"Oh crap," I mutter, hurrying to the table, where the woman is frantically wiping her book with a tissue. She shoots me an annoyed look but continues wiping. I stand there awkwardly, not sure how to offer help. "I'm sorry," I say in English.

Taking a breath, I catch the aroma of her coffee as well as her floral scent. She continues to focus on her task, her hair coming undone and falling onto her smooth skin. Despite her furrowed brows and pouting lips, she remains undeniably striking. Freckles are scattered across her nose like confetti, her ebony lashes frame her eyes beautifully, and her defined nose is large but fits her perfectly.

I reach down, pick up the plastic ball, and throw it to the kids, who are standing nearby. I'm just about to apologize again, but before I can say a word, the woman scowls at me and grabs her small handbag from the empty chair beside her.

"There's even coffee in my purse," she says with a distinctly American accent.

I take a small step back. "I apologize for ruining your table. And your coffee. And your book." I hastily grab it as she moves to clean her purse. I request more tissues from the serving staff, and as I carefully wipe the book, I notice handwritten notes on some of the pages. I also notice that a few pages at the back are taped together.

I have a friend who does this because she can't stop herself from reading the end of a book too soon. I didn't know other people did it, too.

"Let me make it up to you," I say, still holding her book. Some of the pages are warped now.

"Please, let me buy you another coffee. I'd like to buy you a copy of your book, too."

She doesn't look up. "Thanks, but I think I just need some time alone right now," she retorts, as she begins removing items from her purse.

Does she have tears in her eyes? She's not crying over spilled coffee, is she? I crumple inwardly at the sight of the sadness on her face. Her dark eyes are like powerful magnets.

She continues wiping. "You can't just replace a book. It wouldn't be the same book."

A sleek red wallet emerges. She pulls out her driver's license and wipes it with a tissue. "This has coffee on it, too." Next, she pulls a small cube from her bag, its surface covered in colorful squares. It's a Rubik's Cube—the kind I loved growing up. But now, coffee drips slowly from its edges, pooling in the grooves between the tiles.

"I'm sorry," I say, shrugging, palms up. It seems as though I managed to dump most of the coffee into her bag. "It was an accident."

She stops and looks at me with fire in her eyes. "Playing soccer on a street where people are sipping coffee can't be wise."

I look away for a beat and inhale deeply to cool my own irritation. Then I slowly place her book back on the table and step back again. "Again, I'm sorry. Kids have been playing with balls in the streets for generations. It's part of growing up in Istanbul. But now, cafés have taken over their areas. Yes, I kicked the ball into your table, but I apologized. I hope the rest of your day gets better."

She sits with a tiny dip of her head. I return the nod,

my lips pressed together. Without another word, I walk away. The kids have resumed their soccer game. One of them, a boy with messy brown hair, dribbles the ball effortlessly while the other attempts to steal it. Their laughter rings through the air.

Even as a tourist, how can you not notice the joy on these kids' faces? Maybe everything is meticulously regulated in her world. Maybe she grew up with designated spaces to play in. But here in this part of Istanbul, kids tend to make their own playground.

I sigh. What a diva. But a dazzling one.

Chapter 11

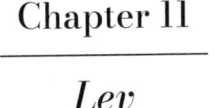

Lev

Before I get into a taxi, I walk for a while. I pause at a tall cube-shaped trailer on wheels with a glass top and a red bottom. The vendor is selling simits. I buy a dozen, one for each team member, and tell him to keep the change.

Today, my team will be busy checking the security systems for the event, which will take place over seven days; most book fairs last only three or four. This book fair is a global event that draws enthusiasts from around the world. The main event will take place in a large hall, but it's just the tip of the iceberg. The rooms with heightened security hold rare books and treasures.

At the entrance points, uniformed guard units will have metal detectors and X-ray scanners to screen all visitors and their belongings.

Throughout the exhibition halls, a network of surveillance cameras will provide continuous coverage.

High-definition feeds will be monitored in a central hub upstairs, enabling swift responses to suspicious activity.

Special attention will be given to the glass display cases housing rare manuscripts and first editions. Each case has alarms, as well as vibration sensors and motion detectors.

Outside, the perimeter will have 24/7 security patrols. Entrance points will have advanced control systems requiring electronic badges or biometric scans for entry, ensuring the integrity of restricted areas. Finally, all security personnel will be equipped with micro speaker earpieces with retention locks for seamless communication during shifts and incident responses to enhance coordination.

The convention center, a structure comprising four major buildings on the edge of the Golden Horn—a major urban waterway and inlet of the larger Bosphorus—is equipped with a state-of-the-art security system.

As I exit the taxi, I tear off a piece of a simit and enjoy the satisfying crunch of the sesame crust before my teeth sink into softness. No matter what life throws at you, in Istanbul, you can always munch away the stress.

The building on the left has two small towers. I find them a tad silly, as they look like they could be from a story about magic, and this is a modern building, but hey, I wasn't the architect.

"Hello!" I call to my head of security, spotting her in the main lobby.

"You know stress is the number-one killer," Frederica says. "Crack a smile now and then."

I shoot her a stern look. *What is it with this morning?*

Frederica is more than just an employee to me; she's like family, and I've come to know hers: her husband, her two sons, and the stories of her grandchildren.

For Christmas dinners and other gatherings, Pera and I have joined Frederica and her family in South London, creating cherished memories that have strengthened our connection beyond just security operations. But she's also one heck of a colleague. I often joke that she could land a role in the next Mission: Impossible movie with her no-nonsense attitude and tech-savvy brain.

"You're early," she says.

"My morning didn't work out as planned," I say, as we head to our operation hub upstairs.

We'll meet the local security contractors later, but for now, my team gathers in one of the large meeting rooms dedicated to security operations. There's a big screen and an L-shaped seating arrangement. I place the bag of simits on the edge of the table and move to the espresso machine to get myself a coffee—strong, bold, black, no sugar.

I take a sip and think of the woman at the café. I hope she ordered another coffee to improve her morning. I smile at the memory despite the chaos and irritation it involved.

One of my team members interrupts my reverie, taking a simit, "Thank you, boss."

Frederica stands tall at the head of the table. "If everyone is finished crunching, shall we get started?"

"I got you one, too," I say, avoiding eye contact with her.

She doesn't like us eating or drinking during these critical meetings, and I usually respect her authority. But sometimes it's nice to enjoy life's simple pleasures. A warm, sesame-covered bagel is certainly one of those.

"I'll have mine after the meeting," she says, her authoritative presence setting the tone. "Okay, team. We have less than two days to get things in order. And we have an hour before the local teams join us. Let's get going."

Our team of eleven flown in from the UK stands ready, a formidable group of individuals with backgrounds in security, law enforcement, and classified operations. I studied criminal justice and hold a master's in information technology. My training also included advanced courses in cybercrime investigation, forensic analysis, and crisis management—plus tactical and field training.

Collectively, we are tactically proficient and have a deep understanding of risk assessment and strategic security planning. But the fact that Yuri, the notorious art thief of Europe, is in Istanbul is a dark, stormy cloud looming over a sunny day.

"Folks, we have an important task," Frederica says, her voice steady. "It's not merely about safeguarding valuable artifacts—it's also about ensuring the safety of those who've entrusted us with their security. The local security team is very competent, but remember, they report to us and expect us to lead the activities."

She clicks a remote and an image appears on the screen: a short blond bloke with a cold expression. His fake-tanned skin is orange, and his blue eyes are like glass.

"Look at this face carefully: this man is known as Yuri. He's originally from Bulgaria, but left his hometown as a teenager. We believe he's made Istanbul his home, though he travels extensively across Europe."

Frederica glances around cautiously before continuing. "Keep in mind, his face may not always look like this. He often wears disguises, and Yuri is as fluid as water. He moves like a shadow and steals in broad daylight with clever tactics, often replacing valuable tomes with counterfeits. He's notorious for organizing illegal book swaps and has an insatiable appetite for rare books."

She stops and looks at the screen for a few seconds. "This event has some of the rarest books in the world, and we have intel that this man is in Istanbul. We're operating on a red-alert protocol."

Chapter 12

Ava

I swing my gaze to Galata Tower, which looms in front of me, and I sit back. Maybe I overreacted a little. But I'd been feeling like a fish out of water, and sitting at the café after a restless night was making me feel a bit better. The now-coffee-stained book is one that Grace had loved, so when I saw it on display in front of a bookstore that was, unbelievably, open at an early hour, I immediately purchased it.

Then, as I do with all my books, I grabbed the final pages and taped them together. I stopped reading the last pages of books when I was fifteen, but pages have a habit of opening up as they wish, so there's always a roll of tape in my purse.

I blink slowly and think of the man. I couldn't help but notice his fit body and big arms, his confident stride. The stubble on his cheeks and his rugged appearance contrasted with his polite British accent and his attire, slightly too formal for a 7:00 a.m. coffee run. I huff, annoyed with myself for cataloging him, and return my attention to the book.

I touch the cover and then carefully begin to peel off the coffee-stained tape, but my hand trembles and my fingers tingle. So I leave it be. Grace used tell me it was silly to avoid the final pages, that sometimes we need to face things head-on. Still, I refused to face the last pages of my books. I miss her—her bubbly personality, her infectious laughter. I often find myself wondering where she is and how she's doing. I never visited her in jail; I was busy trying to survive.

I thought Grace would contact me once she got out. Before moving with John to LA, I left my details with a neighbor in Phoenix. Years later, when I spoke with that neighbor, I learned that Grace had taken my number. But she'd never reached out to me.

I snap back to the present and grab my phone. Thankfully, it had been in my pocket and spared from the hot liquid. I open the front camera to check my appearance. My eyes are red and swollen from jetlag and lack of sleep. I put on my lipstick—a cherry red, the only pop of color on my tired face, then try to pay for my coffee, but the kind woman behind the counter insists it's on the house. She even offers me a refill, but I politely decline. Her act of kindness makes me emotional.

My legs feel heavy and my head spins. I stumble

forward, struggling to find a clear path to breathe in the midst of it all.

What did you do, son?

Tears cascade down my cheeks. I don't even bother trying to hide my emotions, not caring if a stranger sees me breaking down in public, instead focusing on the overwhelming fear I feel. I'm alone with an enormous task.

A set of wide steps connects the street I'm on with another one below. Each step is painted a different color. I descend a few steps and then sit on the edge of one. To my left is some green space. I need a moment to gather myself.

I rummage through my bag and reach for my Rubik's Cube, a three-dimensional puzzle with six sides and nine squares on each. The squares are covered by plastic stickers in various colors, which are worn from my constant rotations. I twist and turn the sections, but they don't move as smoothly as usual. The cube is coated with liquid, making it sticky to the touch. With a sigh, I drop the puzzle back into my bag. "Great," I mutter, annoyed.

I notice a striped orange tabby perched on a narrow windowsill. Then I see a gray cat walking between two buildings, deftly balancing on a ledge. A relaxed ginger cat with a white chest sits at the entrance of the building to my right, enjoying some food from a tray. Next to the food is a bowl of water.

"You guys just know how to be, don't you?" I say to

the ginger cat with a hint of jealousy. "Wherever you are. And I get my morning coffee splashed all over me. Mind you, he was quite a sight. But also arrogant, telling me about kids' right to play in the streets. Of course I know that."

The ginger cat looks up and blinks at me.

"You act like you were born to rule these streets. Back home, I thought I had my own streets figured out. Do you ever feel lost? What would happen if you had to leave your home? Would you still be this confident? I bet you would."

All right, stop chatting with the cats now. Do they note the different languages around them?

With a sigh, I pull out the small U-shaped pins in my hair, letting it tumble free. I shake my head and stretch my neck, which slightly eases the tension there. Then I flip open my small notepad and stare at the neatly written words and crossed-out lines. Everything has gone sideways.

The ginger cat comes close and rubs against my leg, and I give it a few good pets, grateful for its soothing presence. "You speak the universal language, don't you?" I say. "Thank you for that. Just talking things out with you guys made me feel better. I have a lot to learn from you."

First, I jot down my next step. Writing calms my mind. *Focus on one thing at a time*, I remind myself, just as I do when I create maps and flowcharts. *Break it down into smaller tasks.* The book fair is at the top of my list; I need see if I can get a ticket. As soon as I get up, I'll head there. It's about a 20-minute taxi ride away.

Then, with the help of the translation app on my phone, I scribble some questions in Turkish on my notepad. Each question goes on a separate page. I look up the word for "cat" in Turkish—*kedi*.

First, I stand, then climb up one stair, then another, and finally, I reach the top.

Chapter 13

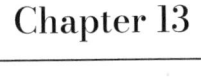

Lev

While waiting for the local security personnel to arrive, I step outside and walk around the grounds. I then head up to the flat roof, located a level above our operation hub, which is situated above the exhibition halls.

On the roof, tables and chairs are scattered around for personnel to relax on. I lean against the waist-high wall at the roof's edge watching and listening intently, scanning every inch of the street and the nearby buildings for signs of unusual activity.

"Hello there."

I turn to see Frederica approaching. "Hello yourself," I say. "I was thoroughly searched at the security checkpoint coming back inside just now."

She chuckles. "Red-alert protocol for anyone entering the main entrance. No exceptions, boss."

My phone chimes, and I tell Frederica I need to check

it. "Maybe it's Pera," I say wistfully. I remove the phone from my jacket pocket, only to see another spam message. I let out a disappointed sigh and slide my phone back into my pocket.

"How is she?" Frederica asks sympathetically.

"She's barely talking to me," I admit. "I didn't think missing her show would be such a big deal—I've missed other things before. She's really upset. I feel like a horrible father."

"Nah, you're a good father."

"I'm not sure about that. Anyway, I hope she'll get over it."

"I know you've always avoided drama, but with a teenage daughter, that's no longer an option," she says teasingly.

I roll my eyes. "Her mood is usually as unpredictable as British weather, but lately, it's been consistently overcast and rainy."

Frederica laughs. "She's a teenage girl who loves her dad," she says, gently patting my back. "I still remember the cold shoulder she gave Serra last year in London. Like an iceberg. Imagine the day that she'll meet an actual date of yours."

"Oh no, that's an absolute no-go," I say, shaking my head. "I'm not prepared to confront that anytime soon. But she accepted Isobel's husband as her stepfather pretty quickly. It pisses me off, but as long as Pera is happy, that's what matters."

Pera doesn't know her mother had an affair with the

man who's now her stepfather, and I intend to keep it that way. I don't want her to resent her mother. I know what it's like—I hold a deep bitterness for my father, for different reasons, and I refuse to let my daughter harbor anything like that. I love and care for her more than I could ever put into words.

Frederica leaves me on the rooftop, and I continue my surveillance. Nothing suspicious or unusual catches my eye. People sit by the water, a few vendors sell food, the city hustles and bustles. But then something does catch my eye.

"Well, I'll be darned," I mumble. The woman from the café is approaching the entrance. Her hair is down now, swaying in the strong breeze.

The convention center is currently closed to visitors. Could she be an employee? The thought of offering her another apology, and maybe even a coffee, weighs on my mind.

I rush down the two flights of stairs, but by the time I reach the entrance, she's already vanished from my sight.

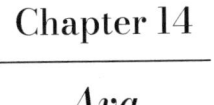

Chapter 14

Ava

The ticket-office attendant tells me that they won't be releasing any more tickets.

Disappointed, I consider coming back in two days—Friday, the first day of the book fair—in case there are any returns, then hurry off to catch a taxi.

My next stop is Sahaflar Çarşısı, the ancient book market I'd hoped to visit yesterday. This market is famous for its collection of rare and secondhand books. I have my questions prepared in Turkish:

> – *Do you have this book?*
> – *Can you recommend other places to visit to find this book?*
> – *Do you know anyone selling rare books?*
> – *Please call me if you come across the book.*
> – *Where can I get some cat food?*

I pause at the entrance of the long alley, taking in the picturesque scene. I'm ready to navigate the labyrinth of shops and stalls and hope to get just one clue as to where I might find the book. The market is heaving: Vendors chat animatedly with customers. Small shops are crammed together, their wares overflowing on display tables outside. The musty scent of old paper fills the air. I intend to visit three particular stores, and I'll pop into a few others while exploring.

The first is a narrow space with shelves reaching the ceiling, each crammed with volumes of all sizes. The shopkeeper, an older man with spectacles perched on his nose who speaks English, listens to my request but shakes his head. "There's an antiquarian book fair in a couple of days, and I'll be going myself. Maybe try there?"

"There are no tickets available," I reply. "But thank you."

The second store is brighter. Expansive windows let in natural light and illuminate countless book spines. A middle-aged woman busy organizing a stack of novels smiles warmly when I walk in. I flip to the page with my question written in Turkish: *Do you have this book?*

Her expression turns to one of confusion, and she glances between the words on the page and me. I realize that I accidentally turned to the page with the cat-food question on it.

Kedi maması nerede bulabilirim?

"Oh, sorry," I say with a laugh, as I flip to the page with the question *Do you have this book?*

Bu kitap sizde var mı?

But she also has no leads.

The owner of the third shop, a cozy, cluttered haven of literary treasures, looks up from the book in which he's engrossed as I approach. He's friendly and knowledgeable but also points me toward the book fair. Each storekeeper takes my phone number and promises to call if anything comes up. One tries to sell me a later edition of the same novel, but I politely decline.

I have to find a way to get into the book fair.

As the day ends, I drag myself into my hotel room, exhausted from my citywide search. The red velvety fabric of the armchair engulfs me, but my pinky toes are blistered and swollen. I had planned to break in my new sneakers during leisurely walks in Hawai'i, not by attempting the Cobblestone Street Olympics in Istanbul.

Tomorrow holds a long list of antique bookstores to visit. I'm also awaiting a call from the collector at a prominent antique auction house. I message Zack, asking if he has any news or updates on the Istanbul contact.

I need a drink—something fun and cheerful. Maybe a tropical cocktail. But first I need a shower to shake off the day. It's official: finding what I'm looking for is like searching for a needle in a haystack the size of this vibrant city.

After quickly stripping off my clothes, I twist the shower knob and lower myself onto the cool marble seat. Each droplet of water hitting my skin feels like a weight dragging me into a pit of despair.

Chapter 15

Lev

I slump onto a stool at the hotel's expansive bar. The day has been like a crash course in how to disrupt a security operation, with our real-life situation serving as the textbook.

It started with the burst pipe in the exhibit-hall bathrooms. Normally, I would have left it to the venue staff and plumbing team to handle, but since we're on red alert, I rushed to the scene. Imagine the headlines: "Book fair sunk by plumbing issues!"

That was only the beginning. Surveillance footage revealed suspicious figures lurking near key access points. The team secured every possible entrance and exit, but just when we thought we had everything under control, an urgent email from our cybersecurity team sent us all into a frenzy again. Someone had attempted to hack into our system through a phishing scam targeting our emails.

As my team tackled these issues, a thought nagged at me: *Is this Yuri's doing?* A burst pipe? Really, Yuri?

I sit back, savoring my gin and tonic. Tiny bubbles rise steadily in my glass. I wonder how Pera is feeling, with her show so close now. She's bubbly and energetic at home but quieter and reserved around people she doesn't know. Being on stage is a big deal for anyone, but even more so for her. I text her:

> You'll be amazing tomorrow, peanut. I'll be watching live.

The buzz of conversation, occasional clinking of glasses, and gentle background music calms me. And then, out of the corner of my eye, I spy a woman entering.

It's her! What are the odds? A faint smile tugs at my lips. *Three different places in one day.*

She heads straight to the bar and sits two stools down from me.

"May I see the cocktail menu, please?" she asks the bartender, her voice soft.

After she examines the menu and places an order, I turn toward her. "Hello again," I say.

Her eyes widen in recognition, but she returns my smile. "Hello."

I want her to keep smiling that smile.

"Can I make up for our encounter this morning by offering you a drink? Consider it my apology?"

She shakes her head, her damp ponytail releasing the

scent of her shampoo—sweet honey. "You've already apologized enough. It's on me for not appreciating it."

"Then how about we drown our apologies in our drinks?" I suggest with a grin.

After a moment of hesitation, she takes the stool next to mine. "Okay then."

"I'm Lev." I extend my hand.

"I'm Ava."

Her hand is smooth and warm in mine, and the sensation lingers.

Her cocktail arrives with a tiny umbrella and a slice of pineapple on the rim. She takes a sip and then places the tall glass back on the bar.

"Long day?" I ask.

"You could say that."

A text notification comes through. I apologize and look at my phone. Pera is telling me she's nervous about tomorrow evening.

"I need to make a brief call," I say. "My teenage daughter has decided to talk to me again, and I don't want to miss this opportunity."

"Of course, please do," Ava responds kindly.

I step outside the bar, and Pera answers the video-call on her laptop. Her knees are drawn up to her face, and she stares intently at the screen with wide eyes. Her hands press against her cheeks. A bright-yellow headband keeps her hair out of her face. I smile, hiding my regret. I should be there right now.

"Dad, I feel like I'm going to forget all my moves," she

says, pulling the headband from her hair. She fidgets with it, stretching it taut.

"Sweetheart," I say softly. "It's normal to feel stage fright. Just take deep breaths and remember, you've practiced so hard. And no matter what, I'm already so proud of you."

She nods.

"You'll do great, I know that."

We chat for a few minutes, and she stops fiddling with the headband. She even smiles at one point. After we say our goodbyes, I feel a bit lighter.

"A teenage daughter?" Ava asks when I sit down at the bar again, her eyes shining with interest.

"Yes, Pera," I explain. "She's fourteen going on twenty-five. She's stressed about performing in a dance show tomorrow evening. She's in London, and I'm here." A cold quiver passes through me, and I take a large sip of my drink.

"A dance show? How awesome." A smile spreads across Ava's face. "Sorry that you're missing it."

"Unfortunately, I had to be here. But I'll still be able to watch it live as her school is streaming it for families. She wasn't too happy with me, but the fear of performing seems to have taken over, so she's speaking to me again."

"Pera is a lovely name," she says.

"It's her middle name, but I like calling her that, and she does too. Her first name is Viola," I say with a soft smile.

"Pera. That's beautiful," she murmurs. "I've never heard it before."

"In Greek, it means 'beyond' or 'across,'" I explain, but I don't mention that it's also the historical name for this part of Istanbul. Then I ask, "Do you have one of those? A child that talks to you?"

"Yeah, I do. I have a nineteen-year-old son. Zack. What's Pera's dance style?"

"London Street Vibes," I say. "Very cool moves."

"How wonderful. I'm sure she'll be awesome." She pauses. "Anyway, this was very nice of you, thanks again, but I'm tired and was planning to take my drink to my room."

"Oh, I see, sure," I say. "Thanks for accepting my apology."

"No more apology talk," she says, wagging her finger with a smile.

As she rises, her knee brushes my thigh. Our eyes meet briefly, and then I watch her leave the bar. I don't want her to leave the bar. A part of me wants to go after her, but that would be foolish. I wonder how long she's staying at the hotel.

Don't be daft, man. You only met the woman this morning.

Hold on. I saw her last night, actually. She was the woman at reception asking about anything being open. That's helpful information. If she arrived only yesterday, there's a good chance she'll be around Istanbul for some time. I hope.

But why do I care?

Chapter 16

Ava

With a yawn, I pick up the ringing phone. "Hello?"

"Hi, Ms. Jenkins, this is Melisa."

Still half asleep, I struggle to free myself from the tangled sheets. "Hi, call me Ava, please."

"I might have some news for you. Could we meet in thirty minutes at the patisserie across from reception?"

"Is everything all right?" I ask, suddenly worried that my credit card was declined.

"Yes, it's all good. It's about a ticket for the book fair."

Hope flickers in my chest. "Okay, I'll see you down there."

I get dressed then call Zack—it's eight in the morning here in Istanbul and late evening in San Jose—and press him for information. Anything that I could use as a lead. A name, a photo. Anything.

"The guy is ignoring me," he says. "But I'll get to him."

"I assume he'll want payment for the information?"

"Pretty sure he will."

My Zack is a social butterfly, has always bounced from one group of friends to the next. Unfortunately, this time he flitted to the wrong people.

"Okay, Zack, then offer him something. But you're paying me back for everything when we get out of this mess. I'm already spending a lot of money here."

"I will. Oh, Mom, by the way, I'm back at home."

I frown. "You are? Why?"

"I just couldn't concentrate on my studies. I'm going to apologize to Elaine, but I haven't gathered my courage yet."

"Alright, I'd rather you didn't fall behind on your studies, but just focus on getting me the information. With each hour that passes, the book could be changing hands, which will make it more difficult to trace. Update me as often as possible. Even if just to tell me there's no update. The last thing I need is for you to be quiet now. I feel like a headless chicken in a lion's cage."

He just nods.

When he's stressed out or sad, he becomes eerily quiet and withdrawn. But he needs to step up; I need him. I'm completely alone in this giant city with millions of people.

After ending the call, I descend the grand, curving staircase and am greeted by famous faces captured in photographs lining the walls. Suddenly, I feel a slight sting on the back of my heel and I wince at the discomfort. I sit down on the staircase, glancing at the red and puffy skin.

Standing up, my gaze shifts to Agatha Christie's portrait. I've always enjoyed her mysteries, the whodunits. Maybe I'm in my own version—a who-has-it. I wonder if she walked these streets extensively while writing her novel. Did she get blisters too? "Alright," I tell myself, "deal with your own now."

As I head down the stairs, I spot photos of other famous people who've stayed here—celebrities, politicians, even royalty. The Swedish-American actress Greta Garbo in 1924, American First Lady Jacqueline Kennedy, Mustafa Kemal, the founder of the Republic of Turkey, and, of course, Ava Jane Jenkins from Beverly Hills—though naturally, no photo of me.

At the bottom of the stairs, I pause to look at the enormous chandelier in the lobby before stepping out to grab a Band-Aid from a nearby store. With what I need in hand, I return to the charming pastry shop tucked into the corner of the hotel. There are three tables positioned by the large windows and two against a wall, creating a cozy atmosphere. A friendly woman with a warm smile greets me from the counter. "Welcome," she chirps in English. "What can I get for you today?"

"Good morning. A latte, please, with an extra shot."

"Have a seat, please and I'll bring it over."

Settling in at one of the tables by the window, I apply

the Band-Aid while I wait for my drink. The display of colorful macarons and delicate desserts glistens under the lights of the patisserie, and the mirrors on the wall reflect the warm light. For a split second, I feel better. I gaze out at the street.

"Isn't this the perfect place for people-watching?" Melisa pulls up the chair across me just as my coffee arrives. She places her order and then dives in. "I made some inquiries about the antiquarian book fair."

"That's very kind of you."

"My friend knows someone who might be able to arrange a ticket. But they want to meet you. If you still want it, I need to call this person right now. And it might be expensive, as it's a sold-out event."

"Please call," I say, hoping I have the financial means to save my boy. "And thank you."

"Before you thank me, I should tell you that I don't know the person selling the ticket. I know you are a book enthusiast, but please be vigilant."

"It's a ticket. They sell. I buy. Right?" A chill runs down my neck. But, desperate times and all.

"Yes, I just want to make sure you know. There are scams out there. Will you be careful?" She takes out her phone. "Are you ready to meet them?"

"Born ready."

Melisa speaks on the phone in Turkish for a few moments. Her left hand rests on the table, and she softly taps her fingers, one after another, as she listens. Time passes. "Waiting," she mouths.

A minute later, she says something else in Turkish then ends the call.

"You're to meet the person in Taksim Square in forty-five minutes. It's a twenty-minute walk from here." She nods in the direction I need to go. "There are florists just before the large square—you can't miss them. Stand by the first one, and he'll come to you."

"Thank you so much for your help," I say, typing "Taksim Square" into my map app. "But how will I know who to talk to? Can't I get their phone number?"

Melisa shakes her head and explains that she already asked—he doesn't share his phone number. "You could always try tucking a rose behind your ear or something," she suggests with a playful smile. "I told them you're wearing a pretty blue shirtdress paired with cream flats."

"I initially packed for a Hawaiian vacation, but that's a long story."

"Works for the city, too," Melisa replies. "Also, the guy you're meeting speaks okay English."

I'm grateful for that.

I head up the crowded pedestrian street lined with stores, cafés, a movie theater, and bookstores. People flow continuously in both directions. I can't stop to admire the charming vintage tram that travels up and down the road; I want to be at the meeting point as early as possible.

A row of colorful flower stalls lines the old brick wall,

with people taking pictures and soaking in the vibrant atmosphere. I stand by the wall, blending in with the crowd. After a moment, I head to a small nearby store and buy a few protein bars to kill time before returning to the flower stalls.

After about 15 minutes of waiting and silently scolding myself for checking the time so often, I spot a man hurrying across the road.

"Hello, are you Ava?" He looks to be in his thirties and has short, curly hair. On his straight nose rest oversized sunglasses that look slightly comical on his face.

"Yes, I am," I say, my voice tinged with nervousness.

"We sit?" He gestures toward a set of benches.

"Sure." His mud-covered slip-on shoes are just the kind Zack loves—light blue canvas with a white rubber sole.

"You want book fair ticket, but it is expensive." His voice is smooth, and he has a thick accent.

"How much?"

He crosses his legs. "Because, a small issue, a discounted price. VIP ticket. Not your name."

Not my name? What does that mean?

He shows me a light-blue ticket with the book fair logo and a name on it—Mrs. Bergström. "Oh, that's not my name."

"No problem, you get in."

I examine the ticket. "Where is Mrs. Bergström?"

He rolls his eyes and sighs audibly. "Want this or not?"

"I do, but—"

"You have this, and you get in, guarantee. No ID check. This ticket is a VIP pass."

"So I can just walk in with this?"

"Yes."

I open the zipper on my bag. "Okay, how much?"

"Four hundred US dollars."

"Four hundred dollars?" I snap my head toward him.

He rises slowly, putting the card into the side pocket of his jeans. "I go if you don't want."

"Okay, how about two hundred dollars? I have two hundred in cash with me."

"Three hundred, last offer. It is VIP."

"But it's not even my name," I insist.

He shrugs.

"Is there a cash machine close by?" I ask.

"Dollar only," he presses.

"Okay. I'll go to my hotel to get money and be back in forty-five minutes." I don't want him knowing where I'm staying.

He nods. "I wait here."

I've traveled here with two thousand dollars in cash. Once I find the book, I plan to secure it with a cash deposit and transfer the remaining funds electronically. Keeping that cash is crucial, but getting a ticket to the book fair feels like a major step.

When I'm halfway to the hotel, pain in my toe forces me to stop. Leaning against a wall, I slip off my shoe. A small patch of dampness stains my ankle sock, and a burst blister on my small toe oozes painfully. I wince, pressing a tissue against it before pulling my sock back on. I walk quickly, determined to save Zack from jail and to see a smile on Elaine's face again.

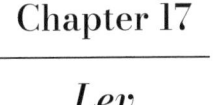

Chapter 17

Lev

Pera's dance performance begins in an hour. She giggled when I mentioned I'd be dressing up to watch her show alone in my hotel room. I'm nervous—as if I'm about to be the one dancing on that stage—so I decide to go for a quick walk. Just as I exit the room, my phone buzzes in my pocket. Pera's name flashes across the screen. I answer the video-call.

"Dad, I can't do this." Her voice is shaky. "I feel sick. I threw up. I didn't want the solo part."

"Look at me, sweetheart," I say, mustering all my calm and reassurance. She wipes away tears and meets my gaze.

"You'll get on that stage and give it your all." I silently curse myself. I should be there, wiping away those tears.

She nods. "Okay."

After hanging up, I take a deep breath and make my way down the stairs. As I pass by the bar, I catch sight of Ava sitting at a table. I head in her direction.

"Hello," I say with a nod.

"Hey there." She grins, her subtle almond-shaped eyes sparkling. "It's dance show night, right? How are you holding up?"

Her genuine interest warms me. "My nerves are shot. I think I have stage fright," I admit with a chuckle. "My daughter just called—she's panicking."

"I just ordered a snack. Why don't you sit down?" she says, gesturing toward the chair.

As I am grateful for the company, I slide into the chair across from her.

"Tell her to come up with a funny focal point—a reason to smile," she says.

I look at her quizzically.

"Growing up," she continues, "I participated in competitions with spectators. I wasn't dancing, but still. Smiling at the beginning always eased my nerves, so I'd locate a focal point—a crack in the wall, an empty seat, something obvious—and think of something funny."

"But she's moving around, dancing."

"The nerves will be at their peak right before she starts dancing. Maybe you could help. Tell her you're wearing silly pajamas. Get her to focus on that, so the brain activates dopamine. You can be her focal point, even though you're not there."

I frown. "But I dressed up for her show—I'm all buttoned-up." I gesture at my shirt.

"That's actually very sweet, dressing up to watch online."

"Okay," I say with a sigh. "Let me call her back and tell her about the pajamas. Anything that might help her."

I stand just outside the bar and call Pera. She answers fast.

When I tell her to picture me wearing silly pajamas, she blinks rapidly, a spark of interest flickering across her face. "Can I give you big ears?" she asks, giggling.

"Of course," I say. "If it puts a smile on your face, I'm in."

She holds her phone above her head, giving me a full view of her outfit. She looks fantastic, rocking a pair of loose-fit cargo pants with bold graffiti-prints and a cropped neon green hoodie. She's also wearing light makeup and colorful beads in her hair.

I give Ava a thumbs-up when I return. "That was really helpful. She even laughed."

Ava claps gently. "A great start."

"What competitions did you participate in?" I ask.

Ava's eyes light up. "Solving Rubik's Cubes, and I was also in a few math competitions. A long time ago."

I'm impressed. "That's remarkable. Rubik's Cubes used to be so popular." Suddenly, I remember she had one in her purse yesterday. I just hope the coffee didn't ruin it. It's hard to believe that the encounter happened just yesterday morning. It feels as if I've known her longer.

Impulsively, I blurt, "Would you like to watch her dance with me?"

Ava hesitates a moment. "Oh, hmm . . ."

"Sorry," I say quickly. "You probably have better things to do."

But to my surprise, Ava smiles, cute lines appearing at the sides of her mouth. "No, no. That sounds awesome."

"Let me see if I can get a meeting room," I say, rushing out.

A few minutes before the show is set to start, we head to the empty meeting room Melisa has just arranged for us, and I set up my laptop on the table. As I sit in the chair, my knee bounces up and down.

"Maybe you should try the focal-point exercise, too," Ava says jokingly.

"I know, I know. I'm typically calm."

She chuckles. "I strongly suggest you avoid entering dance shows." She slides a bottle of water toward me. "I grabbed an extra one for you."

The gesture pulls me back. "Oh, right. You mentioned ordering food earlier," I say.

"It's no big deal. I got it to go, so I'll just eat it back in my room," she says, gesturing toward the small bag resting on the chair beside her.

Then the show begins, and as Pera steps into the spotlight, I hold my breath. She moves confidently and effortlessly, in sync with the hip-hop beats. Then she starts doing daring flips and acrobatics. The audience gasps in awe. I hold still, watching her land each move perfectly and I feel a surge of pure pride. That's my daughter.

When she strikes her final pose, the theater erupts in applause. I leap to my feet, clapping with excitement.

"That's my girl," I say. On stage, Pera smiles. She's shining brightly. Then she bows and flashes a quick V with her fingers.

"Oh, that's for me," I say excitedly. "That V, that's what we do. Our secret message to each other. It means 'I see you.'"

"How cool is that." Ava is also on her feet, looking at the screen and clapping. "She absolutely owned that stage!"

For the first time since receiving that note a few days ago, I feel as if I can breathe properly. I want to hold on to this moment. My daughter achieved something incredible, and she's beaming with happiness. And beside me is a woman with a stunning smile sharing in the joy of the moment. Right now, nothing else matters.

Ava sighs. "Well, I should head to my room. It's been a long day. Thanks for inviting me. She was incredible to watch. Congrats! I wish my Zack had stayed fourteen, but they grow up too fast."

"Thank you," I say.

Ava turns to retrieve her bag, which hangs on the back of her chair, and as she does, her ponytail lightly brushes my face.

As the door clicks shut behind her, I let out a sigh and close my laptop. My fingers rest on the warm metal surface. "You're pretty awesome yourself," I whisper.

Chapter 18

Ava

I 'm in a taxi, on my way to my first antiquarian book fair, clutching Mrs. Bergström's VIP ticket tightly. I'm not sure I can pass for a Mrs. Bergström. I looked it up—it's a Scandinavian surname.

I think about yesterday evening. For the first time since the weekend, I wasn't consumed by my own problems. Instead, I was captivated by a fourteen-year-old girl's performance and her father's overflowing pride. What a great dad he is. A little too attractive to be in a room alone with, but.

As the taxi pulls up to my destination, I straighten out my crisp white blouse. I want to make an impression as I speak with dealers, vendors, and other book enthusiasts.

The convention center is captivating. Distracted, I didn't take it all in when I visited the ticket office a couple of days ago. The expansive modern building boasts a sleek design and occupies a large plot of land. Its outer walls are a blend of light beige and warm sandstone. The entrance faces the blue water, which my map indicates is the Golden Horn, and on the other side of the inlet is the historic center, a city skyline dotted with minarets and domes. Ha, so there are no horns in my room after all!

Standing by the water, I briefly admire the scenery before approaching the entrance, with its distinctive triangle shape and steps leading up to the front. Seagulls soar overhead.

The building on the left is striking, with its two short towers. The architecture with geometric forms catches my eye—perhaps inspired by the neoclassical style. It's charming and full of character.

A buzz of excitement swirls through the air, and the chatter grows louder as I approach the security checkpoint. The line for VIP pass holders is short, but nerves make me shift often. My fingers grip the ticket, the name Mrs. Bergström almost burning into my skin. A slight shudder ripples through me.

But entering the building turns out to be a breeze. Inside, I'm drawn to the triangular ceiling with its square and rectangular glass panels. The long lights hanging beneath the glass cast straight lines, creating a soft glow that mixes with the natural light.

Artwork covers the walls on my left, a mosaic of Istanbul. The crowd slowly moves toward the main hall. Following, I'm soon surrounded by hundreds of dealers in designated stands. The first to catch my eye is a stall with a wooden table draped with a deep-green velvet cloth. It's manned by a gentleman with silver hair, neatly combed back. Leather-bound tomes with gilded edges are carefully arranged in neat stacks. My eyes land on *Great Expectations*.

I think of my youth and the expectations I'd had then. I was alone, without any family, craving a place to belong. I'd expected that being married to John and having a house and home would help me find my place in life.

A woman with silver-streaked short hair arranges vintage maps at a stand labeled Voyages and Discoveries. I make a mental note to return.

Suddenly, all the noise dies as a woman appears on the screens scattered throughout the space. Ahead of me, more people gather, probably where the stage is located. "Hello, and welcome," a woman says, with a warm smile. Her sleek blonde hair cascades down her shoulders, complementing her navy dress. Her accent sounds Australian. "Merhaba."

She enthusiastically welcomes everyone, addressing a few hundred people as though talking with a good friend in a bar. What a confident woman. She discusses the impact that one book can have—how it can transform lives.

"Yeah, you could say that," I whisper dryly.

The hall with the rarest books won't be open for an hour, so I move slowly as the woman repeats her speech in Turkish. There are several aisles with narrow blue carpets. I go straight, breathing in air rich with the scent of dusty leather. The stands overflow with autographed books, photos, and letters featuring notable writers, composers, politicians, actors, musicians, and more.

Turning right at the end of the aisle, I'm surprised to find myself in the 1950s. The aisle is decorated with vintage lights, and there are five stalls: Between the Lines, At the Movies, Storytellers' Corner, and two others with Turkish names. There's a big gold cash register from 1952, as well as a brick floor. It's like stepping back in time—magical!

I stop at various stands to converse with the energetic dealers. I tell them about the specific book I'm after and a few take my number. Having studied the map, I then head for the rooms in a large wing on the ground level. These are exclusive and heavily guarded. I quickly press my palm against my thigh as I get closer and notice another checkpoint. I can only hope I'll be able to get in.

Elaine's version of *Pride and Prejudice*, a Peacock edition, was published in 1894, approximately one hundred years after Jane Austen wrote the story. Elaine had shared with me the antique collectible insurance details:

In excellent condition, bright gilt peacock feather decoration on cover and spine, green cloth boards. All page edges gilt—dark-green endpapers. Inside, there's no toning, foxing, or spotting: first edition thus (first illustrated edition), first printing, octavo (8vo). Illustrated throughout by Hugh Thomson.

Published in London by George Allen, 1894.
Valued at $38,000.

Valued priceless, I think. Elaine and Harold's love story is priceless. It shows how love wins against prejudice.

A woman in a charcoal suit motions for me to show my ticket. My nerves tingle as she takes it from me and places it in a bright-yellow lanyard that features the book fair's logo. She tells me to keep it visible at all times while in designated areas.

I nod and don the lanyard before entering the room.

It's like entering another world. The aroma of aged paper overwhelms my nose.

I love it.

The air here feels different, thick with history and importance. The room is dimly lit, and the soft glow of the lights creates a mystical ambiance.

Some books are behind glass, their covers catching the light and gleaming like jewels. Others sit on elegant stands, their pages open as if inviting exploration. I wander further into the room, drawn to the rare and unique. Some books are from the seventeenth century, some are limited editions of literary treasures—some are even by Jane Austen.

I inspect handwritten lyrics with a signature from 1974. *Freddie*. I read the explanation on the side of the display. It's Freddie Mercury's handwriting. My emotions catch in my throat as I look at the lyrics again. It's "Bohemian Rhapsody."

At a small stage in the back, a woman in white gloves gracefully presents a book.

"This is a compilation of short stories from 1924 by Hemingway. Initially, only three hundred copies were to be printed. However, there was a mistake during the printing process. The frontispiece, a woodcut portrait of Hemingway, bled through to the next page during printing, resulting in the release of only one hundred and seventy copies."

A memory invades my mind. *Mistake*. When I was fourteen years old, I mustered the courage to ask my mom about my biological father.

"Just let it go, Ava," she snapped. "He's gone. It was a mistake, okay?"

I was devastated.

When Grace came home, she sat beside me on my bed.

"What's wrong?" she asked.

"I'm a mistake," I lamented with tearful eyes. "Mom said it."

Grace stormed out and confronted our mother. After their heated exchange, Mom entered my room, her expression softened. She explained that she hadn't meant it the way I'd taken it—she had made many mistakes, but I wasn't one of them. Then she told me she loved me, something she'd said only a handful of times. This was one of those rare moments.

Why have my mother and sister been on my mind so much lately?

I continue moving through the space, surveying the

area and chatting with vendors. After a while, I step out into the main foyer for a quick break, munching on a protein bar before making my way back to the rare books.

In the afternoon, while I'm examining a book with untrimmed edges, some pages shorter than others, a man appears next to me. I've seen him talking to a few people. He has a round face and salt-and-pepper hair, maybe more salt than pepper, and he wears a loud checkered shirt and a belt cinched too tight. He's around my height, five-foot-four, maybe a little shorter.

"That's foxing," he says, pointing to reddish-brown spots scattered across both pages.

I don't remove my eyes from the book. "They're beautiful, almost like freckles," I say. "What causes it?"

"Where it's kept affects it over time," he explains. "The temperature or humidity in the room, the care it receives, or a touch of some mystical elements in the paper."

"I think it adds to the charm."

"I agree," he replies. "Some collectors actively seek out books with foxing."

I think about the book I've kept locked away for over two decades, tucked inside a wooden box in the drawer of a tall dresser back home. It was the last book my mother read before she passed. As she lay on her bed, I took it from her chest and saw that she'd reached the final page. *The End.* I screamed at her to wake up, but she never responded.

I wonder if the book has any foxing on its pages after all these years.

"Are you after anything special here?" the man asks, bringing me back to this book.

With a glimmer of hope, I glance at him. "I am, actually," I say. "*Pride and Prejudice*. A specific edition."

"Which one? I'm John, by the way." He extends his hand.

My shoulders tense. It's funny how the mind works. I wonder how long it will be before I can hear the name and not think of my ex. Another year? A few years? Perhaps never.

"Nice to meet you. I'm Ava," I say. "And it's the Peacock edition."

"Oh, that's a beautiful one," he says. "I may have seen one, but not here."

"Whereabouts?" I ask hopefully.

Suddenly, he shifts and turns. "Excuse me, there's someone I need to talk with." He quickly walks away. *Was he hinting at something?* I wonder, as I debate whether to follow him.

My decision is made for me. A tall man approaches and whispers, "Ma'am, I'm from security. Could you please follow me?" His eyes remain on the book on display.

I point to myself. "Me?" I mouth.

He nods and subtly reveals a badge inside his jacket. "We need a few minutes of your time."

Following him, I scan the room for the checkered-shirt man.

What's going on? My mind spins with a thousand scenarios, and nerves start creeping in—did I ask the vendors too many questions? Do I look like I'm up to something? Maybe it's the ticket I'm holding that isn't in my name. And what's with Checkered-Shirt John? He bolted like he'd just seen his ex at a family reunion!

As soon as we're out in the long corridor, I stop. "Excuse me, what is this? Where are we going?"

"The security offices, please," he says, pointing at the sign next to the elevator: *Security offices, no public access*, followed by Turkish words, presumably saying the same.

"This way," he says, beckoning to the elevator.

We glide up. He steps out first and holds open a door for me. My gaze is immediately drawn to the numerous monitors lining the walls of the rectangular room. They provide live feeds from surveillance cameras positioned throughout the building, an all-seeing view of every nook and cranny. A shiver runs down my spine as I become acutely aware of how closely we attendees are being monitored. My hand flies to the lanyard I'm wearing. At least a dozen eerily quiet dark-clothed individuals make the space feel even more intimidating.

"Hello, I'm Frederica, the head of security," a woman with cropped hair and a sturdy build says. "Shall we have a seat over there?" She points to a room on my right. Through the glass door, I see a cluster of chairs and a sleek table.

I quickly settle into a chair and hug myself. My breaths come in quick, uneven gasps; I detest being in unfamiliar environments. Being in this city is challenging enough, but this area makes my skin crawl.

"Can you tell me why I'm here?" I ask, my words tumbling out.

"Would you like a glass of water?" Frederica asks, instead of answering.

I nod, wrapping my arms even more tightly around myself.

Chapter 19

Lev

I place a bottle of water next to Ava.
Her eyes are fixed on the table.

"Here you go."

At the sound of my voice, she looks from my hand to my midsection to my face. When our gazes meet, she gasps involuntarily. "Oh," she blurts. "Lev?"

I stand tall, not flinching or showing any reaction. This is a security matter.

Her face hardens into a scowl, her chest rises and falls rapidly, and the color drains from her face. "Can we step outside for some fresh air?" she asks, her eyes darting around.

"Frederica," I say, without breaking eye contact with Ava. "Mrs. Bergström and I will take a walk. Shall we?" I extend my arm toward the doorway and take her bottle of water, which I hand to her as we walk.

We climb a set of stairs and reach a door leading to the outdoor space. I lead her to the waist-high wall.

Nearby on the left, a few people are taking their break, chatting casually. Further off to the right, two people are smoking.

With furrowed brows, Ava asks, "Why am I here?"

"This is a staff-only area, but since you asked for fresh air . . . Are you feeling better now?"

"Yes, I'm fine." Her response is sharp. Her fingertips brush her collarbone and her skin turns pink beneath her touch. "I mean, why was I taken to the security area?"

I sigh and look at the water. "I'm responsible for the security measures at this event."

"I see," she says. "And I like books."

During our previous encounters, we hadn't talked about our reasons for being in this city. I tilt my head and focus my attention on her. "Ava Jane Jenkins," I say. "Or Ava Jane Bergström?"

She remains silent. We also hadn't shared our surnames.

"Care to explain what you're doing with a stolen VIP ticket?" I ask.

A strong breeze lifts a lock of her hair. I resist the urge to tuck it behind her ear.

She inhales slowly. "I didn't steal it. The pass was available, and I bought it. Maybe I feel like Mrs. Bergström today."

I turn my body toward her, propping myself against the wall. "Surely you must have considered that the pass was a stolen one when you bought it. Unless Mrs. Bergström handed it over to you?" Irritation fills my tone.

She nails me with a piercing look. "Why are you acting like I've robbed a national treasure?"

I straighten. "Theft is unacceptable, whether directly or indirectly," I reply, my voice razor sharp. "Especially here at this book fair, which is my backyard right now." But as soon as the words leave my mouth, tension grips my shoulders, and a deep unease sinks in my stomach. *What is going on?*

"Listen, I had no choice," she admits. "I was desperate. There were no more tickets available, and I needed it badly."

"You were desperate?" I repeat, raising an eyebrow. *People*, I muse. So many expect to get whatever they desire just because they want it badly. However, I sense that there's more to her story.

"Yeah," she snaps, her dark-brown eyes sharpening, a thunderstorm brewing between us. She leans against the wall, shifting slightly to square up to me. "Look, the ticket was available. In fact, I paid quite a price for it. And today is only the first day. I still have a few days to go with it."

"Seriously?" I ask, tilting my head. "You're not going to be coming back. I'll have to confiscate it and fill out an incident report, which Turkish authorities will collect from us."

This wasn't how this was supposed to go. I curse my luck, clenching my jaw. I liked this woman, but I really don't like this moment, awkward and uncomfortable.

She suddenly places her hand on my arm, her pupils large in her wide eyes. She removes her palm just as quickly, but the unexpected jolt it sent to my body remains.

"Look, I'm sorry. I haven't damaged any books or disturbed anyone here, right? I'm a respectful and polite book enthusiast. Remember, you were the one who ruined my book with coffee."

A faint smile tugs at my lips. "Was that a rare book, your book at the café?"

"What makes a book rare?" she asks, a challenge in her tone, lacing her fingers and placing her wrists on the wall.

"Just wondering if I destroyed a treasure that day."

She pauses. "Yes and no. No, I bought it for under a dollar that morning. But yes, it was a treasure to me for a different reason."

The bellow of a ship horn makes her jump. I instantly place my hand on her back. Her skin is warm under my palm and her shirt. "Are you all right?"

She nods.

I sigh and chastise myself for inhaling her floral scent. "I should really follow protocol and make a formal report. But I won't do that yet. Still, I can't let you wander around with someone else's VIP pass."

"What are you suggesting, then?"

I cackle lightly. "Suggest? I don't think you're aware of the predicament you're in."

"It was available and I paid for it," she snaps. "Now I can't get into the book fair." Her eyes are stormy, her lips pouty.

Again, I curse inwardly. Why did we have to meet here like this? "That's correct. You dealt with someone involved in illegal activities and assumed a false identity at a high-security event—"

"Okay, I get it," she says, cutting me off.

"How about you return the pass to me and leave now? Then this will be the end of it." It saddens me that this will also be the end of our time together.

She tilts her head. "How did you guys know I wasn't Mrs. Bergström?" she asks, her voice softer.

"Does it matter?"

"I'm curious."

"I recognized you. And I saw your driver's license when you were wiping coffee off it."

"But that doesn't make sense. Do you check everyone's driver's license?"

I point at my eyes with my index and middle fingers. "We're watching everyone, Ava Jane Jenkins."

She hugs herself, hands resting on her arms. "Books are magical," she says, locking her eyes on mine. "And I'm after a very specific book." She stands tall, holding her chin high, defiance in her eyes.

I wish there were a way that she could stay, but not on my watch. Especially given our increased security measures. That damn pass isn't hers.

My tone is firm and uncompromising. "You will have to stay away from the book fair for the remainder of the event if you don't want me to report this to the authorities."

She nods coldly in agreement, her brows knitted.

"There are many bookstores in Istanbul that you can explore," I continue. "The old town is a bibliophile's paradise. It's filled with vintage bookstores that will satisfy your love of magic."

"I know," she bites out. "I'd like to leave now."

As we walk, I ask her where she got the pass, but I don't believe her story about someone approaching her outside this morning. Those tickets aren't sold around the convention center grounds.

In the elevator, she stabs the button for the lobby. We descend in silence, our reflections staring back at us, our white shirts reflecting the light. *She is stunning.* I swallow a shudder.

We walk through the corridor, and as soon as she steps outside, she lets out an exasperated sigh without looking at me.

She descends the wide staircase, her stride confident and purposeful. I don't like seeing her this upset, but security is everything. She pauses briefly but then keeps going and doesn't look back.

I'd been hoping to see her again. It's almost amusing how quickly the law of attraction worked in my favor—but with a twist. Earlier, I'd taken over a team member's station in front of a large surveillance camera to give them a break.

A smile spread across my face when I saw Ava. What a coincidence that we'd be in the same building again. She lit up the room with her radiance, even in the dim lighting.

It was impossible to look away. I watched the graceful tilt of her head as she examined books and tucked her hair behind her ears, until the yellow lanyard on her crisp white shirt caught my eye. A name was printed in large letters on the VIP pass: Mrs. Bergström.

My initial emotion was disappointment. We'd talked about our kids but never about spouses.

Then I checked the VIP records on our system. Mrs. Bergström was a woman in her seventies with silver hair. Ava Jane Jenkins was an impostor.

Anyway, now it's done, she's gone. Mild nausea churns in my stomach.

I push open the heavy door to the central operation hub. The air is thick with tension; Serra is pacing. When she looks at me, the furrowed lines on her forehead speak louder than any words.

"To what do we owe the pleasure?" I ask. Serra doesn't usually come to the operation hub in the middle of the day.

"What was that about, Lev? Since when do we let go of someone with a stolen VIP pass?"

Irritated, I motion Serra to the meeting room. It's inappropriate for her to challenge my choices in front of our team.

"Everything's under control," I say, once the door is closed. "We've dealt with it." Though I'm still unsure how Ava obtained the pass.

"And who exactly was she?" Serra demands. "I heard you were on the roof with her. This could have turned into a disaster. What if our book dealers or collectors had caught wind of a person with a stolen ticket strolling through their most prized treasures? Why on earth did you allow her to go?"

"You have to trust me," I insist, looking into Serra's eyes. "This person somehow got their hands on a VIP pass. It's impossible to prevent these things from happening when there's a market for everything. It happened outside the walls of this building, and we intervened within the building. We went up to the roof because she needed fresh air and the well-being of our guests is also our duty, especially if they're in our offices."

"Okay," Serra says, exhaling sharply. "Sorry, I think I'm edgy with everything, this red-alert protocol."

"I know."

Serra exits the room, her heels click-clacking loudly.

Why did I deviate from the protocol? Maybe the gut feeling, or I just wanted to cut her some slack. I think of the regal arch of her brows, of her eyes that blazed with determination one moment and softened with emotion the next. Of her high cheekbones and graceful jawline. She must turn all heads when she enters a room. Well, she entered the wrong room with the wrong pass this time.

Chapter 20

Ava

All my progress has been shattered. I dip my head as I walk away from the convention center. I try to suck air into my lungs, but it comes only in small doses.

Seeing Lev there wasn't just a surprise—it was a real shock. The caring father from last night vanished, replaced by the cold steel of his gray eyes and an irritating, I'm-all-business attitude. Apparently he has a thing about stealing. Well, so did I. But that was before Zack's monumental stupidity.

I replay our conversation in my mind while watching the roads pass by from the taxi. For crying out loud, I didn't steal anything. How dare he judge me! I need to push Lev's steely eyes out of my mind—fast. But finding a quiet corner in Istanbul to gather my thoughts feels like trying to locate silence at a heavy-metal concert. All those musicians are in my head right now.

Out of nowhere, I catch a glimpse of Galata Tower through the taxi window, its shining light winking at me from afar. I can't resist blinking slowly in return.

Reaching the hotel, I quickly retreat to my room and sink into the armchair, where I close my eyes. Once my breathing eases, I splash cold water on my face and reapply lipstick.

What now?

I ponder how to find Checkered-Shirt John. Could I wait outside the building? I could get a wig or something. I shake my head—why should I have to disguise myself to that extent? It's a public space. I'm allowed to be there.

A baseball cap and oversized sunglasses seem like the perfect choice, so I buy them.

The hotel lobby is buzzing with people. Spotting Melisa, I hope she might be able to help. As I approach, she greets me with a warm smile.

"How was your day?" she asks.

"Not good," I say, lowering my voice. "I don't have the pass anymore."

"You don't?" she asks. "Why?"

"When is your next break? Would you have a few minutes to talk?"

She checks her watch. "I finish my shift in twenty minutes. Shall we meet at Pages and Beans Café?"

"Pages and Beans. Cute. Not very Turkish, though."

"It's a new British chain," Melisa says. "You'll love it."

She gives me directions, and I head to the café, which

looks inviting. The entrance, five wide steps down from the street, is positioned at the center of the café. On the right, a floor-to-ceiling window features a tabletop bar with stools, while two smaller windows on the left add a touch of charm. Framing the doorway, two small olive trees in large pots bring a touch of greenery to the scene.

Inside, the café extends to the left and right from the central entrance, gradually opening up into seating areas.

To the far left, a counter showcases an array of desserts and cookies with a mahogany base and glass top. The floor is covered in large white tiles, each featuring a unique black design that adds character to the space. Near the window, sit two small tables offering a cozy spot.

A chandelier draws my gaze up. It's small and modern, boasting four lights, two tiers of crystals, and elegant curves forming a dome. Tiny crystals hang delicately from the dome.

Apparently I still like staring at chandeliers, just not the one back home. Fragments of childhood memories rush into my mind: flashes of a grand house, the sound of my mother's laughter, the embrace of a man who'd lift me and spin me around. But these are strange memories. We never lived in a grand house with a chandelier, my mom wasn't usually so joyful, and the man in my mind has no distinct features. I asked my mom about it once, and she said it was my imagination.

My eyes are drawn to a worn wooden sign that reads "PAGES," hanging above a wide opening leading to a back room on the right. I walk toward it.

Inside, books are neatly stacked on wooden shelves, and a couple of upholstered armchairs sit beneath them.

Then, I perch on a tall stool at the sleek bar counter in front of the expansive window at the front and tell the staff member that I'm waiting for someone.

I keep replaying what happened with Checkered-Shirt John, and the more I think about it, the more I wonder why he rushed off so suddenly. His words echo in my mind: "I may have seen one, but not here."

My chest tightens, and I close my eyes, inhaling the rich aroma of coffee and letting the gentle hum of conversations bring a moment of calm.

Minutes later, Melisa walks in and sits beside me. "So, what happened with the pass?" she says, by way of greeting.

"Day one and I was made."

"What do you mean?" she asks, raising both of her dark, shapely brows.

"The pass didn't have my name on. And they figured it out."

"They figured out it wasn't you? How?"

"Long story, but—"

Our server arrives.

The wrinkles around Melisa's eyes deepen as she smiles at the young woman. "Hey, Yasemin."

Yasemin looks to be around Zack's age. She has a long, straight black ponytail and a white T-shirt emblazoned with the café's name. "What can I get you?"

"Shall we share baklava?" Melisa asks me. "It's delicious here."

"Sure, baklava at Pages and Beans Café in Istanbul," I say. "Why not."

"When are you back at school?" Melisa asks Yasemin.

"In two weeks."

"Yasemin is a medical student," Melisa says. "She helps her mother here at the café whenever possible."

I smile at Yasemin.

"I enjoy helping out here and meeting new people. That's my mum," she says, nodding toward the woman at the counter, who waves at us. I smile and wave back.

After she leaves, I ask Melisa, "Why speak in English? I love listening to Turkish."

"Practice for Yasemin," she says, winking. "Yasemin's mother, the owner, worked as a manager at a nearby restaurant for years before finally achieving her dream of owning her own café."

I watch Yasemin join her mother, behind the counter, and my mind wanders to what Zack might be doing at this exact moment. Does he wonder how I'm doing?

"Yasemin mentioned that they'll soon receive a visit from one of the franchise owners," Melisa continues. "They're both excited and a little anxious. A franchise has specific requirements."

"This place is wonderful," I say. There's something that just draws you in—maybe it's the owner's warm, smiling face. "I feel like I could easily spend the whole day in that armchair in the back room," I add.

"Yeah, it's lovely. It's a very small franchise and each café is required to have a unique local touch, so it doesn't feel cookie-cutter," explains Melisa.

I think of my cookie-cutter routine, my cookie-cutter life.

Melisa's eyes are full of interest as she leans in. "So, you were saying earlier?"

"I have a question. Could you ask your friend to connect me to their friend, the one who sold me the pass? Or ask them if they know someone who knows about rare books in Istanbul?"

Melisa shifts in her chair. Fabric rustles softly. There's tension in her body as she leans toward me.

"May I ask why?"

"I'm looking for something."

"A rare book, like one at the book fair?" she asks, lines appearing on her forehead.

"I don't think it's one of the books displayed at the book fair. I need someone who knows where rare books are sold in Istanbul—I mean anywhere." I leave out the part about searching for a stolen book that's registered to someone in Los Angeles, which makes me doubt it would be at the book fair.

She glares at me.

I shift as well then sit up straight. "Look, I'm just after one rare book. I'm not undercover, and I'm not trying to cause trouble. Just one single book. And I'm prepared to do or pay whatever it takes to get it."

"Whoa." She tilts her head. "Whatever it takes?"

I nod. "It's important."

She's still tense as we allow Yasemin to set down our coffees in front of us and a plate of baklava between us.

"I suppose I could call to see if my friend knows of a friend." As she speaks, she swiftly removes her jacket, draping it over her chair. "But understand that these individuals aren't your typical tour guides or booksellers. Will you be careful?"

"I will. I promise," I say, though I'm unsure of how to keep my word.

I stab my fork into the baklava, cutting through layers of doubt. But before I can savor the bite, thick, sticky syrup cascades down my chin and crumbling pieces of the dessert crash onto my beautiful white shirt.

Chapter 21

Lev

All security personnel as well as Serra gather in our conference room at the end of the day, faces illuminated by the harsh overhead lights, to discuss the events. Yuri hasn't been seen anywhere. The only noteworthy security incident involved Ava.

The meeting concludes. Chairs scrape against the floor as the team leaves. But Serra doesn't move. "I'll walk out with you," I say.

Her eyes narrow slightly. "Lev, I still don't understand why you let the woman go without recording a formal incident."

My irritation flares; security is my domain, not hers. But I force calm into my voice as I explain myself yet again. "It was a minor incident, Serra. Let me handle security."

"I'm not questioning your operation," she replies, her

tone measured but insistent. "I just don't think you've ever let someone go before."

"This is the first time we've ever caught someone with a VIP pass they shouldn't have had," I counter. "And it does feel like you're questioning my decision."

She places her elbows on the table and laces her fingers. "I watched the footage of that woman. There's something about her that I don't like."

"You watched the footage? Why and with whom?"

"I asked Frederica while you were on the roof with the woman."

I nail her with a sharp look.

Serra sighs deeply, running a hand through her hair. "Look, I'm sorry. This is my hometown, and this book fair means more to me than any other. My grandfather may even be coming tomorrow or the day after."

Her grandfather isn't just any businessman. He's among the most influential people in the world. He took his father's company and turned it into an international powerhouse. He's a man Serra admires greatly.

"Just enjoy his visit then," I say gently, trying to reassure her despite my lingering annoyance. "He'll be proud of you."

As I sit at the hotel bar, a part of me—a significant part, I admit—hopes to see Ava. The air is filled with the aromas of various drinks being poured—mixed, just like my thoughts. Her words echo in my mind. *I didn't steal it. I paid for it.*

The salt of peanuts rests on my tongue. I think about how tickets are often transferred or resold for concerts. Even I once bought aftermarket tickets to see my favorite band. They weren't stolen.

If security for the event weren't so strict, I could be understanding, see past the act of paying for someone else's VIP pass. But my mind is rigid when it comes to differentiating between right and wrong. There's no room for leniency.

Still, thoughts of Ava's captivating eyes refuse to leave my mind. She's not a complete stranger; she's staying at this hotel. I even saw her driver's license. I could check her background. We watched Pera's show together and she seemed genuinely enthusiastic.

So what if she went to extreme lengths for a ticket? She's just a book enthusiast. Maybe I need to do something extreme and get her a ticket. Serra would disapprove, but it's ultimately my decision, not hers.

As the night goes on and Ava still doesn't appear, I second-guess myself. Is it even worth it? Maybe it's better to leave things as they are. After all, this city has plenty of bookstores for her to explore. Why am I getting so worked up over this?

After some internal faffing about, I decide to arrange a ticket for her, even if it's just for one day at the book fair.

My mind wanders. I imagine how she'll react when I tell her she can return. I can almost see the excitement shining in her eyes. And that smile.

I could live inside that smile.

Chapter 22

Ava

The taxi screeches to a stop at 8:00 a.m. and I stumble out in front of the convention center once again. It's a bright morning, so the oversized sunglasses don't look unnatural, and my hair is pulled up under the brim of my hat. I'm not inside the building, so I'm not breaking any rules. But thinking of Lev still makes me uneasy. That darn ball that morning at the café—he wouldn't have known my last name if he hadn't kicked it, and I'd be inside the building now. I wish I'd never gone.

I walk through the growing crowd, staying near the water and avoiding the entrance. I scan faces, hoping to see Checkered-Shirt John before he enters the building so I can ask him where he saw the Peacock edition. If he even turns up today.

Minutes tick by into an hour. Sweat beads on my forehead under the rough edge of my cheap hat. Thinking about how much money I'm spending in this city makes me cringe; the fear of going broke gnaws at me relentlessly. I quickly hush my thoughts, reminding myself that it's only for a few days. Still, I've already spent more than expected.

The morning sun is warm now, so I remove my light jacket and enjoy the fresh air blowing through my T-shirt.

Suddenly, I see Checkered-Shirt John, this time in a shirt with dull red and brown lines, climbing the stairs to the building.

Yes! I punch the air slightly. He's close to the top of the stairs as I rush to approach him. I pull down my hat a little and step onto the first stair. I glance up.

My heart leaps. Lev. By. The. Entrance.

He peers at me, his gaze piercing. His dark brows are a bowstring drawn tight, ready to release a volley of arrows.

I freeze momentarily then continue up the stairs quickly. The man I'm after enters before I can reach him. I pause again, unsure of what to do. Lev's eyes are on me.

Summoning my courage, my chin high, I approach him. "Hi, I just need to speak with that man who has just gone inside?" I point.

Lev gives his head a subtle, disapproving shake and stares at me fiercely. I don't flinch. Instead, I meet his stare, my own eyes narrowing in response. My breathing grows heavier as his storm-gray eyes deepen, darkening with intensity. Finally, I turn sharply and march down the stairs, the intensity of our gaze still pulsing in the air.

"Like I just suggested we rob a bank together," I hiss, as I walk away.

After walking for a few minutes, I feel the tension that gripped my body begin to untangle itself, but only slightly. I sink onto a bench. The weight of the city continues to crush my shoulders.

I scold myself. *Be realistic.* I don't even know if Checkered-Shirt John is a good lead. This is an impossible task. I should return to the States, be with Zack, use my savings for lawyers. But what about Elaine's broken heart? And what about my own? How could I bear to watch Zack walk away in handcuffs?

I remove the hat and then the glasses, wiping the sweat on my forearm.

A giant seagull stands on the ground nearby, its sharp eyes fixed on me. "Not your beady eyes, too. Leave me alone." I shoo it away, but it remains rooted to the ground. I spring to my feet and clap furiously, forcing it to finally take flight.

"Yes, you. Go away," I groan, lowering myself to the bench again. I look back at the entrance, now in the distance. "You go to hell too, Mr. All Business," I say, through gritted teeth.

I press my palms against my cheeks. *Okay, what now?*

My phone vibrates in the small yellow cross-shoulder bag lying on my lap.

It's Melisa. "I just got a call from my friend who knows a friend," she informs me. "He said someone is willing to meet with you."

"That's great news! Where and when?"

"There's an old movie theater about a fifteen-minute walk from the hotel. They want you to buy a ticket for the 3:00 p.m. show, go to the upper level, and sit in the last row on the right."

"A movie theater? Can't we meet at a café or something?"

"Not my call. And you said you'd do whatever it takes."

"True."

I replace the Band-Aid at the back of my heel and gather my things before flagging down a passing taxi. I'll visit a few more collectors and bookstores before I meet this person in the theater. It's not that I hope to find it on any shelves, given that the book traveled here only last weekend, but someone might have heard about it through contacts and connections.

By 2:30 p.m., I'm dizzy from the speeding taxis and running around. I've crossed several collectors and bookstores off my list.

Only a few people are waiting for the movie, all sitting on the lower level. As instructed, I sit in the back row of the upper level of the gorgeous old movie theater, which has red seats and cream-and-gold walls. On the screen, a Turkish commercial shows a family enjoying time together. Mom hangs vibrant-colored clothes on the line while Dad and the kid play tag.

The lights dim. A man approaches and sits in the aisle seat, next to me. From the corner of my eye, I observe how enormous he is. His knees touch the seats in front of him. Sunglasses sit on top of his bald head.

"You Jane?" he asks in a near whisper, without looking at me. I had Melisa use my middle name.

"Yes," I reply softly. "Do you know how to find a specific rare book in Istanbul?" *Wow!* I mentally pat myself on the back for my directness.

"Which book?"

I give him the piece of paper I've been showing booksellers all day.

He studies the note. "Information comes with a price, sweetheart."

"It's Jane."

His jaw tightens. "Jane," he says, his voice a low growl. "Five hundred dollars."

"For information only?" I exclaim.

He leans close to me, his eyes on the screen. "You don't want it?" he asks, his accent making the letter *t* particularly prominent.

"What information do you have?" I whisper. "Can you get me the book? Or do you have a specific person, or location?"

"Yes, I can give you a specific person and location. But make up your mind, fast."

I think for a few seconds. What if I offer less? I'll be broke and in debt at this rate. Nervously, I fumble with the strap of my bag, a knot tightening in my stomach. I rub a clammy palm on my thigh before I make the offer. "How about three hundred?"

"Okay," he says. He rises, and the gun at his waist flashes.

"Okay?" I ask. Maybe I should have offered fifty.

But before I can get out the cash, someone else enters the upper level. He whispers into the big man's ear.

"Wait for a moment," the man says to me, and then leaves with the other guy.

The lights dim. The movies starts.

I anxiously wait. A few minutes later, I look up as the towering presence returns.

"Deal is off," he says dryly.

With that, he leaves.

I'm frozen in shock for just a moment before I race out of the dark theater and into the bright upstairs lobby. "Why?" I demand, catching up to him.

"Because it is." His words are cold and final, mirrored by his cold eyes and knitted brows. He doesn't even glance in my direction as he storms toward the grand staircase on our left.

"What?" I shout, trailing him. "But we had an agreement."

"Keep your voice down," he says warningly.

I grab his arm before he can reach the stairs. "Please."

"No," he growls, looking at my hand on his arm.

I let go. An employee, the only other person around, watches us curiously.

I step in front of the man. "I won't tell anyone," I whisper.

He towers over me, making me look up. "No, Jane."

146

He steps past me and heads toward the stairs, leaving me standing confused at the top. I quickly descend and catch up to him again as he exits into the busy street.

"Excuse me," I say, pointing at my cross-shoulder bag. "I have the money here."

He shakes his head and walks away.

Watching him, I feel frustrated, scared, and puzzled. Should I follow him? Maybe not; he has a gun. Who was that other person? The change in his mood happened faster than a bullet leaving a barrel.

The sounds of traffic and people seem muffled. My disappointment hangs in the air like a thick blanket. My shoulders droop, and my steps are heavy as I look for a quiet spot.

I come across a quaint area with stores selling herbs and natural remedies. I touch a few herbs in pots and inhale the scent of fresh rosemary. My mind is still consumed by what just happened. Suddenly, I spot him— the big man—standing a few stores down, watching me.

He's following me. Why? Is he going to try to steal from me? He knows I have cash in my bag. That must be it. He doesn't want a deal, but he wants the cash. *Great strategy, Ava, telling strangers you've got cash in your bag. Genius, you!*

His steely eyes twitch.

My stomach flips. I increase my pace and dart into a courtyard-like arcade buzzing with people. There are restaurants on either side, and tables outside.

Then I spot a bookstore. That's it! A place to hide among

other people. I step through the open door. Numerous bookshelves contain thousands of secondhand books. I linger near the entrance for a moment. *Did he see me enter?*

A man and a woman are having a heated discussion behind some shelves in the corner. I crane my neck. The woman seems visibly upset.

"But Barb," the man says. He's standing behind a small counter with a large cash register on it. "She was meant to be here two hours ago. It's not my fault that she didn't turn up."

"We planned this months ago," the lady retorts.

They both have accents. Their white hair and the deep lines on their faces suggest that they're in their late eighties. The man's wide tie is slightly crooked, and his glasses sit firmly on the bridge of his large nose. Large freckle-like spots pepper the woman's face and forehead. She wears a shawl over her shoulders and black trousers. I wonder why they're speaking in English.

When they notice me, I offer a simple hello and move my attention to the books on the shelf in front of me, hoping they didn't think I was eavesdropping.

"Oh my goodness," the man says. "You're here!"

"Me?"

"You scared us," he continues. "Look, Barb, she's arrived. Go on home, dear; I'll be there soon."

A huge smile spreads across the woman's face. Before I can respond, she flies out of the store like a bird released from a cage.

Seeing my confusion, he begins to speak. Rapidly. In Turkish.

"But—"

He cuts me off, walking slowly toward me, saying many more things as he points at the cash register.

I glance outside and don't see my pursuer. With relief, I turn back to the man. "Can I please—"

He cuts me off again, this time in English.

"This is our sixty-second wedding anniversary. I made a promise to her. I don't want to miss our ferry."

"Ferry," I repeat. My time in Istanbul has been getting weirder by the minute. It's Saturday afternoon already; I can't waste time here. I need a new plan.

I try again to explain to the owner that I'm not the person he thinks I am, but he grabs his black walking cane and puts on a hat. A grin spreads across his face.

"You see, I met my wife, Barbara, while traveling in New Zealand. We've lived all over the world, but we moved to Istanbul when my father needed me. That was over 40 years ago. And every year since, we celebrate our anniversary at our favorite spot—an island not far from here. She loves islands."

He moves slowly. "It's not a busy store, a few collectors here and there. Mind you, Sundays can be busy, but you'll be fine. Everything you need is in this folder, including the Wi-Fi code. There's a small café two doors down; here's their number. When you call them, tell them you work for Mr. Babayan, and they will bring you tea, coffee, anything else you want. Their cheese toast is really good."

Oh, cheese toast, I think. *That makes everything better.* But . . .

A few collectors.

I've been surrounded by books, yet nothing I've tried so far has helped me get close to one particular book. If the key to a bookstore is being offered while I'm looking for a book, maybe I'm meant to take it. The collectors can come to me. Someone might know something that can help me.

And 62 years of marriage—that makes me smile.

Mr. Babayan opens a drawer and grabs a set of brass and silver keys. They dangle from a worn leather key chain like an open book. He holds them out. The cool metal feels heavy in my hand.

"I'll see you on Monday morning," he says, tipping his hat. He slowly makes his way out, relying on his cane for support but maintaining a straight posture. The little chime dings as he closes the door.

I'm stunned. This feels so strange. I barely uttered a word beyond "hello," yet here I am, holding the key to a bookstore. In Istanbul. I peer outside again but still don't see the man who was following me.

A few minutes later, a woman rushes into the store, her cheeks flushed. Turkish streams from her mouth. Realizing I don't understand, she switches to English and tells me she's here to watch the store. I let her know that Mr. Babayan arranged for me to cover as she was late. She apologizes and leaves.

I walk around in the store. Could the book I'm looking for be here? Wouldn't that be a miracle? Am I meant to be here? Should I stay still in this fast-paced nightmare instead of running around? I need to gather my thoughts and get my heartbeat back to normal.

Standing in the middle of the shop, I scan the sea of books arranged in every way imaginable: upright, sideways, piled on the ground, and pressed against walls and shelves.

This place feels otherworldly, a space to stop, breathe, and just be.

Chapter 23

Lev

Ava's return this morning threw me off completely. I'm still peeved about it now, midafternoon, as I walk through the convention center. She'd agreed to keep away but undermined me by turning up nevertheless. How foolish I was even to consider arranging a ticket for her. It was a harsh reminder to concentrate on business, protocols, and procedures. It's black-and-white: no gut feeling or any other nonsense.

Could she be connected with Yuri? Likely not. She seems quite an amateur. Seriously, are we in a cheesy movie? She thinks a hat and sunglasses will disguise her?

And anyone from Yuri's team would have remained composed and detached, whereas Ava panicked when she came to our offices. This morning when I saw her, her eyes darted around and her pulse throbbed visibly at her temple.

Cold and calculating thieves would have walked away as if nothing had happened. There's something different about her. There's no way Ava is a professional thief. Not a chance.

Because I know thieves. I know how their eyes work. I know how calmly they can walk out of a disaster. I know a skilled one when I see one.

Because my father is one.

He's one of the most prolific art thieves in Europe, in fact—a cunning con man who used to take his little son with him to art galleries and museums dressed in roomy jackets. Memories flood my mind, vivid and raw. I'm about seven or eight years old, my small hand enveloped in my father's firm grasp. I recall his glances, his quick movements, a stolen item slipping into the pocket of his large coat, maybe a bracelet or a small book. I detested my dad for what he was doing, for the way he was dragging me into that world. I still detest the act of stealing. Now, I actively work to prevent it.

In my office back home, I still keep the news articles detailing my father's hundreds of operations, written after he was caught. His face was splashed across newspapers and television stations. The papers reported that he'd involved his son but didn't reveal any details about me, since I was just a child.

My father had once been well respected in his community. A family man. A dentist. My wonderful daddy. Then he started taking me on trips to museums and galleries. "Go ahead, son," he'd say, pushing me toward the guards. "Ask about this piece, listen carefully, and then tell me everything you learned."

I would do as he'd asked, trying my best to remember every detail so I could report back to my father. He was always so proud of me, so I began joining him on more of his visits. Sometimes he wouldn't let go of my hand; he'd hold it tightly as we made multiple trips to the same place. I realized later that in these instances, he was scoping things out before the big heist.

One night when I was eleven years old, my mother rushed into my bedroom and told me that we were leaving Istanbul forever—without Dad.

"Honey, your dad has done things that are not okay," my mother said. "Too many people want to know about him and his family, and that includes you. I need to protect you and your future."

I remember confessing to my mom, apologizing. "I know, Mom. Sometimes he'd take me out of school, and we'd visit museums together. He told me to keep it a secret from you—it was a father-and-son thing."

She held me close and told me that it wasn't my fault.

"Maybe he'll stop if we ask him, Mom," I said pleadingly.

"Too late now, hon," she responded, her eyes sad. "Believe me, I tried."

And that was it. I was devastated to leave my dad and my grandma. I loved our life in Istanbul, my school, and my friends.

It still hurts to think about that drive to the airport. I cried my eyes out on the plane. Despite everything, I loved my dad. He was my hero, no matter what. I hoped he'd turn up at the airport, or that he'd stop what he was doing and join us in Britain. But a few years after we left Istanbul, he got caught drilling a hole through a six-foot vault wall, which he'd reached by climbing down a lift shaft.

My mother and I adopted her maiden name, Bowman. I didn't return to Istanbul until I was twenty-one, to visit my grandmother—and the city I loved.

"Your mother took you away from me," my grandmother said, sobbing and holding me tightly.

"No, Grandma, she was only trying to protect me."

Leaving memory lane, I notice the crowd in the convention center is thinning.

I need to get a grip and stop being so bloody upset about Ava. And to do so, I have to find out more about her.

Serra stands by a display, her gaze locked on a manuscript. Her fingers trail over the glass. I pause for a moment, observing her. She's been a consistent presence in my life, though not in a committed way. I often ponder why she isn't in a relationship. She's beautiful, intelligent, and graceful.

As a single father, casual dating works for me. Being head-over-heels in love with Pera's mother hurt me in the end, so no more for me. Serra and I enjoy a sense of familiarity and a nonjudgmental connection whenever our paths cross. Yet on this trip, neither of us has made the effort. For some reason I don't feel the chemistry, and it seems as if this is a mutual feeling.

"Serra." My voice cuts through the ambient noise. She looks to be deep in thought. I get closer. "Serra?"

"Hey, Lev. I was miles away."

"I see that. Is everything okay?"

"Yes. Can we get out of here?"

I check my watch. "Now? The fair isn't over for another thirty minutes."

"I know, I know. But what's the point of having the best teams if we need to be around every second?"

"Oh, okay," I reply, surprised. Serra typically turns up earlier than anyone and leaves after the event finishes.

Minutes later, we're out walking by the water.

"How long are you in Istanbul?" she asks.

"I'll stay for a few days after the fair."

A handful of times over the past several years, I've almost told her about my background—that I'm half Turkish and have a grandmother in Istanbul. But then how would I explain who my father is? Occasionally I feel dishonest, but there's a line, albeit thin, between withholding information and lying.

We head for a covered arcade inside a historical building. There are three restaurants on each side with tables seating four covered in white tablecloths. The arcade also contains a secondhand bookstore and a record shop accessible through a smaller street that connects to shops selling herbs and natural remedies.

Serra and I take seats outside our favorite seafood restaurant, and a server soon fills our table with small appetizers: savory dips, marinated olives, flavorful cheeses, and other bites.

"That was another successful day under your expert guidance," I say, smiling.

She nods. "Thank you, it's teamwork. Actually, there's something I need to tell you," Serra begins, but my attention wavers as a woman emerges from a bookstore. *Oh, my giddy aunt.* Could that really be Ava?

Yep.

She bends down then inserts a key into the bottom lock and turns it. She straightens, uses a second key to secure the top lock, and gives the door a firm tug.

"What's happening over there?" Serra asks.

"I'm not entirely sure," I admit, puzzled.

"What is it?" She turns around. "Wait a minute, isn't that the woman with the pass?"

I nod. "Yeah, how do you— Oh right, you watched the footage."

So Ava works at a bookstore here, but she claimed to be just visiting. *What's going on?*

Ava heads toward the arcade exit, moving in our direction. Nearing our table, she sees me and stops abruptly, a surprised expression on her face.

"Hello again," I say.

The hat and sunglasses from this morning are nowhere to be seen, but everything else is the same. White sneakers peek from beneath the hem of her jeans, and her relaxed blue sweater reveals skin on her left shoulder.

Serra's eyes narrow as she looks up at Ava, and a forced smile rests on her lips.

"Well, well, if it isn't the unexpected visitor." She examines Ava with a piercing gaze. "I don't believe we've had the pleasure of being properly introduced." She extends her hand, and the smile disappears. "I'm Serra, the event director at the book fair you intruded upon."

"Serra, we've already dealt with that situation," I say firmly.

But Ava doesn't back down. Instead, she inches closer to my side of the table so she can look at Serra. "You're the person who gave the welcome speech. It was outstanding. I especially liked what you said about how a book can change us and transform our lives. It's a pleasure to meet you, Sarah."

"Not Sarah. Serr-*ra*," Serra says. "That's s-e-r-r-a. It's a Turkish name."

"Oh, sorry. Serr-raa. I'm Ava." The two lock eyes. "I thought you were Australian. And for the record, I didn't intrude on anything."

"Sure." Serra bats her eyelashes and gives Ava a big, thin grin. "I'm sorry, how rude of us. Would you like to join us?"

Her invitation is unexpected, but I'm okay with it because now I'm even more intrigued by Ava. Who is she? I can't make up my mind about her.

Ava hesitates, glancing at me. "Uhm, I don't want to interfere."

"Please," Serra urges, gesturing toward the unoccupied chair beside her.

"Join us," I say, raising my hand and pointing to the same chair.

"All right, just for a bit." She removes the shoulder bag and sets it on her lap.

I notice how fast she scans both exits of the narrow arcade. Our table sits almost in the middle of it. "The food here is delicious—you really should experience it," I say.

"Thank you, but I won't be staying long."

Serra looks at me disapprovingly. I meet her gaze with a look that says *What? You invited her.*

"Did you just lock up that bookstore?" I ask.

"Um, yes, helping a friend." Ava looks at the dishes on the table. "These look awesome." Her body is slightly closed off, arms folded.

"You must try them all," I say. *Who are you, Ava? Why can't I resist this pull toward you?*

A server places a large dish of stuffed mussels in the middle of the table. The shells gleam with a sheen of oil, and a wave of savory spices fills the air.

"What is this?" Ava asks.

I wait for Serra to respond, as she loves this dish, but her lips are closed, and she gazes away, as if looking at something behind me.

"A cultural treasure," I say. "Midye dolma. Mussels stuffed with aromatic rice, herbs, and spices. You gently break off the top shell, squeeze in some lemon juice, and then use the loose shell as a spoon to scoop the mixture. Take one, please." I pass her a small plate.

Ava takes a mussel and brings it close to her face. Her eyes light up. "It comes with its own natural spoon."

I point out the empty plate in the middle of the table. "That's for the shells."

"So, Ava, what brings you to Istanbul?" Serra asks, with an obvious frostiness. She deftly cracks open a mussel.

"Visiting," Ava replies, her voice guarded.

Serra's eyes narrow ever so slightly, and her thin smile doesn't quite reach her eyes as she continues her meticulous mussel extraction.

"Visiting who?" Serra asks.

Ava hesitates. "No one in particular."

She gestures toward a yogurt dish with dark-red flakes and a single roasted chili pepper. "Is this spicy?"

"It's the hottest; it takes courage to eat," I say, attempting to defuse the palpable tension oozing out of Serra.

Ava nods, scoops an overflowing amount onto her fork, and takes a big bite.

"Whoa, be careful," I exclaim, chuckling and watching her expression. "That is seriously hot."

"I like it," Ava replies, with a cough and a slight cringe. Adorable.

Two musicians, one with a clarinet and another with an accordion, mount the stage inside the restaurant. I point to them. "There will be live music soon."

Serra cracks a mussel with an aggressive snap. The shell lands on the table close to Ava.

Ava picks it up and drops it on the shell plate.

Serra turns her head toward Ava. "Did you pick up a rare-book interest while visiting Istanbul, or have you always had it?"

"As you said in your speech, books change us, whether rare or not," Ava responds. Her lips curve up, and small lines appear at the edges. Her eyes crinkle at the edges. I admire how confidently she's handling Serra's interrogation. And I quickly chastise myself.

"So, where are you from?" Serra asks.

"LA."

Trying to steer the conversation to neutral ground, I ask Serra, "Didn't you used to live in LA?"

Serra waves a hand dismissively. "Yes, I did. A long time ago, when I was studying."

Ava grabs her small bag from her lap and stands. "Thank you both for inviting me to your table. Can I help with the bill?"

I lift my hand to stop her. "You're our guest."

She smiles warmly. "Thanks again. Enjoy the rest of your evening."

She holds my gaze for a brief moment before turning and making her way to the exit.

"I'm not following, Serra," I say, once Ava is out of earshot. "Why invite her if you're just going to be unfriendly?"

"Are you into her?" Serra asks, her tone frosty.

"That's a ridiculous question."

She frowns. "I don't like her, Lev. She's trouble. You should steer away."

"Then why did you encourage her to join us?"

"Just curious."

"Curious or not, you don't treat a guest at your table with hostility. That's not very Istanbulian."

Serra cracks another mussel.

"Are you planning to win this battle with these mussels anytime soon?" I say teasingly. "Anyway, you were going to share something with me earlier. What was it?"

"Doesn't matter," Serra says firmly, then lets out a quiet, exasperated sigh.

I lean back. My mind is a whirlwind.

How can I see Ava again?

Chapter 24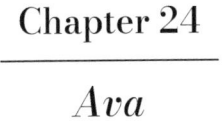

Ava

Taking a long route to my hotel to calm my head, I stop at a local grocery store. *I need a fig.* My mouth waters as I imagine sinking my teeth into the oddly shaped, succulent, flavorful fruit instead of the usual produce sold in big chain stores back home. Here, there's a whole section dedicated solely to figs. It's the little things. They're what I need right now. In this colossal mess I'm in.

As I approach the entrance, a tiny ginger kitten atop a chair to the side of the entrance catches my eye. "Oh!" I exclaim softly, drawn to the adorable little thing. "Is this your chair?" I ask. The cat stretches comfortably in response. I stroke its soft fur. "Thank you," I murmur to the kitten, feeling slightly uplifted.

Sensing someone watching me, I nervously look up. To my relief, it's not the big man from earlier, but it's Lev. He holds a small plastic bag with figs inside.

"Well, what a coincidence," he says with a smile.

Despite his hospitality earlier at the restaurant, I'm still irritated with him. "Yeah, we meet again, as rare as winning the lottery twice in a row! Here to get some figs," I say coldly. His friend Not-Sarah was ten times colder.

"Figs taste different here," Lev explains. "The owner brings them from his orchard. Would you like to try one?" he asks, holding up his bag.

"Thanks, but I'll get my own."

But he persists. "I'm walking back to the hotel. Shall I wait so we can walk together?"

I pause and look at him. He stands there like a towering oak, and I feel an essence of earth and green. "Sure," I reply, realizing that a part of me actually preferred walking with him. After all, the thought of the big man from earlier still unsettles me.

When I return, he offers to carry my bag of figs, but I decline.

"Apologies for earlier, on behalf of my friend," he says. "She's stressed out about a few things at the book fair."

"No worries," I say. I'd accepted their invitation so that if the man from earlier was around, he'd see that I was with friends. I'd also thought that building bridges to the book fair I want to attend might help, but Serra's cold eyes were in the way. I wonder if she's his girlfriend.

I steal a glance at him; he seems warm now, but his eyes were steel this morning.

"How is your daughter?" I ask.

He smiles. "She's over the moon about her performance. Thank you for watching a teenager's dance show when you could have been exploring Istanbul."

"It was my pleasure. She was really good!"

"How is your son?"

"He's okay," I reply glumly. "Thanks for asking."

I concentrate on avoiding stepping on cracks in the concrete. He'll probably think I'm superstitious, I just don't like standing on the lines.

"Have you seen much of the city yet?" he asks.

"Some." I wish I were just here visiting.

"So what do you do, Ava?" he asks, as we move onto the pedestrian-only cobbled street.

"Back home? For work?"

He nods.

"I run my own business, primarily working for a major home-gadget company. I design user experiences and create manuals for their electronic devices."

"Interesting. Where is the company based?"

"They have offices nationwide, but Seattle is where my main client is based. My office, though, is at home. I work remotely, and it suits me just fine."

"Sounds like bliss," he replies. "My business is intense, leading a large team of skilled professionals. It's fast-paced, full of risks, and requires being in the thick of it."

I nod. "They asked me to join their leadership team, but that would have meant traveling to their sites, so I declined," I say. "How did you get into security work?"

"That's a long story," he replies. "You wouldn't believe it if I told you. How about you?"

"My story is pretty funny, actually. It all started when I purchased a fancy robot vacuum cleaner."

"A robot vacuum?"

"I'd just started studying part-time to get my degree in graphic design. My son, Zack, was in junior high."

"That's brilliant."

"Yeah, when Zack was little, we'd create games together and loved working with visuals and colors. Then he had a school project where he had to create a magazine, and I loved helping him with it. That's how my interest in graphic design really started."

I pause for a beat, noticing his intense listening. But it feels good to talk about my accomplishments.

"The instructions that came with the robot vacuum read like a textbook in a foreign language. When I turned it on, instead of gracefully navigating around the room, it spun out of control like a drunk party guest." I chuckle. "I wrote an email to the company, and a few days later, a representative asked me to join their focus group. Then they offered me a contract, working from home." My voice quivers on the last word.

"Are you all right?"

"Home," I say with a sigh. "Feels a world away right now."

"Yeah, LA is far."

It's not the distance, I think.

He points at our hotel. "Did you know Agatha Christie stayed in this very hotel? I have her room right now."

"I know," I chirp. "And you have her room? That's so cool. I love her books," I add, even though I never read the last chapters so I never know whodunit.

"I might be able to arrange a peek sometime," he offers. "If you want, of course. How long are you here for?"

I hesitate for a split second. "A few more days."

We step into the lobby. "This might come across . . ." He hesitates, the enormous chandelier above him shining rays of light on his face. "When you start a sentence with 'this might come across,' it's almost a guarantee that it will . . ." He trails off again with a laugh.

He steps a little closer. "So here it is. Would you be interested in an evening tour of Istanbul? With me as your guide? I know this city like the back of my hand."

I look at him with questioning eyes.

"Just a friendly offer."

"But, you're from London," I say. "And why an evening tour?"

"I am from London, but I spend a lot of time here. And I'm busy during the day, but this city offers an exciting experience at any hour."

My lips curve into a gentle smile. He is the gatekeeper of my book-fair entry. And I didn't expect to see him again after this morning, yet we've already bumped into each other twice. *Go with the flow*, I tell myself. My pulse seems to chime in, too.

"Maybe a short one?" I say. "Tomorrow, after 5:00 p.m., when I lock the bookstore."

"That would work. We can do a short evening walking tour."

"Yeah, why not?"

I get off the elevator on my floor with a tug in my heart.

"Call Zack, find the book," I mutter to myself. "Book." That's all.

But I can't help it—my steps feel lighter.

Chapter 25
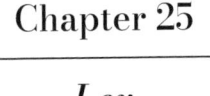

Lev

"There's an issue," one of my colleagues announces through my earpiece. At the main entrance, a man in his forties is arguing with a local security guard, and a small crowd has formed to watch. My mind races as I hurry toward them. Things are never as they seem in our world; this could be a distraction. My father often employed this tactic. Frederica broadcasts a warning to the entire team and instructs everyone to stay alert.

I think of how my father effortlessly charmed his way past museum guards. Sometimes, he'd take my hand and say, "My son is interested in becoming a guard." With that simple line, the guards were happily distracted while my father's friends did whatever they needed to do. A few years later, when I was a teenager, I made up my mind to protect the kinds of things my father stole.

I arrive at the checkpoint to find the man waving a

book in the air. He's becoming increasingly agitated as my team member tries to placate him. I announce myself as the director of security. "I understand there's an issue. Can we discuss it calmly in my office?"

Once the two of us are settled upstairs, he explains that the book he's carrying is rare but that he refused to register it at the entrance. "It's my book," he says. "Why should I have to jump through hoops just to bring it in? All that paperwork is a waste of time."

I calmly explain that the rules and protocols are in place for the benefit of everyone and everything involved, including the literature. After some hesitation, he agrees to register his book per the guidelines.

My shoulders ache with tension. I instruct the team to stay on high alert and report anything suspicious, different, or unusual. I head to the small, dimly lit room where the rare page Yuri previously tried to steal is displayed. Frederica, a few other specialists, and I had many meetings and discussions about this page and how to protect it after what happened in Paris. The aged parchment, slightly yellowed, rests under a protective glass cover. Shakespeare's handwriting sprawls across the page in a mixture of neat script and hurried annotations, the ink varying from deep black to a faded gray.

Satisfied that everything is in order, I find a bench outside by the water and savor a cheese-and-tomato sandwich and some freshly grilled corn from a nearby vendor. It makes me feel nostalgic.

When I was growing up in Istanbul, my grandmother

and I would often buy corn on the cob together. My parents had met in London but made their home here after marrying. Our small family spoke my mother's native tongue, English, with one another, and while living in Istanbul, I attended schools where everything was taught in English. But I'm also fluent in Turkish, having spent so much time with my father and grandmother.

My maternal grandparents, both esteemed barristers in the UK, would never purchase street food, though they spoiled me in other ways; I cherished our Christmases at their Hampstead house, now my home.

I was a happy child, oblivious to the brewing disaster. I spent countless hours playing football in the streets of Istanbul until dinnertime called me home. When my mother whisked me away, life took a sharp turn. We stayed with her parents, who welcomed us with open arms. They had never fully approved of their son-in-law and disliked the idea of their daughter moving away.

But my grandmother in Istanbul never forgave my mother for taking me away, and my mom still harbors serious resentment toward my father. "Family," I muse, shaking my head.

It's only 1:00 p.m., which means there are several long hours until I meet with Ava. Just a hot minute ago, I was upset with her for turning up at the book fair. Now I'm looking forward to seeing her. She's confusing, and all my self-imposed rules are losing their grip. A subtle warmth stirs in my chest.

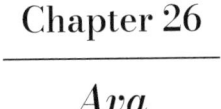

Chapter 26

Ava

I twist the key in the lock of the bookstore while looking at the table where I sat yesterday with Lev and his too-cool friend Not-Sarah. The door doesn't budge. With more force, I push against it but only hurt my arm. *Oh, right, the second lock.* Of course, I locked both yesterday.

The atmosphere of the bookstore is serene, a contrast to my buzzing mind and sore arm. I have a full hour before I need to open the door. It's unlikely that Elaine's book will be here on a shelf just waiting for me, but I still look for it. Hope is a wonderful source of strength.

I grab the folder Mr. Babayan left behind. Yesterday, I followed the instructions inside to close up the store since no customers showed up. It was straightforward—no cash, no sales.

After a few attempts, I get the register to work and then take a cloth from the back office to dust the shelves.

I perch on a comfy chair, engrossed in creating my plan. I list my options:

–Today, speak with customers and collectors about rare books and where best to find them.
–Find someone else to go to the book fair and ask them to inquire for me.
–Find Checkered-Shirt John, somehow.

The store is quiet. Only a handful of people come and go before 11:00 a.m., and no one makes a purchase. Each time a customer enters, I feel uneasy. How will I help them if they don't speak English? I'm in Istanbul. It would be silly to expect people to speak English.

I end up using the translation app on my phone to help one customer find what she's looking for. After I ring up the purchase, the receipt doesn't print out and the cash drawer doesn't open—I must have pressed the wrong button.

"Sorry," I say, flustered.

But she kindly helps me figure it out, and we laugh.

Ha! I'm becoming a master of communicating without words.

After the customer leaves, I create an easy-to-follow flowchart for Mr. Babayan so that someone filling in for him in the future will be able to follow his instructions more easily:

1. Opening tasks
2. Lock-up tasks
3. How to work the register

As the day progresses, I continue helping customers. Being surrounded by thousands of books calms my nerves.

I ask every customer what they would recommend if I were looking for a rare book. Some speak English; others communicate with me through my translation app. I jot down the names of a few collectors in the city who weren't on my original list. I'll add them to my digital list on my laptop when I'm back at the hotel.

Late in the afternoon, I grab a Turkish translation of an Agatha Christie book from the shelf. Is it the same story when told in different languages? If not, what changes? The emotions it incites?

The little bell above the door chimes, announcing a visitor and snapping me out of the pages. A local boy, maybe fourteen or fifteen years old, strolls in, his worn-out sneakers softly scuffing the polished wooden floor.

He's wearing a Nirvana t-shirt, and his hoodie is tied around his waist. He seem out of place as he navigates the neat stacks of carefully arranged books. He stops by a display of vintage classics, and his fingers lightly trace the weathered covers.

I greet him with a warm smile as he heads toward the

counter. "Merhaba," I say. "Do you speak English? Or I can use this?" I show him my phone. My translation app is open and displays the words "How can I help?" in Turkish.

He looks up with a hesitant and shy expression. "Um, I wanna find somethin' good," he says, with a Turkish accent. "English book." His voice is soft, and his lashes are so long and defined it's as if he's wearing mascara.

I nod. "You've come to the right place. What kinds of stories do you like? Adventure, mystery, fantasy?"

He scratches his head. "Adventure."

I grin, and my hands navigate the shelves. "Ah, the magic of exploring new worlds through books! I have just the thing for you." I hand him a YA fantasy. Zack liked these books, and I read them too, to connect with him. "It's a series."

My young customer examines the book, eyes widening with curiosity. "Are there detectives?"

"Hmm. Okay. Let's see what we have for adventures with detectives." I continue searching the young adult section. "How about this?" I pick up a book with a colorful cover: *Agent Kate and Max: The Secret Door*.

He takes it, turns it over in his hands, and nods. "I like. How much?"

"Let me check," I say, quickly reading the back cover, making sure the book about a detective and her dog is age-appropriate. I tell him the price and do the currency conversion in my head. Eleven dollars is a lot for a used book, but I've noticed English books are more expensive here.

He looks unsure as he continues to examine the book.

"May I gift this book to you?" I ask.

"I got money." He takes out a few notes.

I take the smallest of the notes. "Now you've paid."

"Thank you," he says with a grin. "You work here? I come, but not see you before."

"I'm visiting. I like books so I'm helping the owner. What's your name?"

"Umut," he replies.

"Yours?"

"Ava. Nice to meet you, Umut."

His eyes twinkle. He holds up the book, corners of his lips turning up in a shy smile. "I know Istanbul and all bookshops."

I smile. My young, sweet customer knows all the bookshops in Istanbul, and I'm looking for a book in many bookshops. "I'll come to you if I need help finding a book," I say.

He leans toward the counter and points at the pen. I nod, and he grabs it. I hand him the notebook I recently bought, red and letter-size, which I found in the small stationery part of the store, and he writes down his phone number. How charming.

After Umut leaves, I get my purse from the little back office and pay for the rest of the book. Then I return to the comfy chair behind the small counter, Agatha Christie book in hand. We both like detective stories, Umut and I.

I flip through the pages all the way to the end, then go through them once more. My fingertips glide over the last few pages as I quickly scan the Turkish words. I start reading a few aloud—words I don't understand. The more I read, the faster I go, speeding through with a strange mix of excitement and silliness. It feels . . . good. Silly, but good.

A few pages from the last chapter, I close the book and whisper, "Thank you," so softly it's barely audible, as I slip it into my purse. I ring up the sale and put the cash into the register.

Glancing at my phone, I realize time is ticking. Less than an hour remains until I meet Lev. He's always so put-together, with crisp shirts that accentuate his broad chest and shoes that match his tailored suits. Not many men can carry a scruff that well.

The irritated, logical adult in my mind is grilling me: "Why on earth are you looking forward to seeing Lev? And why is the thought of spending a few hours alone with him has your stomach fluttering."

What I should be focusing on is how I can get him to help me. I don't think I'll ever tell him my son stole a book. Zack isn't a thief, and I won't label him that way. He's just a silly boy who made a big mistake.

I begin lock-up preparations, first counting the cash and then placing it in the safe in the back as per Mr. Babayan's written instructions. Finally, I walk around the store to make sure everything is in order. All seems fine, but a nagging feeling of restlessness gnaws at me, so I take out my Rubik's Cube.

My sister was my cheerleader when I was competing,

always jumping up and down to support me. My mother couldn't care less. "Why waste time on some stupid puzzle?" she would say dismissively. At age thirty-eight, I still like having it in my hand.

Zack's father didn't understand why I wanted to keep this colorful cube close to me. He acted as if my existence started the day I met him. He'd often stop me from talking about my mother or sister. "I'm your family now." In hindsight, I wonder if perhaps he liked the fact that I had no parents and a sister in prison. It gave him the freedom to shape me as he wanted. He reveled in being the only thing that mattered to me. Well, he's no longer the center of my universe. I'm done with him.

As I twist and turn the cube, aligning the colors, a memory surfaces. I was eight years old, and we had just moved to a new neighborhood. "This one is better for you girls," Mom had said.

I liked the new school, and when I found out they had a Rubik's Cube competition, I signed up at once.

On the big morning, a Saturday, the school gym was transformed into a small competition hall. I made it to the final round. Winning meant representing my state, California, at the national level and receiving a cash prize. I dreamed about surprising my mother by giving her the money to contribute to rent.

The judges timed how quickly participants completed the cube. Every millisecond counted, and I'd achieved a strong average time across multiple rounds. If I could finish the final round in under twenty-five seconds, I'd win. Just before the round began, I stepped outside to clear my mind.

A group of boys a few years older than me approached, and one of them got right in my face. "So, you think you're smart just because you can solve some puzzles?" he said with a sneer. "That's pathetic. You're pathetic."

The school grounds were empty, just the three of them and me.

I turned to walk away. But before I could take a step, he shoved me hard in the arm.

"Hey, stupid, I'm talking to you."

My Rubik's Cube fell out of my hand and landed in a murky puddle. As I bent to pick it up, he shoved me again, this time with more force. I fell face-first into the slimy mud.

They laughed. "Ava the mud nose!" they sang.

I raced away from the school and ran all the way home. Collapsing onto my bed in the room Grace and I shared, I aggressively twisted and turned my Rubik's Cube, but no matter how hard I tried, the squares refused to move correctly. There was too much mud in the cube.

I hurled the cube against the wall and screamed.

Grace rushed in. "Ava, what happened? Ava, talk to me."

I knew she wouldn't understand what I'd just been through, the torment I faced outside these walls. Everyone adored her. She was so pretty and popular.

"Leave me alone," I snapped.

Maybe that boy was right, I thought. *Maybe I am pathetic.*

"Hey, look at me." She lifted my chin and stared at my mud- and tear-streaked face. "What happened?"

My eleven-year-old sister pulled me into a tight hug, and just like that, I started to feel better. That's when I broke down and told her what happened.

"They called me 'mud nose.' I hate my nose," I sobbed.

"Your nose is cute, and you're beautiful," she said, comforting me.

When Mom appeared in the doorway, Grace relayed the story.

"It's a silly competition anyway," Mom said dismissively. "I don't get why you're so upset about it."

"It's Ava's dream," Grace said, her voice trembling with anger. "We don't question your ridiculous Hollywood dreams, do we?"

Mom yelled. Grace yelled even louder. I lay on my small bed, covering my ears against the chaos. In the end, Grace was grounded for the weekend, forbidden from seeing her friends or leaving the house. "It's okay," she said once our mom had left. "I like being here with you."

Our mother had big aspirations of becoming a Hollywood star. She was stunning and landed minor roles in movies. Dad had agreed to move from Arizona to LA so she could attend auditions, but Grace once told me that Dad had never found his place in LA. He'd left behind all his family and friends.

After Dad passed away, Mom was still determined to make it big. She paid for memberships to social clubs on credit cards to infiltrate the inner circle of the industry. She registered with numerous casting agencies and bought better outfits while working at a bar. She owed both friends and, eventually, loan sharks, and the mounting debt weighed heavily on her. We rarely stayed in one place for more than two years. Either our landlords would kick us out or Mom would have other reasons to move.

When I was twelve, we crammed all our belongings into Mom's dark-green station wagon and moved to Phoenix. We drove for seven hours and all sang together despite the bruises on Mom's face. She claimed she was hit while trying to break up a fight, but I never fully believed her.

Her face eventually healed, but the shadow in her eyes never faded. She left her Hollywood dreams behind in LA, but the disappointment cast a permanent shadow on her demeanor.

Chapter 27

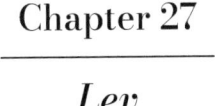

Lev

I step into the bookshop. Ava is wholly absorbed in whatever precious treasure she's holding.

"Afternoon," I say.

"Hello," she says, with a surprised smile. She rises and makes her way toward the entrance. "Is it that time already?"

"I'm a bit early."

Her eyes dart from the top of my head to my brown shoes. She's wearing white cropped trousers that accentuate her figure. Her sandy-colored top is neatly tucked in and drapes over the smooth skin of her shoulders. Her hair is styled in a loose bun. Her scent dives through my skin, stirring my sleepy blood awake.

My gaze focuses on the cube in her hands as she lifts it toward me. "This is the same one from my childhood—the one I used in all those competitions I mentioned. It knows so much about me," she says, a faint smile touching her lips.

"That's remarkable," I reply. "I used to like these, but I was never any good at solving them."

"Practice makes perfect," she replies, handing me the colorful cube. "Although, this one needs a bit of extra muscle to turn—someone spilled coffee in it a few days ago." She grins.

"Sorry," I mouth.

"White opposite yellow, blue opposite green, orange opposite red."

Some of the colors have faded, and the edges are soft. I turn the squares, unsure what I'm doing.

"So, opposites guide you to the correct alignment?"

"Yes," she says. "I was only five years old the first time I completed one."

"No way!"

She nods. "Then I won a few competitions—the ones where I used a funny focal point."

"Oh, I see," I say. "Well, nice to meet you, Ava, the child prodigy!"

"Not at all," she says with a chuckle. "Let me just lock up. I'm almost done. It's not a busy place."

I hand the cube back to her. "Is there anything I can help you with?"

"I'm good, thanks," she responds, walking toward the small room in the back.

"I'll browse while I wait," I say. "When will your friend be returning?"

"What friend?" she calls from the back room.

"The owner of this bookstore?"

"Oh, him. He'll be back tomorrow morning."

No walls are visible. Books are everywhere. There's an order in the crowded space, though. Books are organized by genre, but it feels like an arrangement only someone with a true passion for literature could maintain. Faded bookmarks peek out from between some of the pages, and handwritten notes adorn several of the preloved volumes.

"I'm ready." Ava emerges from the small room holding a dark-blue jacket and her handbag.

"Great." I meet her by the door. "What have you seen in the city so far?"

"Not much."

"Here's the plan, then. Let's start with Galata Tower and the neighborhood and then walk up to Taksim."

"Sounds great," she says, putting on her jacket.

"It's good that you have comfortable shoes." I hold open the door for her and then she locks up.

"One of my favorite things to do is rediscover Istanbul —or London—through the eyes of someone who's never seen it before," I say, my gaze lingering on her. Her eyes, already captivating me, sparkle with curiosity as she listens. "There's nothing quite like seeing a place for the first time, the wonder in every detail."

A slight smile dances on her lips. For a beat, our eyes meet. I get the sense that this will be a whole new kind of adventure.

We stroll through the cobbled streets for about 15

minutes. When I ask if she grew up in LA, her replies are short: yes, up to a point, then Phoenix, and eventually back to LA.

We continue walking in silence until we reach Galata Tower. "This was originally built as a watchtower," I explain. "It's been standing since the fourteenth century and has served various purposes, from being a prison to being a lookout point for fires in Istanbul. Nowadays, it's a museum."

Ava touches a few of the weathered light-brown bricks of the exterior. "There's something romantic about towers, especially this one," she says. "The top seems to reach the sky."

Her neck stretches as she gazes upward. "It's only been in my life for a few days, but this tower already grounds me."

She inhales and leans on the wall of the tower, facing me. "As soon as I see it, I feel better somehow. It's sturdy. And you can see it from many angles in the city, too. Maybe it's the familiarity in an unfamiliar environment. I can rely on it. There are no surprises. I feel connected to it. And the conical top with its blinking light is just so cute."

"All that in just a few days."

Her eyes narrow as she points and says, "That's where we first met—the café."

"Yes, Wednesday morning. I wasn't supposed to be here until the Friday, but an emergency changed my plans and I ended up interrupting your coffee that morning. Did I apologize for that, by the way?" I ask teasingly.

"Funny," she says, her gaze on the road. "My trip to Istanbul definitely wasn't a planned one."

"Is that so?" I ask, intrigued.

"Yeah," she dismisses with a casual wave, then adds, "Time to explore more of this city now."

We pass the café and walk through the neighborhood of Galata. "Did you know that the world's first coffee shop was here in Istanbul?"

"Seriously?" she asks, placing a hand on her chest. "Where? How old is it?"

"It doesn't exist anymore. But it wasn't far from here. It was a social gathering place. I think it was built in the fifteenth century."

We wander onto İstiklal, a pedestrian avenue.

"How cute is that," she says, as we watch a vintage red tram with just one carriage approaching. "Would you mind taking a photo?"

I take her phone and snap pictures as it glides past her. Its bell rings out, filling the air with a sense of nostalgia.

"I can practically feel the heartbeat of this city," she says, looking at the photos. "They turned out great!"

"Quite a sight," I say, watching her.

"Do you speak any other language?" she asks, as we continue walking.

"Yes, I do. English, Turkish, German, Spanish. I studied for a few years in Germany. Do you?"

"Wow. Four languages. No, I don't. This is my first time visiting a non-English-speaking country, although I'm familiar with Spanish, living in LA and Phoenix. Growing up, I had Mexican American friends who taught me some Spanish as well. Here, I love playing a guessing game."

"Guessing game?"

"Yes. When I hear two people talking, I guess who they are to each other and what they're talking about."

"Sometimes even speaking the same language isn't enough," I say with a chuckle. "I trust my senses more than words." I point to a bench and suggest we sit for a moment.

"Being here has made me realize how fluid culture is," she says, as we sit on the bench.

"In what way?"

"I thought culture was a fixed thing. But that's not true. It changes. It moves. You and I are sitting here. We add to the culture of this area. It's collective."

"I like that," I say with a nod. "Yeah, this city is like a bridge connecting many things—opposites, two continents. You can feel the contrast between East and West." *And between the two of us*, I think. She and I are worlds apart, yet she feels so close.

"Sounds like Istanbul and I have something in common, both straddling different worlds."

"How so?" I ask.

"Lately, I've been reflecting on my world and the choices I've made—where I stand in life. My mind tells me one thing, but I feel the complete opposite." She pauses, looks up, and then adds with a grin, "Anyway, this street is awesome."

"So have you played your guessing game about me?" I ask mischievously, relishing her attention.

"Hmmm." She twists toward me and puts her index finger on her cheek.

You can stare at me like that all night and make every guess in the world.

"These built-up arms are likely the result of being part of the security world."

She touches my right biceps briefly, and all my muscles tense.

Her eyes return to my face. "The millimetric slant of your nose to the left tells me you broke it some time ago. And there's a thin, faint line here."

Her fingers trace the tiny scar above my right eyebrow. A bracing shiver runs through me.

"I don't think this was a fight. I think you're skilled enough to avoid a good old-fashioned brawl. I'm guessing a sports injury."

I take a deep breath, the impact of her touch lingering. "Impressive," I say, my voice slightly unsteady. "I played rugby professionally, but that was a long time ago."

Excitement flashes across her face as she brings her palms together. "I knew it!"

Then she crosses her legs and leans back. "What about me? Dare you play the guessing game?"

"I can try," I say. *I've been playing it since we met.*

I take the opportunity to scan her from head to toe. My gaze lingers on her lips, and I imagine what kissing them would feel like. She opens them just a bit and glances down.

"You're recently separated or divorced," I remark. "You're an avid reader." I continue, my voice softening. "And I bet your hair is soft and silky." I tuck a wavy lock behind her ear.

She blinks slowly then inhales deeply, her eyes locking on mine as my hand lingers behind her ear for a long moment.

A slow smile spreads across her face. "Okay, Mr. Intelligence. I think you did a background check on me, so that's how you know about my divorce. Also, it's a given that I like books. You kicked me out of a book fair. I'm still upset about that, by the way."

I shake my head. "No. Your skin is lighter at the bottom of your ring finger. And I noticed a dog-eared page in your book at the café, even though you had just bought it." A few beats pass. "And I was right about your hair."

"Yeah, the book was from a secondhand store. I left the dog-eared page just as I'd found it."

Then she looks away. "And yes, recently divorced. I took the ring off when we separated, more than a year ago, after wearing it for almost twenty years." She lifts her left hand. "I wonder if it will ever disappear, the line."

"I'm sure it will with time." I show my own left hand. "Look, no trace."

"Good to know." She takes my hand and caresses my ring finger, sending shockwaves through my body.

"No line left," she confirms, still holding my hand. When she releases it, my hand feels a pang of sadness.

"This street is great," she says. "I thought I didn't like crowded places, but watching people is fun. Maybe traveling changes the filter in your eyes. A crowd is no longer a crowd but individuals with stories."

"I like that."

"What's your story with Istanbul?" she asks.

"I'm here protecting books. Doing what I do."

Ava looks into the distance. Then she clenches her hands and speaks softly. "Protecting." She blinks a few times, her voice barely above a whisper. "I see how fragile everything can be in life." She pauses, her eyes reflecting the weight of her words.

I want to know more, to understand what she meant— what exactly is so fragile in her life?

She says, "I'm sorry. I don't usually open up like this. Things have just been a lot to handle lately."

"I don't mind at all," I say.

"Maybe we can grab a quick dinner before we return to the hotel?"

I readily agree and suggest one that's on our way to the hotel. As we head for the restaurant, she exclaims, "Oh, there's Umut!"

Who's Umut?

Five teenaged boys sit on a low concrete wall in front of a school.

"Hey, Umut." Ava walks over to them.

The boy's face lights up. "Ava." He hops down from the wall.

"Are you a musician?" she asks, pointing at the clarinet.

"My friend plays it, but I can play too," he responds eagerly.

"That's totally cool. I'd love to hear you play sometime."

He nods enthusiastically. Then Ava turns around. "Lev, this is my friend Umut. Umut, this is Lev. He's my tour guide for tonight."

Umut fixes his eyes on me and raises an eyebrow. "Tour guide," Umut repeats, as he looks me up and down.

"It's nice to see you again," Ava says, as she gives Umut a hug. He grins shyly.

"How do you know him?" I ask, as we walk away.

"We met earlier at the bookstore."

"He has a serious crush on you," I say with a chuckle.

She laughs. "I don't think so. We met a couple of hours ago."

"When you're a teenager, sometimes that's all it takes," I say, pondering how long it takes when you're forty-five.

Chapter 28

Ava

After a long, hot shower, I wrap myself in a towel and ease into the chair by the window with my laptop. The time with Lev was an unexpected escape from my anxiety, and I have to admit I really enjoyed it. I'll keep that to myself.

I spend nearly an hour reviewing the bits of information about rare bookshops I gathered from customers today and add them to my ever-growing list. Then, I slip into leggings and a T-shirt and begin pacing around the room, trying to shake off the restlessness.

What else can I do? Where on earth is the book? In a city of 15 million people, with hundreds of bookstores, countless book markets, and a large antiquarian book fair, the idea of tracking it down feels almost laughable. I knew when I agreed to come to Istanbul that this would be a near-impossible task. But I've maintained a flicker of hope, a fragile flame in the darkness. Now, more than ever, I need that hope—I can't let it be extinguished.

I video-call Zack. It's Sunday morning in California. Since I told him off a few days ago, Zack has called every day with updates, but nothing useful has come up so far.

He picks up on the first ring. "Hi, Mom. Are you okay?"

"I'm holding up. You're up early."

"Yeah," he says hesitantly. "So I went to Elaine's last night. I was dreading it, but she was cool."

"You're lucky that she really loves you."

"I know, Mom. Her table was full of pictures. She said she had so many photos, both in print and digital form. I offered to help her scan them and sort them into albums and folders, so she can easily find any picture she wants. She seemed pleased with the idea."

"That's good, but you're still grounded forever," I remind him sternly.

"Okay," he says, in a defeated tone. "Any updates, Mom?"

I let out a deep breath. "I'm trying, but I'm desperate for any information from you. Do you have any leads? We've got to narrow our search."

"I'm still tracking the guy down, the one who passed the book, and reaching out to others, but it's tricky. They're really shady."

"No kidding," I reply sharply.

"I'm sorry, Mom, for everything," he says. "I promise to make it up to you."

He blinks slowly, a habit he gets from me, something we do when our eyes sting. I feel a wave of compassion for my son. "Zack, we're in this together. We'll be okay."

"Uhm." He pauses. "So Dad came round and woke me up."

"He did?" Is he finally stepping in?

"Yeah, he told me that Julianne is expecting."

"Oh."

"They're going to get married soon." Zack swallows audibly. "I'm happy but also somehow sad."

The news floods me with conflicting emotions. I'm happy for Zack, but there's also a hint of sadness. I had yearned for a second child, but John had been opposed to the idea. He was an only child and critical of my sister's and my upbringing. He eventually convinced me.

I take a deep breath. "Well, you always wanted a sibling. Aren't you happy?" I force my cheeks up, trying to craft a smile.

"It's a boy."

"Oh, they already know," I say dryly. "Well, congratulations to you, darling."

Zack shrugs, but I know he'll be an exceptional older brother.

"Did you talk about the book?" I ask.

"Yeah, I told him you were in Istanbul, and he was surprised you'd traveled there on your own."

After we end the call, I step onto the balcony. The gentle air brushes against my skin. I lean against the cool railing and bite into a juicy fig, the bitterness of my desperate search lingering in my mouth. I tilt my head back, breathing in the sea breeze and looking at the bright moon.

The life John and I built together now seems meaningless. Not knowing how to heal the wounded teenager I was, I crafted a life with John, choosing to overlook his self-centeredness. Now, he doesn't even care about what's happening to his own son.

My blood boils. "Of course I can travel alone, you disrespectful shithead."

I'm unsure of how much time has passed when a knock on the door startles me, causing my stiff neck muscles to protest. Cautiously, I crack open the door and peer out.

Lev stands in the hallway holding a small gift bag. "I know it's late, but I have something for you. I hope you don't mind."

I hesitate for only a moment. "No, come in. I was on the balcony." I open the door wider.

"I don't want to bother you. I just wanted to give you this." He hands me the bag, which is about the size of my hand.

"It's okay, come in," I say. "There's a lovely breeze outside. We could sit on the balcony."

"Sure, for a little while."

As we settle outside around the small marble-topped

table, we take our seats, both chairs facing outward. I ask, "How did you know which room I was in?"

He points up to my left. "That corner room is mine. I saw you down here."

"Oh, and you knew exactly what room this was? I hope you haven't been knocking on many other doors," I say teasingly.

"Occupational hazard." He grins. "I was pretty sure this would be the room. There are only fifteen rooms on each floor. I just popped out to get you something." He points at the small bag in my hand. The metallic paper shimmers under the soft lights of the balcony.

I open it to find an oval-shaped glass pendant with a small loop at the top, about the size of a coin. The outer layer is a deep, dark blue, followed by a bright white circle, a smaller vibrant light blue circle, and a tiny black dot at the center.

"You just popped out to get me this?" I ask, surprised.

"Yes, it's an amulet known for its protective energy."

I touch the smooth glass. "It's beautiful, but I can't accept this."

"It's nothing. It was really cheap, if that helps. Just from a gift shop in the area. It was either a key ring or a pendant. This reminded me of the liquid culture you were talking about earlier. It's a nazar bead—a protective symbol in Turkish culture, also common across Mediterranean or Middle Eastern regions. Now, you're part of it."

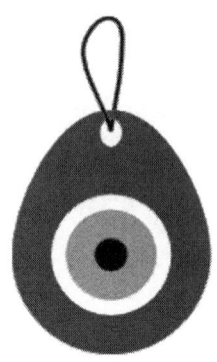

"Thank you," I say, hugging the pendant against my chest.

"It's known as the evil eye, but it's there to protect you from the evil eye —keeping negative energy away."

"A protective symbol. I really like it," I say.

As he rises to leave, the scent of soap wafts toward me. A hint of stubble still dusts his jawline, and his crisp white V-neck T-shirt hugs his toned physique.

"Would you like to see the Agatha Christie room now?" he asks.

"Really, you don't mind?"

"Not at all."

The pendant clinks as I drop it beside my earrings on a small plate resting on the side table in the room. I feel my chest crack just a little.

Chapter 29

Lev

Ava's beautiful eyes light up as she takes in the décor of my suite. She moves like a breeze through tall wildflowers, gently touching a velvet armchair. "I can't believe Agatha Christie stayed here," she whispers. She runs her fingers along the edge of a vintage mahogany desk beside the balcony door.

"She's one of my favorite mystery authors," I say, entranced by Ava. I'm glad I left my room tidy. It was a spur-of-the-moment invitation. "Would you like a drink?"

"I don't want to intrude on your evening," she says quickly. "Just a quick peek at the room would be great."

"I don't mind at all," I reply. *Please stay.*

"Okay then."

I open a bottle of wine and pour two glasses. She takes hers and then moves to the couch in the room. "Imagine her sitting at that desk, watching Istanbul and writing," she says.

I sit beside her on the couch and raise my glass. "To literature."

She raises her glass to mine, and as we sip, I glance at her lips.

"There's a rumor that she wrote *Murder on the Orient Express* in this very room," Ava says. "There must be countless stories hidden within these walls."

Her presence melts away the tightness in my shoulders. "I stay in this room whenever I can," I sigh out. "It's like my Istanbul home."

We talk for what feels like hours, our conversation flowing effortlessly with anecdotes about London, LA, and Istanbul. I pour more wine.

"Growing up, we moved a lot," Ava says. "In each place, I'd finally not be the new girl. But every time I started putting down roots, my mother pulled them out." She takes a sip. "I'm sorry. I don't know why I'm bothering you with this."

"Please, keep going. I really want to hear more." I want to know everything about her.

"Is this wine from the minibar?" she asks, closing her eyes for a beat after a sip.

"No, I got it at duty-free. It's from Tuscany."

"It's bold and flavorful," she says, swirling the red liquid in her glass. "I've never had a strong desire to travel before, but I should get to Tuscany just for this wine. How incredible would that be, right? I visit my son in San Jose and always think about driving to Napa Valley, wine country, but I've never done it. And here I am, talking about leaping over to Tuscany." She laughs, a sound that's like music to my ears.

"But enough of me. Do you travel a lot?" She asks.

"Yeah. I travel extensively for business, but we also spend holidays in the Mediterranean. Pera loves the beaches, my mother loves reading by the pool, and I love both. I also like flying." I remember the excitement of watching my parents dress up for a flight, with me also wearing a button-up shirt, which was the thing to do in those times.

"Zack has always been into planes," Ava says. "I've always preferred driving. It's not that I'm afraid of flying, but there's something reassuring about knowing I can go home on my own terms without depending on a pilot." She chuckles with a playful shrug. "After a trip to Florida when he was only eight, Zack said he wanted to study planes."

"And now you're in Istanbul."

"Yeah," she replies, her voice almost a whisper.

"I'm pleased you are." My voice is suddenly raw.

Ava's chin dips as she gazes at her wine glass. She then looks up, and our eyes lock. Her chest rises and falls with each breath, causing my mind to wander. A faint flush spreads across her cheeks as her eyes linger on my lips for a brief moment.

I reach out to her chin. "You are stunning," I whisper.

She takes a deep breath. "Thank you," she says, blinking slowly. Then clears her throat. I withdraw my now-tingling finger.

We both take sips from our wines, but mine is audible. *What was I thinking?* But I just gave in to the pull she had over me, drawn like a moth to a flame.

Her head turns toward the balcony, eyes drifting outside. "Could I see your balcony? The view of the Golden Horn must be incredible from the corner—I'd love to see what Agatha Christie was gazing at."

"Of course," I reply.

"You know, when Melisa told me I was staying in the Golden Horn Room, I thought maybe there'd be horn decorations or something."

We laugh as we stand and step out onto the balcony, which curves around the building.

"Same little table on my balcony," she murmurs, her fingers brushing the smooth surface of the small marble top. "Back home, my bathroom is covered in Turkish marble—I'm surrounded by it. But somehow, this tiny piece feels more . . . noticeable. More beautiful." She drifts to the edge of the balcony and leans against the railing, a distant look in her eyes.

I also glide my fingers over the cool top of the table. "Have you seen the Bosphorus yet?" I ask. "It's the main strait between the two continents, while the Golden Horn is just an inlet."

"Only from a distance."

"I have a friend here with a small boat. I usually meet him for a quick boat tour and catch-up. Seeing both continents from the water is something else. Would you like to join us? He wouldn't mind."

"Thank you," she says. "I'm not sure how my days will work out, but I'll let you know if I can."

"Great, let me give you my number."

"I didn't bring my phone." She extends her arm. "Write it here."

"Are you sure?"

She turns her palm up.

I fetch a pen from inside, steady her arm with my hand, and scrawl my number on her wrist. I know her floral scent so well now. I yearn to be closer to her. The city night stretches around us, a vast scene of rooftops and lights.

Placing the pen on the small table, I lean against the railing beside her.

She turns toward me, her teeth sinking into her bottom lip. A spark ignites in my chest, my body reacting to the sight of her teeth marks on those soft, full lips. I never realized how tiny this balcony was. She moves closer. I grip my wine glass more firmly, my fingers itching to touch her. I can feel the warmth of her skin, only inches away.

Then she balances on the balls of her feet and places her lips on mine. My mind goes blank, overwhelmed by the earthiness of the wine and the sweetness of her lips.

As we pull away from each other, I take our wine glasses and place them on the table. Then I move to stand in front of her and place my hand on her heart. It beats in rhythm with mine.

She grabs me by the shirt and pulls me to her for another kiss. I tenderly hold her face with one hand and trail my other hand down her neck to her back, where I trace patterns.

She sighs softly. My body responds, pressing against hers. The night breeze carries a hint of cinnamon and secrets.

I crave her. I want to spend the entire night here, lost in her kiss. Our lips part, noses brushing. "Ava," I growl.

"I want you," she whispers. Her pull is forceful, her kiss insistent. I sense that she needs me just as much as I need her.

"Mmm, I want you, beautiful" I rumble, letting her guide me, enjoying the demands of her touch, her kisses, her body. The scent of the sea breeze mixes with that of Ava's velvety skin, making me dizzy with lust.

She runs her fingers through my hair and down the back of my neck, igniting every nerve ending in my body. We stumble back into the room, lips locked, tongues dancing, exploring and tasting each other with intensity.

She sinks back on the bed, her hair like a silken waterfall across the white bedspread. I move my body over hers, cradling her cheek, my thumb tracing gentle circles along her earlobe. Her lips are tinged with color, adding to her beauty. Our eyes meet. I breathe in her expression. "What are you doing to me?" I whisper.

Our mouths collide again, feral, and I cup her breast through her soft T-shirt, finding the lace of her bra and the firm bud beneath it. I trail kisses down her neck. Her skin is salty and intoxicating. She moans and her body arches, inviting me to continue.

We shift, turning until she sits on my lap, her legs wrapped around my waist. As we strip, our bare chests press against each other, sending heat and electricity through my body. I hold her tightly as I lower her back onto the bed. Then I reach for my wallet and use my teeth to rip open the foil packet.

Our bodies fit like two puzzle pieces finally coming together.

Chapter 30

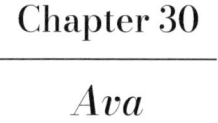

Ava

I slowly open my eyes, feeling Lev's dark chest hair brushing against my eyelashes. My last memory is of gradually drifting off to sleep after several rounds of passion, each one longer than the last.

His slow breaths caress my forehead. I savor the warmth of his embrace for a few moments, feeling as if I'm being carried by a gentle wave.

When I start to move away, he stirs. "Stay," he pleads, pulling me closer and placing a gentle kiss on my collarbone. His stubbly beard tickles my skin, bringing back memories that make my body tingle and send heat racing to my cheeks.

His desire for me sets my whole being ablaze.

Last night, on the balcony, I craved more of him, and boy, did I get more of him. I felt wanted in a way I'd never felt before, even though I'd only ever been with one other person. Being with Lev was exhilarating and unfamiliar but also somehow natural and comfortable. His touch made me feel beautiful. I never knew the touch of a man could evoke such sensations within me.

I curl into his arms, inhaling his unique and comforting scent.

"Remember this," he whispers. He lifts my chin to lock his eyes on mine before placing a kiss on my lips. As his thumb caresses my cheek, the gentle kiss turns into a deep one. I close my eyes and let go.

"Just remember," he whispers in my ear, his warm breath tickling my skin.

"I will," I purr, feeling his arms tighten around me.

Finally, I peel myself out of his embrace and sit on the edge of the bed. He attempts to get up too, but I stop him. "Please, stay in bed."

He turns to look at the clock on the nightstand. "It's only 6:00 a.m."

"I have to go get ready for the day."

"Okay," he responds huskily, and props himself up on one elbow. I feel him watching me as I dress.

As I open his door, I glance back. His eyes are hopeful, his head tilted. "Just remember," he says, blowing me a kiss.

With a smile, I nod and step out. I close the door quickly. I'm terrified of how badly I want to return to his arms.

Chapter 31

Lev

Please remember, Ava.

Chapter 32

Ava

A couple of hours later, I walk quickly to Pages and Beans Café. I need my morning coffee—and to find a way of not thinking about last night. I don't know what to do with how my body is responding to the memories.

After bursting through the door, I take a moment to check out the selection of pastries then beeline for a table by the window.

"Good morning," says the owner. "Welcome back. We'll be with you in a second."

"Good morning," I reply. "No worries."

I take a deep breath to clear my mind. I finally let myself enjoy a moment in life—well, many hours. *Woohoo!* My cheeks flush as I lightly touch my wrist. His phone number is smudged. I want to keep the faded pen marks on my arm for a while.

I touch my collarbone, remembering how gently he

kissed it this morning. The pink patch of skin there, the one I scratch when I get nervous, tingles.

"Just remember." How could I forget? Kissing has never made me melt like that. *I remember!*

But I need to focus on why I'm here. I can't be distracted. I have a son who stole a book, and Lev has strong feelings about theft. Last night is just a memory now. It was likely just another night of lust for him anyway.

I open my red notebook to a blank page then realize I left my pen in my room.

"What can I get you?" says a man with a British accent. "The special today is a mosaic cake." I look up to see a guy wearing an apron with the name of the café on it.

Another Brit?

"May I borrow a pen, please?" I ask.

"Sure, do you take it with milk and sugar?" he asks, his warm smile reaching his eyes.

After a split second of confusion, I laugh. "I'll have a latte, please. With an extra shot."

He's back in a flash, placing a pen on my table. "Here you go, and your coffee is on the way. Anything else I can get for you?"

"What's the cake like?"

"Oh, it's delicious, made with dark chocolate and biscuits."

"Sounds good."

"Perfect, I'll bring those right out for you."

I can't stop thinking about last night. It's like my brain

is a broken record, replaying every moment on a loop. It felt as if I were on a stage in someone else's life, on a romantic balcony with quite a hunk. Then there was the rest of the night . . .

I turn my arm and jot down the fading numbers in my notebook. One could be a 3, but it might also be a half-erased 8. My cheeks heat as my skin reminds me of the intense moments with Lev. Drops of sweat mix with the ink. I take a deep breath to steady myself.

I'll probably feel silly about it all in the future. Asking him to write his number on my arm (what was I thinking?). Having fantastic sex until dawn as I realize how tired I am. "Sleeping is overrated," I mumble with a goofy smile. It was otherworldly—how could I feel regret?

I gaze out the window, and my eyes dart from person to person: a businessman in a hurry talking on his phone, a mother leading her child by the hand, a teenager scrolling through their smartphone, obsessed just like Zack. For our son's eighteenth birthday, John and I splurged on the newest smartwatch.

"Mom, look, it'll alert you if I fall off my bike!" he exclaimed. He'd traded skateboarding for mountain biking with a girl he liked in his class.

"Here you go." The British guy sets down my coffee and cake.

"Ah, I see why it's called mosaic cake." The triangular piece of chocolate cake looks like a mosaic.

"And you'll soon understand why it's your new favorite cake," he says. "Are you visiting?"

"Yes, from Los Angeles. And you?"

"How lovely! I'm also visiting. I'm from London, but I actually live in Hawai'i."

"You're visiting but also helping out here?" I ask, surprised.

He smiles. "Ah, these two fantastic ladies here are my business partners." He gestures toward Yasemin and her mother behind the counter. "Pages and Beans is a London-based franchise. I own the original, in London. I'm Roy," he adds, extending his hand.

"I'm Ava," I say, shaking his hand. "Nice to meet you. Quite a distance between London and Hawai'i."

"Love and family know no boundaries when it comes to time and distance," he says with a gentle smile. "Enjoy," he says, and joins the women behind the counter.

Love and family. I wonder how Grace is, where she is. Does she think of me, her little sister? I wish she were here with me.

The flavors of walnuts and bitter chocolate explode in my mouth. I take a sip of my coffee. The delightful combination on my taste buds instantly makes my morning feel brighter.

Then my mind drifts to thoughts of my Hawai'i trip. If everything had gone according to plan, I'd be lounging in a luxurious hotel on golden sand at this very moment. Instead, I'm seated at a café on the opposite side of the globe chatting with a Londoner who lives in Hawai'i. It's almost comical.

I wonder if Grace ever made it Notting Hill. I make a

mental note to create my first bucket list. London first, then maybe Tuscany. Mom loved watching movies set in Italy.

A horn outside jolts me, and then my phone vibrates on the table. It's Zack.

"Hello darling," I say. "Please tell me you have some news?"

"I do, Mom." His voice is ecstatic. "I'm texting you a photo as we speak. My friend and I managed a breakthrough. I have a photo of the man who has the book in Istanbul. As of yesterday he still had the book, apparently."

My heart flaps like a hummingbird on too much Turkish coffee. "How did you get it?"

"It's a long story, Mom. I'll send you everything else I found out about him."

After we hang up, I open the picture Zack sent, and as I zoom in for a better look, my hand flies to my mouth. Checkered-Shirt John! John Klein is his name.

I frown, staring at the photo. I don't want to be thinking about one John—my ex—while I'm busy chasing another. Of course, I'd end up with an ex who has one of the most common names. It's bugged me since I met him a few days ago. So, I decide to rename Checkered-Shirt John as "Kleinman." If I can't change the situation, I'll just change a variable. Ha!

At long last, I have a solid lead. Reaching for my jacket, I stand but am unsure what to do.

I feel Roy's eyes on me from the counter.

"Is everything all right?" he asks.

"Um, yes," I say, an idea forming. "I thought I had somewhere to be, but it can wait."

I hang my jacket back on my chair and dial Umut's number. He answers right away. "Umut, it's Ava. So you like detective stories, right?"

For half an hour, I try to come up with a plan. I need to be ready when I see Kleinman. This explains why he bolted as soon as he saw security approaching—he was handling a stolen book. I analyze my finances and calculate how much I can offer him for the book. I shovel the last piece of cake in my mouth. The thought of being penniless sends a lump down my throat; I remember my teenage days, when I often survived on just bread and butter.

But that was when I was young. Things have changed and so have I. It's time to stop dwelling on the past and focus on retrieving the damn book. Then I can deal with whatever consequences come my way.

Sensing someone approaching my table, I look up to see Melisa. "Hey there," she says.

"Hi," I reply with surprise, setting down my pen.

"I came to see how Yasemin and her mom are doing," she says quietly. "The franchise owner is here now." She checks her watch. "I have a few minutes before my morning shift starts. Can I join you?"

I nod but hope she'll leave soon. Otherwise, I'll need

to change my meeting point with Umut. It's not that I don't trust Melisa, but she already knows a lot, and it would be better to keep Umut out of her sight.

Yasemin comes over to take Melisa's order, and she tells us the franchise owner is really nice.

"I met him earlier," I say. "Roy. He suggested this delicious cake."

"The mosaic cake?" Melisa asks with a smile, as Yasemin heads back to the counter.

"Yes, that's the one," I say, subtly checking the time on my phone. "It's delicious."

"You know, I make that at home," Melisa says. "It's surprisingly simple, a no-bake creation with crushed biscuits, cocoa, some dark chocolate, butter, nuts and a little vanilla extract. Maybe you can come over one day when I'm off work and I'll show you how to make it?"

"Thank you, that's very kind of you. But I think I'll be leaving Istanbul soon. I'm still looking for the book, so I need to stay focused on that." The truth is, I have no idea when I'll actually be leaving. Darn, I've got to extend my stay at the hotel.

"I'm sorry, normally I wouldn't invite hotel guests into my home. I didn't mean to be too forward."

"Thank you. Maybe next time I visit." I am intrigued by her invitation. "Do you live alone?"

"I share with a couple of flatmates, but I'm getting ready to finally move to my own place very soon." She beams. "On my day off this week, I have a few appointments to see apartments."

"How wonderful!" Being able to afford one's own place in a big city must be incredibly challenging for a young professional.

I check the time again. "What time does your shift start?"

"In thirty minutes."

Okay, change of plan. "I just have to make a call," I say, grabbing my phone. I can't risk sending a message. Umut might not see it in time.

"Don't worry," Melisa says. "I should go now anyway. I'll get my drink to go."

I put down my phone, relieved. "By the way, would I be able to get a few pages printed at the hotel?"

She says yes, and after she leaves, I email her the flowcharts that I created for Mr. Babayan.

A few minutes later, Umut walks in. He's wearing a faded yellow T-shirt with an image of a tiger on it.

"Hello," he says, approaching my table.

I invite him to sit, and we order tea, çay, and a breakfast sandwich for him.

"How much time do you have, Umut?"

"All day," he says with a grin.

"I'd like you to be my detective today. A paid detective."

"Really?" His dark eyes brighten.

"Yes," I say, as he takes a huge bite of his sandwich. "I'm looking for a person, and I'm hoping you and I can team up to find him."

"Okay," he says seriously. He reaches over the table, and we shake hands. As he leans back, his eyes sparkle.

"How old are you, Umut?"

He flashes a bright smile. "Fifteen."

When Zack was fifteen, he skateboarded with his friends, played computer games, and rode bikes.

When I was fifteen, my entire world was torn apart by one single decision. If only I hadn't stayed behind. If only I'd gone home as usual. If only. I wouldn't have to live with the constant what-if. I wouldn't have to wonder, every day, what could have been if my mother were still alive.

I silence every what-if and concentrate on the here and now, flashing a smile at Umut. "Let me explain my plan."

Chapter 33

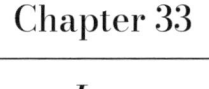

Lev

I pluck a strand of Ava's long hair from the bedspread. It floats out of my grip as I exhale. Every part my body holds a trace of her.

I impatiently check my phone to see if she's sent a message then scold myself for acting like a clueless teenager. All I want is to hear her voice, see her smile, feel her skin against mine, inhale her scent, and taste the sweetness of her lips.

I hop into the shower reluctantly, wishing I could keep the feeling of her sweat on my skin. As warm water cascades over my body, my mind wanders. Sure, kissing her sent thousands of mini shivers through my body. Just thinking about last night stirs a physical response in me. Yet, this is more than physical attraction.

Every time we've bumped into each other—and blimey, it's happened too often to be just a coincidence— something inside me has shifted and I like it.

And on her balcony last night, I could feel her sadness, and a strange, twisting feeling churned in my gut.

As the water washes away the remnants of our night from my skin, my walls are already crumbling, slipping away with every drop. The truth flows in my core: meeting her was something I hadn't known I needed. And the moment her lips touched mine, I knew I'd never be the same. I choose my battles wisely, and there's no point in resisting her pull and whatever is happening to me right now.

On the rooftop of the convention center, I check my stubbornly silent phone again. It's difficult to fathom the situation. No one has ever stayed in that room with me before; it's always been my sanctuary, my home in Istanbul.

Just before she left, I saw a dark cloud in her gaze— maybe doubts about our night?

I can only hope she remembers how it feels when we lock eyes, touch each other, taste each other. There's no shadow, no uncertainty, no doubt.

Please remember, Ava!

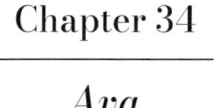

Chapter 34

Ava

After a quick stop at the hotel, I extend my stay, I'm relieved to keep the same room for another seven days. If I get the book sooner, so be it. Then we head to the bookstore to give Mr. Babayan the keys, along with the documents Melisa printed for me.

He thanks me repeatedly and tells me to return anytime.

Once situated in the back seat of the taxi Umut and I are sharing, I remind him of his task. "Your only job is to let me know if you see him. We'll stick around the convention center for maybe a few hours. Is that okay?" It's a big area, and four eyes will be better than two.

Umut takes my phone and studies the photo of Kleinman closely. "Send me this photo?"

"Sure," I say. "But delete it later. If you do spot him, just call me and I'll come and speak with him."

"When I call, you don't answer, you call me back."

"I don't answer?" I ask.

"Yes, hmm . . . My friend move to Germany. I know it's expensive . . . uh . . . ." He checks his translation app. "I will get a big phone bill if you answer."

"Oh, sure," I say. "It must be costly to make international calls. Thank you, my friend, for helping me."

The convention center grounds are relatively quiet when we arrive. Most of the attendees must already be in the building. I remind myself that I'm in a public area, so I'm not breaking any rules.

Lev must be here already. I gulp, and my chest thumps as I remember our evening again, but I remind myself to focus.

I sit on a bench that faces one of the exits and take in the scent of the water. Umut made his way to a side exit. It's a cloudy but warm day. The city bustles around me and the waves relentlessly pound against the shore. Two hours pass. I move to a bench with tree shade when the midday sun becomes too intense.

I call Umut, who's on the other side of the building. "Is there shade? You're not sitting directly in the sun, are you?"

He assures me there's shade.

As the day winds down and large numbers of people start leaving the book fair, I start to lose hope. It might be too crowded to spot Kleinman. Suddenly, my phone rings briefly before stopping. Umut. A tingle of anticipation runs through me as I dial him back.

226

"He is out," he says. "I follow."

"Okay, I'm running toward you," I say, holding the phone tightly to my ear. Why is this convention center so enormous?

"No, no, man getting in taxi. Come to road."

I turn right, still running. "Heading toward the road now." It's busy with cars and buses, and the air is thick with the smell of hot asphalt. Moments later, a taxi pulls up beside me. Umut is practically bouncing in his seat, waving excitedly for me to jump in.

"You're good," I say, buckling up.

Umut points to the taxi we're following, a few cars ahead of us. We weave around countless other yellow taxis, our driver trying to catch up. When we reach a changing light, Kleinman's taxi zooms through the intersection just as the light turns red. My hopes sink, but our driver refuses to give up.

We catch up to the other taxi shortly after the light turns green.

At a large intersection, Umut points to the right. "That's Galata Bridge."

My breath catches in my throat as the other taxi's turn signal comes on. The vehicle slows down at the curb. "They've finally stopped!" I yell.

We stop too. "Teşekkürler," I say to the driver, handing him a few bills—more than necessary.

Kleinman is crossing the busy street on foot. A tram station surrounded by flashing lights looms in the middle of the chaotic intersection. The smell of exhaust and gasoline fills the air.

We cross the street as well. The sidewalks are decorated with colorful art and inviting cafés. The cheerful chatter of people dining and drinking adds to the lively atmosphere.

"Where are we?" I ask Umut, jogging after him.

"Galataport."

Another Galata.

Kleinman is still ahead of us.

"Umut, please stay here. I'll go talk to him, okay? I'll call you when I'm done, and we can meet up later today or tomorrow," I say, quickening my pace.

But then Kleinman stops beside a building about fifty feet ahead, and a figure steps out to meet him. "You've got to be kidding me," I say with a scoff.

It's the big man from the cinema. My mouth suddenly feels desperate for a drop of water. I swallow nervously.

I scowl as Umut appears beside me. But before I can scold him for following me, the big man's eyes lock on me. "Hey!" he yells, his lips twisting into a snarl.

"Run, Umut!"

He doesn't hesitate, and I'm close behind.

As we weave through the crowd of commuters and tourists, Umut points toward a set of steps. "Under bridge."

We descend to an area full of shops selling everything from bikes to shoes and herbs. I glance back but don't see the men. And I've also lost sight of Umut.

228

I barge into a spice store and pretend to browse so I can gather myself. Scents overwhelm my nostrils—cumin, coriander, and turmeric. A couple of minutes later, I step out of the store and look around. Where is Umut? Nerves kick in. Could he be in danger? I decide to head back and look for him. If it means confronting the man directly, I will.

But then I see Umut waving. He gestures to a different set of stairs. I take a deep breath and follow him up and onto a narrow street.

"I was scared I'd lost you," I say. "Can we find a quieter spot? Maybe a café or something? And I need to use the restroom."

"I know one place," Umut says. "This way."

We make our way to a street composed of small rectangular bricks and narrow sidewalks on each side. I initially step over a few cracks then start walking without checking where I step. It's a strangely quiet street, given that we just left an area with thousands of people. A man sits in front of a small store selling telephone gadgets. A cat roams between buildings.

"Where are we going?" I ask, as the street becomes a T-junction.

"Here," says Umut, stopping in front of a single-story red brick building at the end of the street. Patches of green peek out from between the weathered and cracked bricks.

I frown with confusion.

He leads me to a door hidden in a small alley beside the building. Stepping through it, I find myself in a large dusty room with a dome ceiling. Golden-hour lights pour through numerous small circular glass windows from the dome and illuminates the raised marble platform in the center of the room.

"What is this place?" I ask, in awe.

"It's hammam."

"A hammam?"

"Turkish bath."

I take a few steps across the floor. "I've never been to one."

A cozy small sofa is tucked away in a corner. There are four large sinks positioned around the walls. I approach one. It's made of marble, with a rounded basin and smooth, polished edges. Above it, a spout—likely crafted from brass—features delicate flower motifs.

"And toilet," he says, pointing to a door across the room. "But wait." He heads there himself.

"Sure, go ahead," I respond as I step onto the central marble platform, standing in the heart of the room. I pause, taking in every detail around me. *Wow!*

I hope he hurries, though. I need to pee.

Umut emerges from the bathroom holding a plastic container.

"Ready," he says, with a shy smile.

"Thanks," I say, realizing he's been cleaning. Does he live here?

When I return, he's sitting on the sofa behind a stream of light.

"Man can't find us here," he says.

"Good idea. Interesting place. And quiet." I sit across from him on the raised marble structure. "Let's rest for a bit."

On the surface of the cool, smooth marble is a jagged edge. A piece has broken off. I unzip my handbag. The crystal shard from my chandelier fits somehow in the space. What are the chances?

"Do you know the saying 'Trying to push a square peg into a round hole'?"

Umut shakes his head.

"Well, I think it also depends on the size of the hole. Sometimes I get fixated on finding the perfectly shaped peg. But in life, it doesn't work like that, right?"

"Huh?"

"Never mind." I smile as I place the piece of crystal back in my bag. It fits, but it doesn't belong here. "So, how do you know this place? Who owns it?"

"Dunno. Always empty. My friend's sofa, and I gave this." Umut points at the worn-out rug in front of the sofa.

"Do you go to school?"

"I gone, but no more," he says, looking down.

I want to ask him why, but his body is closing up; he's taken a sudden interest in his shoes.

"Your help was great today," I say instead. "Thank you. But I need to continue by myself." Losing Umut earlier made me uneasy.

"The man, he knows where the book is?"

"Um, I think so."

"What is the name of the book?"

"*Pride and Prejudice.*"

He frowns. "What is prejudice?"

I think for a moment. "It's when someone makes up their mind about another person without bothering to get to know them first," I explain. "*Pride and Prejudice* is a novel, a very important one in literature, and this particular copy is important to my friend."

"You wanna steal a book?" he asks.

"No, I don't want to steal it. I want to return it. It's already been stolen." By my son. My chest tightens.

"Ah, wanna steal a stolen book."

I laugh softly. "I prefer to call it 'relocating.' But no. I'll try to buy it, first."

He puts his hands in his pockets and seems to be thinking.

"I'll pay you for today's great work," I say. "And for the two other days we agreed on."

He just nods.

"Where is your family, Umut?" I ask, unzipping my purse.

"My father. Hmm. Away. I work."

"And your mother?"

"Married again. I got brother and sister. Hmm. Stepfather doesn't like me. But I work and pay sister and brother some school."

"You pay for their school?"

"No, pay for schoolbooks and things. I help."

"You're an amazing brother, Umut. What kind of work do you do?" I ask curiously. "And where is home?"

He shrugs. "My uncle has a shop, I carry things, fix things. I help him. But not every day. I stay with uncle."

"Well, today you were a great detective," I say, handing him a hundred-dollar bill. "Here, take this." We'd planned on thirty for each day.

His eyes widen. "But I only done one day." He comes to sit on the marble next to me.

"No argument," I say. This is the first time I've spent cash in Istanbul without feeling guilty or questioning my decision.

"I hope I go school one day," he blurts.

"That's excellent!" I say. "Hope is a great first step. I went back to school, too."

He tilts his head with a smile. "My name is hope."

"Your name is hope?" I repeat, unsure what he means.

He types something into his translation app and then shows me.

"Oh I see. *Umut* means *hope*. I love your name, Umut."

He nods, a grin spreading across his face, his eyes gleaming.

I've had hope with me all along!

He braces his hands behind him on the marble and leans back. I mimic him.

Dampness and dust fill my nostrils as the sun warms my cheeks. A calming, earthy embrace. My heartbeats have slowed since we stepped into this unusual building. What a strange but comfortable moment.

A small laugh escapes me. So much has happened in the last few days.

The memory of Lev's arms around me holds me close. Can I hope? Nope, not that far. We're worlds apart.

Chapter 35

Lev

I t's Wednesday, the day before the final day of the book fair. The nonstop activity—watching monitors, scanning the halls, running an effective operation—hasn't bothered me, but I'm frustrated that there's been no trace of Yuri.

I'm also bothered about the fact that Ava never called. It's been three days. I hope she's okay. Maybe I should initiate contact to check, and then I could see her face, too. *Curses!* Well, that's it. I'm completely smitten, and there's no turning back now.

On her break, Frederica joins me in the small meeting room at the back of the operation hub as I sip my coffee.

"What's bothering you?" Frederica asks, sitting in the chair beside me.

"The most notorious bibliomaniac in the world is in the city, yet everything has run smoothly," I say with a scoff.

"There's nothing strange here at all." *And the woman I yearn to see is ghosting me.*

"Give your team credit. We're running a tight operation with double the security, and I'm sure he knows that."

I give a slight nod. "But what was his motive? Why did he even bother sending me a note? Was his only intention to provoke me?"

"I don't know. Criminal minds?"

Yuri is an exceptional criminal. Almost as good as my father. I'm the son of the greatest thief in Europe. What a thing to be proud of. I stifle a laugh.

"Frederica, I'd like to share something with you, but please don't ask questions."

"I'm all ears."

I shift my weight, and the chair creaks beneath me. "My father is Rasim Sertel," I say, the words tumbling out before I can change my mind. "A renowned art thief."

I fix my gaze on the window, which offers a view of the other side of the water. "I was about eight when I first realized it. He slipped a vintage bracelet under his jacket while we were in a museum."

I pause, but Frederica remains silent.

Avoiding her eyes and run my finger along the rim of my coffee mug. "My father was in hiding when my mother and I left Istanbul when I was eleven." I clear my throat. "We moved to London, changed our surname, and continued life as if he never existed. But I'd scan newspapers, searching for any mention of him. Then—" I swallow. It's hard to talk about him. "He was caught during an elaborate heist: heavy-duty drills, a tunnel into a museum vault. A guard, following a hunch, was inside the vault. My father and two others were apprehended."

I steal a glance at Frederica. Her expression is soft.

Encouraged, I continue, detailing my return to Istanbul years later and my father's release. I tell her that he begged for my forgiveness. "Despite everything, I forgave him. I loved him and believed he'd left his criminal past behind, yadda yadda. But just before Pera was born, he vanished again with authorities in pursuit. I had already told him I was going to be a father. And he still just left. I was in my early thirties, but it hurt as much as leaving him when I was eleven. About to become a father myself, I couldn't understand his choices." My voice turns hoarse. "I was already running this company, with you beside me, when he was sentenced again." I lower my head. "Now you know."

A brief silence fills the space.

"I'm proud of you," Frederica says softly, "and grateful that I work for you. Most of the time, anyway."

I chuckle. "You get to call me boss, but we know who the real boss is around here."

Frederica practically runs this company. "So you're not upset that I kept this a secret?"

"Why should I be? It's your story. You get to choose what you do with it. Your fa—" She stops, eyes widening. "Oh, I see. Yuri's note. That's what he meant when he said 'I know exactly who you are.'"

I nod. "But it's day six and he's nowhere to be seen."

"You know, boss, maybe Yuri didn't mean what you think he did. Maybe he's saying that he now knows not to mess with you because you chose this path despite your father. I think he's scared of you."

I exhale and laugh wryly. "Thanks for the vote of confidence. I appreciate your listening." I stand and place my palm on her shoulder before I leave the room and head for the monitors.

Tomorrow is the last day of the book fair. Then I can finally go see my grandmother, the only other person who loves my dad despite who he is. I can't wait.

Years after Pera was born, my father dared to reach out again, telling me he wanted to see his granddaughter. He explained that he'd moved out of Istanbul and was now working as an advisor to law enforcement and the National Crime Agency. But I refused to see him. Too many broken promises. Too many scars. For me, that chapter is closed.

I'm also looking forward to seeing Pera in a few days. I have a few things in mind to clear away her pout. She can't refuse a dad-daughter weekend in London. I miss my daughter, my peanut.

Later that same day, representatives from various teams sit around an extravagant table. The local security team, IT support, Serra's logistics crew, PR staff, event coordinators, and vendor relations all gather together, indulging in conversation as they reflect on the day's progress. The warm glow of candlelight illuminates our faces as we engage in conversation and share stories about the event.

Serra looks stunning, but the air between us is as frigid as a Siberian winter night. Everything feels off-kilter, as if I'm in an alternate reality where nothing quite fits the way it used to.

Then there's Ava. Her silence lingers in my mind, an ever-present undercurrent. I could easily find her contact information, but I resist the urge. Maybe she doesn't want to see me again. Once again, I push that nagging thought aside.

I quietly step out onto the expansive terrace at the back. The beautiful sunset casts a warm glow over everything, but even the sun's heat does little to reach the cold ache of her absence in my chest. I hope she remembers.

Chapter 36

Ava

I t's been ten days since Rayner, Elaine's son, gave his ultimatum. The setting of the sun marks the end of another day that's slipped by in a blur. I've been rushing around the city like a whisk in a mixing bowl.

It's possible that Kleinman has already sold the book, so I've been visiting as many collectors as possible. But my search has been utterly fruitless so far.

Once more, I leave the hotel and head toward Galata Tower, which is all lit up. I've become familiar with every nook and cranny of this street and am heading for a light dinner at a small family-run place. I haven't eaten much in the last few days, and I had a dizzy spell earlier.

Today, only two cats sit on the wide stairs—a gray one and a brown one with a hint of orange. I enter a small gift shop then return to the cats, fill their containers with food, and sit on the staircase to greet my feline friends.

"How are you guys?" I murmur, as the gray cat walks toward me for a stroke. "Cute kedi."

I glance at my wrist. Lev's phone number is no longer there. I haven't called him, but I repeat his number to myself often. The right thing would be to shut these thoughts down and focus on the book, but part of me yearns to be in his arms. My heartbeats are erratic whenever I think of him. I'm terrified by how much I want to see him. I've begun dialing his number a few times only to stop before completing the call.

From the zippered pocket of my bag, I remove the oval-shaped pendant and slip it onto the chain I just bought at the gift shop. They meet perfectly. With some effort, I secure the chain around my neck and let the pendant drop onto my chest. I gently touch it, whispering, "Protection."

I wave off the thoughts of Lev and envision going home without the book. My eyes sting. Why won't these tears listen to me and stay away?

I call Elaine. She picks up right away. It's lovely to hear her warm voice.

"No news yet, but I'm still looking," I say apologetically.

"Oh, darling. I know you're trying. Zack comes around every day and gives me updates. He's helping me with my computers and all my tech issues."

"I know, he told me. After what he caused, it's the least he can do."

"Let me tell you something interesting, I remembered

that Harold got me that book when he traveled to Istanbul."

"Really?" I say, surprised she hadn't mentioned this before, and equally shocked that the book had once been in Istanbul.

"Something had been nagging at the back of my mind, but I couldn't quite put my finger on it—until now."

"Oh, I see," I reply.

"Perhaps this is how it was meant to be," Elaine muses. "For some reason, maybe it had to return to Istanbul. Fate? Maybe it has a reason that we're unaware of."

"Perhaps," I reply hesitantly. Could it be fate that the two people I love most will be in handcuffs over twenty years apart?

"You get home safe and sound," says Elaine.

"I will, but I'll stay a few more days."

After the call, my shoulders slump as I ponder the situation. Who am I against all the odds? I dial Zack's father. As expected, he doesn't pick up, so I leave a voicemail message.

"John, you need to call your lawyer. Now. Without a delay, please. Our son, your son, is in deep trouble, and he needs all the help he can get."

The past rushes in. I was instantly smitten when I met Zack's father. He was a smooth talker. Looking back, I can see that I needed someone to hold on to. After all, I was a lonely teenager still trying to find my place in life.

After my mom and sister and I moved to Phoenix from LA, Mom found a job at a bar. Life for our family of three improved for a while. We went to the movies. I even considered a girl in my class my best friend forever. Then my mother's reliance on prescription painkillers began. She'd been suffering from headaches ever since we left LA.

One day when I was fifteen, I stayed at school a little longer than usual to chat with my friend. I loved having a close friend. I ended up missing the school bus and had to walk home. I should have been home by 4:00 p.m., but I didn't get there until 4:45 p.m. My mother's time of death was registered as between 4:00 p.m. and 4:30 p.m.

My heart dropped at the sight of her still body on her bed. Sobbing, I called for an ambulance and gingerly removed the book from her chest.

The End.

If only I'd caught the bus. She'd taken more painkillers than she should have. Intentional or not, my sister and I never knew. We later discovered that they were cheap, illegally manufactured drugs she'd bought from someone.

Our household became eerily quiet after her departure. I even longed for her drunken episodes.

Since that day, I've made a few attempts to read the last chapters of books, but each time, my chest tightened, and my breath came in short gasps. So, I started making up the ending for every book I read.

At the time, Grace, who was eighteen, worked at a department store and was able to provide enough for us to continue living in the small apartment. I'd have nightmares about running to save our mother and would wake up to

Grace holding my hand, whispering, "Not your fault, Ava."

I got a part-time job at a fast-food chain, and Grace and I grew to love our simple life. We managed to pay the rent each month. We had a lot of grilled-cheese-sandwich-and-tomato-soup dinners, but we didn't mind. I often daydreamed about attending college, becoming a math teacher like my dad, having a better life and a bigger house, and hosting holiday dinners my sister and her family could attend.

She was sent to jail two years later. I was shocked, heartbroken, and scared that child protective services would place me elsewhere, as I was still a minor.

I applied for emancipation, a court order that would allow me to live on my own, following the steps of a work colleague who'd done so. Thankfully, it was granted. Rent took up most of my wages. I could have rented a room for less, but I didn't want to live in an unfamiliar place that held no memories of my mom and Grace. I kept my mom's bedroom door closed most of the time but looked at Grace's bed every morning as soon as I opened my eyes.

Another year passed, and then I met John, who was eight years older than I was. He came in for lunch and sat alone at a table. Whenever I glanced at him, he smiled at me. I liked the attention. After that, he returned regularly, and we began chatting. I always looked forward to seeing him.

I smile sadly at the memory.

As we got to know each other better, his compliments

became more flattering, and I hoped he'd ask me on a date. But a few weeks later, he came in and told me he was returning to LA. He was an accountant for a large firm, and his position at the Phoenix office had been only temporary. I was sad. Once again, someone was leaving my life and I had no say in it. He promised to come back, but I didn't believe that things would work out that way for me.

He did return, though, a few months later for some additional temporary work. He eventually became a partner at the firm, a position he still holds today. Mind you, his ego grew larger than the entire firm.

We didn't go through the typical stages of dating; there was no first or second date. Instead, our relationship fell into place through conversations during his lunch breaks. Soon enough, he became my boyfriend.

Then came the unexpected pregnancy. We used protection. "But it's never one-hundred-percent," he said.

We got married quickly and left Phoenix, as his job was pulling him back to LA. It was agreed that I would stay home to care for our baby and I loved it.

After living in his condo for a few months, we bought a small house. I'd shopped for the chandelier first. He thought it was silly but went along with it. I made sure the house fit the chandelier. Then I tucked the wooden box securely away in the spare bedroom.

Eventually, we bought our home in Beverley Hills, where my mom had dreamed of living one day.

Chapter 37

Ava

Maybe it's time to accept defeat and just go home, I think after a quick dinner as I sit in the armchair of my hotel room, my laptop open. I can't stop my mind from racing through all of my options. I recount every detail of my trip so far, analyzing each event and examining my actions. I check the spreadsheet I've been using to track my visits—to bookstores, collectors, and an auction house. Unfortunately, no one has returned my calls yet. My finances are draining day by day.

As I begin looking for a flight back home, I realize I need to spare some time for my friend Umut. A warm feeling fills my chest as I text him.

> How about early breakfast tomorrow morning?

> Meet me at the front of the hotel at 7:30 a.m.?

Okay

There's a knock on the door. I open it to see Melisa standing there with a smile. She's holding a small envelope. "Ava, I have a delivery for you."

"Thank you," I reply, taking the envelope with my name on it. "Do you know who left this?"

"Someone gave it to the concierge outside."

I thank her and close my door. Inside the envelope is a note.

Come to this address NOW if you want your book. ALONE!

Staring at the note, my mind races. Huh? Now? Alone?

I rush out of the room and catch up to Melisa at the end of the hallway. Showing her the note, I watch as her face lights up.

"That's good news, right?"

"Maybe, but why the secrecy? Tonight, and alone? It's already after eight. I'm not sure about this."

Melisa studies the address in the note. "It's a gift shop, not far from Taksim Square. I wouldn't worry about it. Most stay open late, and it's a busy area. Call me if you need anything."

"You think I should go?"

"I think so, but it's up to you," Melisa says. "Do whatever you're comfortable with."

I quickly reapply all my Band-Aids, wincing as I cover each blister. Grabbing onto a sliver of hope, I rush out of the hotel. It's a thirty-minute walk ahead.

When I reach İstiklal, the busy pedestrian street, I increase my pace. Just as I was giving up, my luck is finally changing. Clutching my cross-shoulder bag tightly, I maneuver through the crowds walking in both directions as if there's an invisible force pulling me, guiding me along the path to my son's rescue. Taking a deep breath, I break into a jog; even though my feet are on fire, I'm determined to reach the store as quickly as possible.

The gift shop is nestled among other businesses underneath a wide red building. The street is alive with shoppers. *Nothing to worry about*, I think, as I enter. My hand flies to my necklace. There are nazar amulets of all sizes and shapes in this store.

A friendly young man greets me.

"Hello," I say. "Merhaba. I'm here about a book."

He nods and guides me toward the back of the store. He raps on a door and opens it. I approach but hesitate before entering. *It's okay*, I tell myself. One more step. This is a rare book; a back office makes sense.

Inside is a small sofa and a large desk. In front of the desk are two chairs with a low coffee table between them. A short, slender man with dark-blond hair stands from one of the chairs and approaches me with an outstretched hand.

As I reach out to shake it, I can't help but notice his orange-tinged skin.

"Hello," he says. His grip is tight, and he doesn't let my hand go. He locks his glass-blue eyes on mine.

"My name is Yuri. What a pleasure to meet you."

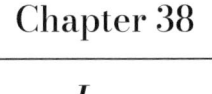

Chapter 38

Lev

Rain has just begun to fall on this final day of the book fair. I stand on my balcony, taking in the moment before making my way to the convention center.

I'm looking forward to visiting my grandmother this evening. I'll then catch a flight home tomorrow evening as I want to get home as soon as possible. Pera seems over the moon but still a little offish with me.

My phone vibrates in my pocket. It's a message from an unknown number. *Probably a scam*, I think. But then I receive another message from the same number.

Ava is on my phone. I freeze. It's a photo. She's walking toward the camera in a white shirt, her head bowed. She's on the convention center grounds. I zoom in on the picture, and my jaw drops as I recognize myself standing at the entrance behind her. It's from the day I asked her to leave the book fair.

"What the hell?" I snap.

I stare at the second photo. It captures the moment Ava locked up the bookstore before we embarked on our small tour, when I told her I was looking forward to discovering the city through her eyes. I zoom in, examining every detail, feeling the blood rush to my head. The picture captures the moment our eyes are locked.

Yuri? No, no, no. I curse under my breath, wanting to throw my phone into a wall.

I send a reply to the number.

> What is this? Who are you?

I sprint out of the room and, knowing how slow the lift is, dash down the four flights of stairs. Umut, Ava's friend, is in the lobby, soaked and having an animated conversation with the concierge.

"Mr. Lev," he yells, as soon as he sees me.

I head over, telling the concierge I know him.

"Ava and I plan breakfast, but she not come," Umut says.

"Speak Turkish," I say in Turkish, hoping to communicate faster.

He looks bewildered for a second. "Okay," he says, switching languages. "Ava and I were supposed to meet for breakfast this morning, but she didn't turn up and her phone won't ring." His words are rapid, and his arms move frantically.

He looks at the concierge and snarls. "He doesn't

believe I'm a friend of Ava. I just want someone to call her room and see if she's okay." He's almost shouting now.

"Okay," I say. "It's just after 8 a.m., and maybe she's running late?" I say, hopeful.

"She would call," replies Umut.

"Why don't you go into that patisserie and I'll make some inquiries?"

"I'll come with you." Umut wipes the raindrops from his face with his sleeve.

"Please," I say firmly. "I'll join you in a few minutes. Order anything you want."

"I don't want anything, but I'll wait for you there."

My throat tightens as I ask the receptionist on duty to call Ava's room.

"Of course, sir," she says, but unfortunately, she seems to be the slowest-moving person in this fast-paced city.

She types something on her computer, her hand not on the phone.

"It's an emergency. Can you make the call now? Please."

"I was just checking her room number."

I nod and give her a forced smile. *Calm down*, I tell myself.

She finally picks up the phone and dials. I watch her face. Her expression remains deadpan.

"No answer, sir," she says, returning the phone to its cradle.

Panic rises in my throat like bile. "Can you tell me when she was last in her room?"

The receptionist shakes her head. "I can't do that."

"It's an emergency. I'm also a guest here. Staying in room 411. I've been staying here for years."

She still seems hesitant but types something else into her computer. She tells me Ava's card was used last night just after 8:00 p.m. I'm outwardly calm. Very calm. Inside, I'm screaming.

It's Melisa's day off, but the receptionist fetches the duty manager. Together, we ride the elevator up to Ava's room. My mind races. What does all this mean?

As we approach her door, an icy sensation spreads across my neck.

"Please wait here," the duty manager says. He knocks on the door a few times, calling her name repeatedly. Finally, he opens the door. My heart sinks as he confirms what I already knew: Ava isn't in her room.

The duty manager leaves me in the hallway. I call the unknown number that sent me the photos, but no one answers, so I text.

> What do you want? Who are you? Leave her alone. She has nothing to do with me.

The response only fuels my desperation.

> Aw, pretty boy! That photo tells me otherwise!

I feel like a pawn in Yuri's twisted game. Another text message arrives.

Wait to hear from me!

I run down the stairs to join Umut at the patisserie, calling Frederica as I go to let her know I'll be late for work.

"No problem," she says. "Everything is under control here."

Umut is looking at me with bulging eyes when I hang up. "What's going on?" he asks in Turkish.

"I don't know," I say, pulling a chair across him.

"We had a plan. Something's wrong. And those men— I didn't like them."

"Men?" I ask, my brows shooting high. I lean forward. "What men? Umut, you need to tell me everything."

He crosses his arms.

"I'm also her friend, remember? You saw us together, right?" *Come on mate, help me out here.*

"I met her at the bookstore," he says. "Then, a few days ago, she called and asked for my help, and I said yes."

I try not to frown. Why would she ask for his help and not mine?

"I was a detective for Ava," Umut continues. "We followed a man from the book fair."

"When was this?"

"Umm, on Monday."

The day after we spent the night together. I swallow hard. "What did he look like?"

Umut tells me that the man had a belly.

255

"That could be anyone," I say.

"Short guy. Kleinman. Umm, I have a photo of him." Umut grabs his phone.

"Show me," I say impatiently, my voice louder than intended.

"I deleted it, but it will stay in my Deleted folder for a while," Umut says. He passes his phone to me. "Here, but I can't send it to you. Ava asked me to delete it."

"Okay, buddy," I say, more softly. "I appreciate your loyalty. Just let me have a look." I peer at it.

Umut fills me in, animatedly pointing at the photo. "We followed this guy—he went toward Galataport, then started talking with a tall, bald, big guy. But then Ava told me to run because the bald guy yelled at her. She got really scared."

I sink back in my chair and force some air through my nostrils. *What are you involved in, Ava?*

"Where did you go after Galataport?" I ask.

"An old Turkish bath," Umut says casually.

"A Turkish bath? Really?" I scoff. "Is this story not strange enough without throwing a hammam in it, my friend?"

Umut raises an eyebrow. "It was nearby, and she needed a quiet place. And to use the restroom, okay?" He shrugs.

"Okay, let's head to Galataport and start from there. Would you recognize the tall man if you saw him?"

"Yeah, I would," Umut replies confidently. "He is very

tall and very bald, and I remember what building he came out of. Just before the port, the older part of the area."

"That's helpful," I say. "But can you promise me that if I ask you to step away, run, or leave, you'll do it?"

Umut pushes up the sleeves of his sweatshirt and gives me a curt nod with stormy eyes. "'Kay."

"Give me your number, just in case."

I've realized just how much Ava means to me, and how far I'm willing to go to find her. I'm scared of my fury.

Where are you, Ava?

Chapter 39

Ava

"**Z**ack," I whisper, as I try to open my eyes. They move only a little.

Where am I?

It's dark here.

A soft pattering sound fills my ears. It's like tiny fingers tapping gently on the glass.

Rain?

Why can't I move my hand?

Chapter 40

Lev

Umut points to the entrance of a building before
Galataport and dashes ahead of me. I follow
him through the heavy rain toward the old
five-story building with a weathered stone archway. It sits
about three hundred feet from the waterfront. The actual
Galata shipport is farther away, housed in newer buildings.

I catch up to him. "You run like a cheetah."

As we move through the archway into a sprawling
courtyard, I remove my jacket. My drenched suit feels
heavy. We walk past a pharmacy, a coffee shop, and a
medical supplier on one side and a real estate agency and a
hair salon on the other. The walls are adorned with plants
and flowers. There is no tall and bald man.

"He's not here," Umut says, a hint of panic in his
voice. "But, he came out of here on Monday," he adds,
hanging his head.

"The chances of seeing him here were small," I say, placing my hand on his shoulder.

There's a loud ding in my pocket. I take out my phone. It's cold against my fingertips. Umut shuffles closer to me, trying to peer at the screen. I give him a look, and he steps away.

> Join a tour at 11:30 a.m. at Topkapı Palace. You'll get instructions on what I want you to steal for me.

> Seriously? You jackass!

I immediately regret my words. *Calmer, man. No point provoking him.*

> You don't want to play, pretty boy with a bad mouth?

> Okay, I'll play. Whatever you want me to do. But let me know she's okay.

> She is okay. COME ALONE.

"What's wrong?" Umut blurts.

"Nothing, I'm making a plan," I say. If I don't lose it first, my breathing is getting faster and more shallow.

"What plan?" Umut asks. I look at him. His eyes are glistening. "Is she all right? Why do you look worried? What's the text saying? Where is she? How can I help?" Exhaling, he adds, "I'm calm."

"We're both handling this very well, aren't we?" I say.

"Come here." I wrap an arm tightly around his shoulder. "You need to go home and dry off. Here's some money for your taxi fare."

He nods but doesn't take the money.

"Can you please send me a photo of the guy? I promise I'll delete it. But I might need it to find our friend Ava."

Umut agrees and shares the photo. Then he turns and walks away slowly, as if it's not raining cats and dogs.

A small kiosk-like place by the water sells newspapers, magazines, and snacks. I wander over and sit at a small table as the cover shields the tables from the rain.

The palace is across the water, at the top of a hill, a twenty-minute drive away. Topkapı Palace is located on what is known as the first hill of the city, in the historic area. Once the home of sultans, it's now a museum filled with priceless treasures.

I curse under my breath. Yuri has a laundry list of crimes when it comes to paintings and rare literature, but holding someone against their will? I'm a tad surprised, to be honest. This is unusual behavior. It's said that he sees himself as a connoisseur, even an artist. But a kidnapper?

I'm familiar with every nook of the palace, as my father often took me there. My family-man father, scoping out the museum to plan a theft while holding his child's hand.

I've returned to Topkapı Palace many times since starting my security business. I've guarded numerous artifacts during private exhibitions. And each time, I've silently apologized on behalf of my father.

My eyes sting, and I grit out another curse. The last time I cried was when Pera was born.

My shirt clings to my body, and I shiver a little. "Get a grip, man," I say. I'm the epitome of calm under pressure —except, of course, when a psycho decides to hold someone dear to me hostage.

Staring across the water, my gaze as sharp as a blade, I remove my phone from my pocket, gripping it tightly to keep my hand from shaking. Only one person in this world can help me now. The same person I swore I'd never call again.

Rasim Sertel.

My father.

Chapter 41

Ava

My head is too heavy to move, but my eyelids lift a fraction.

Daylight falls on my hand.

I recognize the office and this sofa.

I see slip-on shoes covered in mud by the wall.

My lids shut again.

I hear children's voices in the distance.

Chapter 42

Lev

My father answers after one ring.

"Hi, I need your help," I say, in Turkish.

"Hello, son." His voice is exactly as I remember, warm and familiar.

"I need your help," I repeat.

"I'm texting you a number for a secure line."

I hang up and then call the number. He answers on the first ring. "I need to steal something from Topkapı Palace," I say.

"You what? Are you out of your mind?"

"Were you?" I ask bitterly.

"Um . . . I . . ."

I suppress the emotions his baritone voice stirs in me, holding back the longing to hug him. I clench my hand into a fist. "Do you still know people from the art-theft world? Bibliomaniacs and all?"

"Who are you after?"

"Someone called Yuri." I spit his name through my teeth.

There's a long silence on the other end of the line. "Yuri."

"Yes, Yuri," I say impatiently. "Do you know him? I don't have much time."

More silence, for what feels like an eternity, broken only by the sound of his heavy breaths.

"Do you know him?" I repeat.

"Yes, I do. I know him well. What did you get yourself into, son?"

"Just make the calls, Dad," I say. Damn, I just called him Dad. I stopped calling him that years ago.

"I suggest you be careful with Yuri. He's unpredictable."

"Gee, you think?"

"Okay, I'll make the calls, but you need to tell me everything."

I brief him, explaining that a woman I know has disappeared and I'm now receiving messages from Yuri about what I need to do. "Another man might be involved. I'm sending you his photo now. Not sure if he's connected to Ava's disappearance."

"Who's Ava to you, son?"

"A close friend," I say, my chest thudding. "Do whatever you can. Please . . ." My words taste sour, as if I've just chewed half a lime marinated in rancid vinegar.

He inhales. "I need to tell you something about Yuri." The line goes quiet for a beat. "I, um, trained him. He was kind of like a son to me in those years."

"Bollocks." I lower the phone from my ear for a moment. "You're responsible for his training?" I grind out each word as if it's coated in molasses. "A *son* to you?"

"I'm not proud of those years. And Yuri always envied you. I talked about you a lot, but he didn't know who or where you were. A few years ago, he approached me with a big plan, wanting me to join him. I refused because I'd made a promise to you. He said I was foolish, that whoever my son was, he didn't want me in his life. I begged Yuri to leave that life behind, but he wouldn't listen. After that, I never heard from him again. He must have uncovered the truth: that you are my son."

I shake my head in frustration, and the anger in my chest boils over. "Your *son* is in serious shit with me," I snap. "I won't give up until I find him. But first I have to locate Ava."

"I know you're angry, and I'm sorry, son, but let me make the calls."

"Great." *Bring it on*, I think, ending the call.

Yuri and my father. Yuri was like a son to him. Meanwhile, I had a big black void in my life.

I call Frederica. "Can you get a couple of people from the plainclothes team onto the tours at Topkapı Palace?"

We have a couple dozen of them stationed throughout the book fair.

"Yes," she says. "Is everything okay?"

"I don't know," I say. It's far from okay. "It's just the usual for them: be vigilant, look for anomalies."

"I'll send them over now."

Now what? I could return to the courtyard, or I could—

Suddenly feeling someone watching me, I turn around. There's Umut, who's supposed to be at home drying off. He's waving toward the building, the courtyard.

I grab my jacket and sprint toward the building.

"The last office!" Umut shouts. "The real estate agency on the left—he's sitting in there."

We run together.

"That's him, that's him! That's the man!"

"Wait outside, I say. "Please, I need eyes out here." I hope this request keeps Umut out of the small office with a potentially dangerous man. "Don't come to the front—he shouldn't see you." The shop front is glass.

He nods. "'Kay."

I walk in, closing the door behind me, and stand in front of his desk. Even sitting, the man is clearly tall. And bald.

"Merhaba," he says.

I don't beat around the bush. "Hello," I say, speaking Turkish. "My name is Levent. I'm not here for trouble. I need to find a man called Yuri, and I think you may know him. Do you know where I can find him?"

His brows pop up. "This is a real estate agency, not a Yellow Pages directory."

270

I suck air through my nostrils. "Okay, big chap, on Monday, you spoke to a man outside this building." I show him the photo on my phone. "Remember him? Then you saw a woman, and you yelled at her. Tell me why you yelled at her. And who was that man you were talking to? Tell me and I promise I'll leave quietly."

"Who are you to come into my business and question me? I don't know what you're talking about."

"I think you do," I say calmly, fixing my eyes on his.

He stands, chest swelling.

I'm acutely aware that his office is away from foot traffic.

"Leave my office," he barks. "Now."

I hear the door open behind me and see Umut out of the corner of my eye. Without looking at him, I motion him back. "Wait outside," I say firmly, not taking my eyes off the man.

I hear the door click.

"Last chance," I say, my voice low. "Just answer these questions and I'll leave you alone. No trouble."

The man rounds his desk. "Get out of my office!"

Fluidly, I retreat a step, creating enough space between us to grab his left triceps, just above the elbow. Simultaneously, I grab his left wrist with my other hand and execute a sharp, controlled pull that draws his upper arm backward: the armbar maneuver.

His elbow locks, and under the pressure, his upper body jerks forward, sending him crashing to the ground—facedown. He lets out a cry, his breath coming in sharp gasps. I can feel the tension in his muscles as the back of his neck flushes red.

"Look, big guy," I say quietly, my grip on his arm tightening. "I don't want to do this, but I know how to handle your type. It's what I do. And right now, I have enough anger to break your arm."

The man whimpers and nods frantically. "I don't know where Yuri is."

"How are you involved with him? Why did you scare Ava?"

"I don't know who Ava is, man," he says, wincing.

"Let's jog your memory." I push his elbow down.

"I'm no— Ah! Do you mean Jane?" He grunts. "She told me her name was Jane. We met before."

What? I release the pressure again. "You met before?"

"She wanted a rare book, and I was going to give her a contact. Mr. Klein. The guy in the picture you showed me. But then Yuri's associate told me not to make any deals with Jane."

It sinks in. Ava was searching for a rare book. Why didn't she just ask me?

"Let go of my arm now," he growls.

"When did you meet her? What day?"

"I don't know, man, it was last week!"

"Dig into your memory," I say, pushing his arm down.

"Okay, okay, yes. It was Saturday. There was a matinee at the movie theater."

"What happened after?"

"The associate told me not to make a deal with her. But I got annoyed, so I followed her a little to see where she went. Just in case."

"Just in case of what?" I shout, my anger boiling over.

"I don't know, man, it was a spur-of-the-moment thing."

"I have one more question," I say, eyeing the office exit. Umut is outside the door, mouth agape and eyes wide.

"What was happening on Monday, when you yelled at Jane?" *Ava Jane Jenkins.*

"I was about to get the book from Mr. Klein. *Pride and Prejudice.* But then your Jane appeared."

"Anything else?"

"Yuri's man came here after and asked me to call Mr. Klein. They talked, I believe he agreed to sell the book to Yuri instead. I don't want anything to do with that book. It's bad news."

I sigh. "I see. I'm going to release your arm now, but don't do anything silly. I'm going to show you another photo before I go, okay?" I increase the pressure.

"Okay, okay!" he shouts.

I let go of him and move to stand by the door, where I hold up my phone. "Is this my Jane?" I ask, as he clutches his arm. *My Jane. My Ava Jane.*

"Yes."

With that, I step out of the office and shut the door. "Run," I say to Umut. I follow closely.

Is Ava in danger because of Yuri's twisted vendetta

against me? He saw us together when I took her for that guided walk, but the first photo? She was walking from the convention center.

Why was he targeting Ava only a few days after her arrival? What don't I see?

Chapter 43

Ava

"Hello," I whisper. Am I alone?

There's someone in the room.

"Hel— "

I swallow. My throat is dry.

"You have been a very good girl," says a man.

I recognize that voice.

Me? A good girl?

"Thank you," says a woman.

I recognize that voice, too.

Chapter 44

Lev

"**A**s fast as you can, please," I say to the taxi driver.

I roll down the window. The air is thick with exhaust fumes. Now that the rain has stopped, the sun shines brightly. The tram rumbles down the middle of Galata Bridge, its wheels clanking.

As the taxi weaves its way across the bridge, I feel as if my chest has joined the city's pulsing artery. A few people are fishing, a young couple is taking a selfie, and another person is capturing a photo of the beautiful scenery. I envy them all.

I'm sorry, Ava. This is my fault.

I keep looking at the pictures of her. Her beautiful face is downcast as she walks away from the convention center. Then there's the other one. The one where we're smiling at each other. "My Ava Jane," I murmur, shaking my head.

What should be a ten-minute journey between

Galataport and the historic area takes thirty, but walking or running would still take longer as it's uphill. I'm not late, but I'm anxious to get there. As the taxi screeches to a halt, I quickly pay, throw open the door, and rush toward Topkapı Palace.

I join the queue of people waiting in front of the ticket office. Twenty-five minutes until the tour. My stomach coils, twisting and turning.

Right before the tour begins, a kid with scruffy hair—barely a teenager—approaches and hands me a note. He tries to run away, but I grab his arm. "Hey, young man, what is this? And who are you?"

"Let go of me!" he squeaks. "A man asked me if I spoke English. Then he showed me your photo and paid me to give you a note."

"When? Where is he? What did he look like?

"Dunno, a while ago. A man with a mustache."

Sighing with exasperation, I release the kid and then open the note.

Go to Basilica Cistern. Get in – NOW!

Surprised by the new instructions but relieved I don't have to steal anything from the palace, I crumple the note in my hand. "Yeah, I'll play your scavenger hunt, you maniac," I grumble under my breath.

I move swiftly toward the Basilica Cistern, passing the iconic Hagia Sophia along the way. In the near distance, the Blue Mosque stands tall. It only takes me a few minutes to reach my destination.

I wait in the queue, quietly scanning my surroundings. Then, I buy a ticket, my frustration growing. Yuri must be amused watching me hop from one attraction to the next, but I suspect that his spies are around, so I do as he asks. Standing in the queue at the entrance to the Basilica Cistern, I gaze around but wear a calm expression, trying to blend in with the crowd.

At the bottom of fifty-two stone steps, more than three hundred colossal stone columns come into view, rising from the water. The vaulted ceiling adds to the eerie and otherworldly feel.

Basilica Cistern

The last time I was here was the summer before last, with Pera and my grandmother. Pera still talks about it.

She couldn't believe this was the structure that had provided water for the whole city for centuries.

Once I'm out of this mess—and out of a sixth-century underground chamber—I'm going to plan a vacation to a remote Scottish village where the only sights are an unobstructed sky, an endless ocean, and rolling valleys.

The awed crowd snaps pictures and ventures down narrow paths. The area is illuminated by lights that cast a green hue over everything. I look around, not sure where to go now. The air is heavy and damp. My pulse races.

I step onto a narrow walkway between the columns and move toward the two stone Medusa heads. One is upside down and the other is on its side, revealing only half her face. Their origins are mysterious, and legend has it that if you look directly into Medusa's eyes, you'll turn into stone.

The light changes from green to red. What does Yuri want me to do next? I'm certainly clear about what I want to do to him. Turning him into stone would be justified right about now.

Chapter 45

Ava

The woman in the room faces away from me.

Long curly hair. Lots of it.

She turns around.

"Melisa?"

She walks toward me, smiling.

One side of my mouth twitches upward.

I see a man standing behind her.

He smiles. His name is Yuri.

They both smile.

Fear floods my veins.

My fingers curl.

My skin feels cold.

Chapter 46

Lev

I stand as motionless as the Medusa heads, waiting, until a man in his twenties approaches me.

"Messenger here. A man over there"—he points to the entrance—"told me to ask you to jump into the water and get out of this place. He said he'll only give you your next clue if you follow his instructions."

"Let's get even more ridiculous," I say, weighing my next move. The place is full of people.

"Will you jump?" asks the messenger with a grin. "Is this part of a show?"

I shake my head. "No, mate. You wouldn't believe it if I told you. Thanks for the message, though," I say, then hop over the railing, landing in the knee-high water with a splash. Several people gasp and snap photos. I quickly climb back out, photobombing a few shots. I dart past a guard.

"I'm sorry," I call, as two more guards give chase,

shouting. "I promise I'll come back for a talk and get the fine."

I'm out, on the street. What now? I look around for another messenger. "C'mon man," I groan. "You've had your fun. Got me chased by guards."

My phone pings. I take one large gulp of air before I look at it.

> If you want her, get me WHAT I want.

"What do you bloody want, man?" I hiss, staring at the screen.

Another message arrives.

> You know, the one that got away. In Paris.

"Bloody hell." I grit my teeth. He wants the page. The page from an early draft of *Hamlet*. The one I stopped him from stealing. He's getting me to do his dirty work for him.

"Like father, like son," I say.

"He was like a son to me."

Fury engulfs me.

My phone pings again.

> U have 2 hours. Take the page to the location I send you. Put it in the red car and leave. I'll tell you where she is when I get the page. Tell NO ONE if you want to see her beautiful face again.

I text back.

> I need more time!

Another message comes through seconds later with a Google location link.

> Sure thing, I'll extend your time. You now have two hours and five minutes!

> TO BE OR NOT TO BE?

> TO STEAL OR NOT TO STEAL?

> That is the question, pretty boy!

Chapter 47

Ava

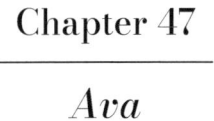

S omeone is shuffling papers and pushing things around. The sounds are sharp, setting my nerves on edge. Then footsteps, deliberate and heavy, approach. A chair scrapes across the floor, making me cringe.

"I hate your boyfriend's guts," says the man. Yuri.

Boyfriend? I don't have one. I keep my eyes tightly shut, the lids squeezing so hard they might never open again. Cold sweat gathers at the back of my neck.

"Look at me. I'm a pretty boy," he says mockingly.

What? Who's a pretty boy?

He continues to taunt me, his breath warm against my ear. "He thinks he's better than me, but now he knows not to mess with Yuri."

The foul odor of his breath hits me—a stale, smoky stench of cigarettes.

The door creaks open, and the light tap of heels echoes.

I inhale deeply, sensing Yuri moving away from me.

"Once I get what I want, what shall we do with her?" Yuri says.

"Leave her with me," says a woman. My scalp prickles. *Melisa?*

"You're not just a pretty helper. You'd kill for me?"

"I'd do anything for you," Melisa replies with a giggle.

"I like that," Yuri says with a laugh. "For now, give her more drugs, keep her quiet. Pretty boy is wrapped around my finger."

I hear footsteps. The door closes.

A warm hand touches mine, and I jolt.

"Ava, it's me. Melisa." Her whisper is urgent.

I keep my eyes closed. There's a sour taste in my mouth.

"I didn't give you drugs last time," she continues, "so I know you can hear me."

I slowly open my eyes and meet her gaze.

"I'll help you, but you need to help me too. Just pretend to be asleep, all right?" she says softly, revealing a small needle. "I won't administer any more, but you need to act like you're sleeping so I can help you."

I give a weak nod in agreement.

"I didn't know how dangerous this man was. I'm looking for an opportunity to get away with you, okay?" She glances over her shoulder nervously.

I nod again. I have no other option.

Chapter 48

Lev

I hail a taxi. "I'll triple your fare if you take me to this address as fast as possible," I say to the young driver.

A mischievous grin spreads across his face, and then he revs up the engine, throwing me back into my seat. I strike a deal with the driver, offering a generous amount for him to stick with me for the next couple of hours—Two hours and five minutes.

As I make several phone calls, we zoom through the streets and quickly arrive at the convention center.

"Wait for me here," I say, before rushing inside.

Thirty minutes and several activities later, I return to the taxi, clutching a bag under my arm.

"Here's the address," I say, jumping into the front seat this time. The location is a car park. It's only fifteen miles from the convention center, but with the city traffic, it could take forever. The driver enters the location in his navigation system and presses down on the gas pedal again. I'm thrown around in my seat as we take sharp turns.

When we eventually arrive 25 minutes later, I see the red car. Its license plate is caked with mud, making it impossible to read.

I do as instructed, leaving the bag inside, and swiftly return to the taxi. "Back to the convention center," I inform the driver.

Given Yuri's erratic behavior, I couldn't risk negotiating for more information about Ava's whereabouts. He holds all the power.

Or so he thinks.

As the taxi drives off, my father calls.

"Son, I'm sending you an address. I think she's there. I'm on my way, too. I finally got a lead from one of my old connections. There's a gift shop near Taksim Square. Best Gifts."

"Genius name for a gift shop," I say with scoff, before giving the driver the new address. "I am not far," I add.

"Me neither. Apparently, Yuri hangs out there a lot. The owner is also from the same town. He's bragging about something big. We need to be careful, like shadows." He pauses. "We need to call the police, too."

"They already know," I say, my stomach twisting. "They're tracking me, this call and the page right now."

"Oh, okay. Apparently, he's been fixated on revenge since your last encounter," my father continues. "His girlfriend is still locked up. Now that he knows you're my son, too . . ." He trails off, and I can almost hear him clenching his jaw.

The taxi weaves through the roads. I check the address again. The buildings blur together. My anxiety grows.

When we finally arrive, I hand the driver a wad of bills, thank him, and jump out in front of a fast-food restaurant nestled underneath a four-story red building with fading paint.

On my left, next to the restaurant, is a beauty shop, and next to it is the gift shop. I inhale sharply. Its windows display a variety of souvenirs: ceramics, colorful lamps, textiles, and nazar amulets in different shapes.

Then my father emerges from a taxi that has just turned onto the street. He has more silver hair and lines on his face than I remember but still wears the same old charming smile.

My pulse zings. I'm tired of hiding and pushing down emotions. We embrace for the first time in years, a solid hug that dissolves years of distance and silence.

"Good to see you, son," he says.

I nod. "Good to see you, too." Surprisingly, it does feel good.

"The gift shop is there," I say, gesturing. "But let's check the back first."

Behind the building stretches a wide, long alleyway. In front of each of the five doors at the back of the building sits a large wheelie bin. At the far end, three kids, about 9 or 10 years old, are playing with a football—of all places.

There's a man standing near a door in the middle of the

building. He's smoking a cigarette and has his back turned. My father and I keep out of sight, peering around the corner.

Then I spot her—Melisa, talking to the guy with the cigarette. She's facing in our direction.

My blood boils, anger surging through my veins, and I feel my Adam's apple rise and fall, tightening with each breath. "Is she fucking involved in this too?" I say, trying to keep my voice down.

"Look at her left hand," my father replies calmly.

Melisa leans against the wall, her weight on her right side. She repeatedly curls her index finger, gesturing for me to come closer.

"She's distracting the guy," my father whispers.

I nod, stepping lightly. Melisa's voice grows louder, and her laughter echoes through the alleyway. I sneak up behind the man, ready to pounce.

Chapter 49

Ava

I clench and unclench my fists. My strength is coming back but my arms and legs feel weighed down. I tilt my head up and flinch. The overhead light is bright. The door on my right is closed, but there's no one in the office.

I need an escape plan.

I slowly move each one of my limbs—all intact. Then I hear footsteps. I shut my eyes and hold my breath. Each thump of my heart seems to echo in the quiet space. The door swings open.

"Ava, I'm getting you out of here," Melisa says, quietly but urgently. "Can you stand and walk?"

My throat is dry and metallic. "Yes," I manage to say, the word feeling like dust.

"Let's go," Melisa urges. "Hold my arm."

I shake my head as I stand. "I'm fine," I say. My blisters are throbbing, raw and hot on my swollen heels and toes. I ignore the pain and move. There are thuds and shouts as we burst out of the office into the gift shop. My eyes bulge at the scene before me: Lev and an older man pinning another man down.

Lev runs toward me, and I melt into his arms. His forehead and part of his face is crimson. "Your head!" I exclaim.

"Only a small cut. All that matters is that you're safe."

Then, I spot a man emerging from the back door, gun raised and aimed directly at us. "Watch out!" I shout, and Lev yanks me to the side. We tumble down, pain slicing through my shoulder as chaos erupts around us. Sirens wail in the distance, and everything fades to black.

Chapter 50

Lev

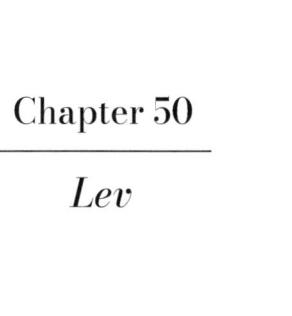

I sit beside Ava's hospital bed watching clear liquid drip slowly into her arm through an IV tube. Her left shoulder is heavily bandaged and immobilized in a sling. Dark circles under her eyes mar her pale, beautiful face. A monitor beside the bed flickers with green and blue lines, and each beep matches the rise and fall of her chest. The ninth-floor room has a large window revealing a cloudless morning.

My father enters quietly, holding a cup. I stand to greet him, and we step into the hallway.

"How are you holding up?" he asks gently.

"Terribly," I reply, through clenched teeth. "I can't believe I let her get shot."

The bullet grazed her shoulder, tearing through muscle and fracturing her upper arm bone on its way out.

"She's safe now, so stop torturing yourself," my father

says, resting a comforting hand on my shoulder. 'That other guy came out of nowhere."

I just nod bitterly. "Any news about Yuri?"

"No, son. It appears these guys were just hired hands. No one from Yuri's actual circle was caught. He's too careful. Even the shop owner, the one who shot Ava, was just a pawn."

Before returning to Ava's room, I use the bathroom. The right side of my forehead is stitched and bandaged. I shudder at the memory. Yesterday, as I lunged at the man Melisa was speaking to, she yelled, "I'll get Ava," and ran inside. I grappled with the guy, but he broke free and followed Melisa in. Giving chase, I sent him crashing into a shop table. He swung a broken chair leg at my head. I managed to block most of the blow with my arm, but the leg grazed my forehead. Seconds later, I had him facedown, arms behind his back, and my father helped hold him down.

I push away the memory and hurry back to Ava's room. After a while, she stirs.

"Ava, I'm here," I say, taking her hand. "I'm here. I'll call the nurse now, okay?"

Ava, groggy, gives a slight nod as I press the button to call the nurse.

The nurse arrives promptly.

"Where am I?" Ava asks, barely whispering.

"In a hospital in Istanbul," says the nurse in English. "Everything is fine. I'm your nurse, and you're on some painkillers. Can you tell me your name, miss?"

"Ava," she responds weakly, then gestures toward me. "And that's Lev."

The nurse smiles. "That's great. Let me check a few things and I'll let your doctor know you're awake."

When the nurse leaves, I move closer to her bed. "Hey, you," I whisper.

The slight smile tugging at her lips is the best sight I've seen in a while.

"How are you feeling?" I ask.

"Confused," she says, glancing at her left shoulder. "What happened? Am I in danger? What's happened to your face?"

"No one can get close to you here," I assure her. "And it's just a few stitches."

A doctor enters to check on Ava, so I step outside. My knees buckle with relief; I've been waiting all night for her to open her eyes, refusing to leave the hospital.

I lean against the wall. "She's okay," I whisper to myself. "She's awake, she's safe."

A few hours later, Ava is awake again and sitting up in the bed. It's Friday afternoon. I didn't get to the book fair on its last day—well, I did, but not for security operations. I curse under my breath.

"The doctor was here again," Ava is saying. "I'll be out tomorrow. My shoulder and arm will take six to eight weeks to recover, and I might need some physical therapy

297

afterward. It's not bad, I suppose." She blinks. "Zack. My son. I need to call him."

"He knows," I say. "I spoke with him. When he rang your phone, I answered. He knows you're in the hospital but also that you're okay. It's very early in LA now."

"He must be worried," Ava says softly.

"Yes, he was. He called several times, and I answered each time. I even stayed on a video call while you were sleeping so he could see you. He knows you're okay."

"Thank you."

"Of course, but could you please talk to Umut briefly? He's driving me bonkers."

I video-call Umut and hand my phone to Ava.

They talk for a while—mostly, Umut tells Ava how worried he was—and then I tell him she needs to rest. With a dramatic sigh, he tells me in Turkish that he should have protected her better.

Warmth bubbles up in my chest. This kid. "The important thing is that she's okay now."

"I'll make sure to see you before I leave Istanbul," Ava says to Umut. "We'll have our breakfast date."

"Leave?" says Umut, looking as though he just discovered a triangle with four sides.

"Well, I need to go home sometime, you know."

After hanging up, she tells me, "You know, meeting Umut was one of the unexpected highlights of this trip."

She's the only highlight of mine.

"How is Pera?" Ava asks.

"I expected a tantrum, but she was incredibly

understanding when I told her what happened and why I was staying. Most of what happened, anyway."

"How sweet."

"She thinks her daddy is a superhero now," I say with a chuckle.

"He is," she says, making my heart flutter.

"But you were the one who noticed the guy and shouted. It's you who saved us."

"Thank you for coming after me," she says, turning her head to the side and pressing her cheek into the pillow. "I was terrified in that room," she adds softly."But I could hear children playing soccer nearby. Their happy voices were calming among all the scary ones."

"I'm sorry you had to go through all this."

Her hand flies to her neck. "Where's my pendant?"

"It's here." I smile and remove it from my pocket. "Hospital staff took it off when you arrived, and it was with all your other belongings."

She takes it and holds it in her fist.

"The police are coming to get your statement," I say. "The doctor is allowing it, but only if you're up to it."

She nods. "But first, can you tell me what happened? Do you know what that man, Yuri, wanted from me? And where is Melisa?"

I pull my chair closer and, after a big exhale, tell Ava about my history with Yuri, leaving my father out.

"So," I say, finishing, "he wanted to hurt me. He knew I was staying at our hotel, and he paid Melisa a lot of cash to be his informant."

Ava turns her head and looks out the window. "I liked Melisa. I still can't believe it," she says, sadness drenching her voice.

"I'm just as surprised as you are. She's in custody now, cooperating with the police. Melisa told Yuri we met at the bar and then watched Pera's show together. That's how you ended up on Yuri's radar."

"Oh," she says, a look of realization crossing her face. "That was right at the start of my trip. Mrs. Bergström's pass, the VIP ticket . . . She told me she made inquiries."

"All seems to link back to Yuri and his men," I say.

"Melisa told me she was excited to finally be able to afford to move into her own place," she says. "But then why did she help me escape if she was working for Yuri?"

"Apparently she agreed to help Yuri but didn't know the full extent of his plans and had no intention of causing you or anyone else harm."

"I remember—she asked me many times, 'Will you be careful?'" she says quietly, wrapping her arm around herself.

"Also, it was Yuri who ordered that big guy to stop negotiating with you at the movie theatre."

"Oh, yeah. That was really strange."

"I have a bone to pick with you for meeting with shady people, but that's for another time," I say teasingly.

"I was desperate to get the book." Ava's voice softens, her words trailing off as if their weight is too much to carry.

"I'm sorry, it seems Yuri now has the book you were after."

Ava's long eyelashes flutter as tears roll down her cheeks. Having a teenage daughter, I've come to learn the importance of embracing all emotions, but it still pains me to see Ava in such a state.

"That's it then. This story ends here. I failed."

I gently grasp her hand, and a shiver runs through me. "Perhaps that story comes to an end, but there might be another one waiting somewhere."

Ava's gaze shifts to our hands, and she blinks rapidly.

I ask, "Why didn't you mention the book, and your urgency to get into the book fair? Why were you desperate? I just want to understand."

Her chin drops, and the shadows under her eyes seem to deepen. "It's not you—it's me."

"Are you breaking up with me before we even start dating?" I ask, cackling. "Get ready, because I'll do whatever it takes to convince you to go on a date with me. I'm ready to pick you up with flowers, my hands trembling."

But she doesn't laugh. "I was already having a hard time as a mother, Lev. When we were at the top of the convention center, you told me in no uncertain terms how you felt about theft. And . . . well, my son stole the book I was after. Admitting that to you would have felt like forever branding him as a thief. One instance of stupid judgment on his part brought me to Istanbul."

I feel a pang of guilt for being happy that she was led to Istanbul.

"Do you know who he stole it from?" I ask.

"Oh yes, our lovely neighbor and close friend, Elaine. Her late husband, Harold, got her the book as part of his proposal over seventy years ago. In Istanbul, actually."

"Wow, that's one romantic gesture. Go, Harold." Then I sigh. "As far as your son, well, people, kids, make mistakes." I clear my throat, which is suddenly as dry as sandpaper. "My confession time. I lived here in Istanbul with both my parents until I was eleven, when my mother left my father and we moved to the UK. Turns out my father is— well, was, I hope he's not anymore . . ." I clear my throat again. "Anyway, he *was* a known art thief. It wasn't a one-time mistake. It was many, many years of stealing."

"Come again?" she says, with a confused expression.

"My father. The old guy you saw at the gift shop, that was my father, a former art thief."

"Oh, wow," she says, her voice a whisper.

I shrug. "Yeah, who's afraid of being judged now?"

Ava sits up straighter. "And you run a security company?" She tilts her head. "I thought my childhood was traumatic enough. I focused on getting a house in life with a stupid chandelier."

"We all have our stories." I pause. "Speaking of theft, Yuri had a ransom demand. He wanted me to steal a rare page from the book fair in exchange for your safety."

302

"What?" she asks, her eyes as vast as the universe. "You didn't actually do that, did you?"

I lock my gaze on hers. "Of course I did. I'd do anything to keep you safe. But, there is more."

I give her the rundown. Before the event, Frederica worked with specialists to create a decoy of the page. We also placed microchips on certain protectors as precautions. The chips are tiny, practically invisible without a microscope. I never imagined that I'd be the one doing the stealing.

I contacted the police, who quickly sent a Special Crimes Task Force. After I shared everything I knew about Yuri, they agreed it was best to use the actual rare page, knowing he'd easily spot even the most convincing decoy.

"Really?" exclaims Ava.

"Yes, I wasn't about to handle this on my own, not with your life at risk. We devised a fast but careful plan. We couldn't just give Yuri the page and hope for the best —we needed a way to track him, find you."

I pause, taking a deep breath. "Then my father called, saying you were likely at the gift shop."

As the Special Crimes Task Force tracked every movement, they intercepted the red car just as it was leaving Istanbul, once they confirmed Ava was safe. I had planted a microchip in the car when I left the page behind. The driver insisted he didn't know anyone named Yuri and claimed he was merely delivering the item to a taxi, having been paid in cash.

"Mind-blowing," Ava says, shaking her head in

disbelief. "I'm really sorry for all the trouble. I'm just so relieved you have the page."

"No apologies, remember?" I reply with a wink.

"Was Not-Sarah upset?" she asks, and immediately her eyes widen. "I'm so sorry. I meant Serra. Please ignore what I just said—it must be the medication I'm on."

"Not-Sarah?" I repeat with a grin. "Anyway, Serra wasn't upset. She worked with me and dealt directly with the collector who owns the page. Oh, and she came to the hospital to see how you were doing."

"I'm sure she came to the hospital to check on you," says Ava. Do I sense a little jealousy? Maybe it's my wishful thinking.

"No," I say firmly. "She's a friend. She's been in a happy relationship for months." I say. Something I learned only a few days ago.

Serra is dating one of my team members, a colleague from London who's also here now. Apparently, she's wanted to tell me a few times but never found the right moment. They probably weren't sure how I'd react, but of course, I'm happy for them. I recall Serra trying to say something during the meal when we met Ava.

I fill Ava on everything else. She cracks up when I tell her that Yuri sent me into the water in the Basilica Cistern.

"I'm glad you find it amusing," I say wryly. "Your laughter is the most beautiful sound I've heard in a while."

Ava blushes. After a few moments of silence, she asks, "So, what now? Where is that man?"

"Still at large," I say, as a sharp pain twists in my gut.

"With Elaine's book?"

"I'm afraid so," I reply, my chin dipped. My voice steady and controlled. My jaw tightens ever so slightly, and a pulse throbs at my temple as I hold back to contain the quiet storm inside me. "But, just focus on getting better, please," I say, standing. I brush her cheek for a moment, starting to pull my hand away when Ava leans in. She presses her face into my palm and covers my hand with hers. Her smile reaches her eyes, lighting up the room. She holds my hand there, and the warmth of her touch spreads through me like sunlight, melting away the tension.

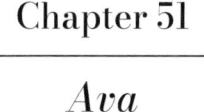

As night falls, I recount every moment to the police. Each detail drags me deeper into sadness and anxiety. After they leave, I lean back in the chair and close my eyes. What a mess!

Moments later, I hear the door open, followed by Lev's gentle voice. He takes my hand. "It's done now," he says softly. "Let's get you back to bed for some rest."

I nod. Just as I sit on the bed, my phone starts ringing. "It's Zack!" I say, beaming at Lev before answering. "Zack, sweetie?"

"Hey, Mom. I was losing my mind worrying about you."

"It's so great to hear your voice," I say. "I want to see your face. Turn the video on." I move to sit in the chair by the window.

Lev stands next to me. "Do you want me to give you privacy?" he asks quietly.

Shaking my head, I reach for his arm, wanting him to stay.

"I'll video-call later," Zack says. "I just woke up."

"Zack, please turn the camera on," I insist. The thought of seeing my son's face again kept me strong when I was drugged and helpless in that office.

"Okay, but just so you know, I'm all right."

I gasp as the video flickers to life on my phone screen. "Oh. My. God." Deep, dark bruises frame Zack's right eye. His lip is swollen, and his cheek is scratched.

"What happened? Are you okay?"

I can feel Lev watching me.

"I'm fine. When I didn't hear from you, I drove back to San Jose and found the guy who originally took the book from me. He's the one who passed it on to someone else. He stopped taking my calls after I paid him for the photo of that guy."

"You paid him? With what? Did your dad help?"

"No, I sold a few things online and offered him everything I had. Anyway, when I didn't hear from you, I went to see him in person. I threatened to go to the police if he didn't tell me more about what he knew about Istanbul. He insisted he didn't know anything; I punched him, and he punched back."

My hand flies to my mouth and I look at Lev.

"That was before he got ahold of me," Lev says.

"Don't worry, Mom," Zack says, as I stare at his battered face. "The other guy looks much worse." He laughs, but I don't join in. I'm panicking.

"Are you in danger? Should we call the police? Did you call your dad?"

"No, no, and no, Mom. Look, I'm back home now. See?"

The background, my living room, seems as though it belongs to someone else. "Just keep out of trouble, okay?" I plead. "Will you?"

"What do you think?" he asks rhetorically.

"Good," I say. "What did you sell?"

"My phone. I'm using an old one, but it still works. I also sold my smartwatch and my bike and a few more things."

"Oh, darling."

"I don't care, Mom. You're okay. That's what matters. Although you and Lev don't look much better than I do."

We all burst out laughing.

After I hang up, tears skid down my face. Seeing Zack hurt is overwhelming.

Lev sits on the edge of the bed. "He was looking out for you," he says. "He's a good lad."

"I know," I say, proud of my son. I realize I've missed being proud of him. With a smile, I picture him. On the call, he was wearing his favorite T-shirt—the one that he loves wearing with his slip-on shoes.

"The shoes!" I yelp, suddenly remembering.

"My shoes? What about them?" Lev asks, lifting his foot.

"Not your shoes," I rasp. "The office where they kept me—there were shoes. The guy who sold me that VIP ticket, he wore them. Those exact ones. White soles, blue canvas slip-ons."

"Are you sure?" Lev asks, standing.

"The mud patterns . . . " I swallow hard. "Yes, those are the exact shoes. The officer told me to call them if I remembered anything else, even the smallest detail."

After I finish speaking with an officer on the phone, exhaustion washes over me, and I close my eyes for a moment. Each time I lift my lids slightly, I catch sight of Lev—sitting in the chair, standing by the bed, or leaning against the wall, his gaze fixed on me.

When I finally open my eyes, I see his lips twitch into a smile as he gently touches my

"How are you feeling?" he asks.

"Tired, but okay," I reply.

"Elaine called a few minutes ago," he says.

"Oh, let me call her back." I start a video call, and Elaine's face soon appears on my phone screen. "Oh Ava, what happened? Zack told me you're in the hospital. I'm so sorry I asked you to go to Istanbul. This is all my fault." Her eyelids are red and puffy.

"I'm fine, Elaine. Please don't be upset. But I don't think I can get your book back," I say, hanging my head.

"You just worry about getting better now, my dear girl."

Tomorrow morning can't come soon enough. I'm anxiously waiting for the doctor to give me the green light to leave the hospital. I can't wait to see Zack. I'm dreading receiving the bill, though. I forgot to buy insurance before this trip. *You can't dwell on that now*, I remind myself. *You were in a bit of a rush to get here.*

In the morning, I sit on the edge of the bed, just finishing my small breakfast. There's a soft knock on the door, and Lev enters. I told him to go and get some rest last night. He protested, but in the end, he agreed.

He moves the breakfast table aside and stands next to me. I inhale his outdoorsy scent—earthy, sturdy.

"How are you this morning?" he asks.

"Ready to leave," I say. "The police came by again this morning. They want me to work with a sketch artist to identify the guy with the shoes. How's your head?"

"I'm great—I've assigned you a personal bodyguard."

"Bodyguard?"

"Yeah. Me." He tilts his chin up.

I can't help but grin at him.

He steps closer, smiling from ear to ear. His hand brushes my cheek—soft and caring. Closing my eyes, I lean into his hand and let out a contented sigh. We stay in the stillness for a moment, then a rustle stirs within me, like the whisper of leaves in a quiet forest. *One last time being close to his skin.*

I lift my head and sit up, even though I want to stay in that moment. Reminding myself that we are worlds apart.

Slowly, he lets his hand fall away. "You look much

better," he says softly. "Did you sleep well? Any discomfort? How's your shoulder?"

I nod. "I'm much better. Like I said, ready to get out of here."

"Zack called," he says, his tone casual.

My brow furrows. "Why? Is he okay?"

"He said he was sending a family member to check on you."

I frown and rack my brain. "Who?" Then it hits me, and I groan. "His father? No, no, no. He's not family. I don't need him."

I hear her voice before I see her. "You know, you do have another family member besides Zack."

I look up. There she is, standing by the door. Grace. My sister. My mouth falls open and my pulse races.

She comes to my side. "No sister of mine is going to be alone in a hospital in a foreign country." She kisses the top of my head and then carefully hugs me, avoiding my shoulder. Lev quietly slips out.

"Grace." I nuzzle into her neck as tears streak down my face. "I can't believe you're here," I say, my voice muffled against her.

"Zack found me on social media," she says. "I took the first flight."

After staying in her embrace for a while, I sit up and take her hand. "Let me look at you," I say.

She wipes her eyes and stands back. Her light-yellow blouse is almost the same shade as her hair, which falls

312

just above her shoulders. Soft waves frame her face, and she has a side bang across her forehead.

"Give me your hand," I say, pinching the top of it. "Are you really here?"

"Hey, you're supposed to pinch yourself, not me," she says with a laugh.

"Touché," I say with a grin. "You still have that infectious laugh."

Lightness floods my limbs.

"I want to know everything. Are you happy? What have you been doing for the last twenty years? Where do you live? Do you still love tacos?" I frown and add, "I should really be angry with you, but I'm just so happy that you're here."

"Yep, you're ready to get out of hospital," she says with a chuckle. "I live in Seattle. I'm happy, I'm married to a wonderful woman, Katie, who can't wait to meet you. I still love tacos. There's so much to catch up on, but let's get you better first. And I really missed you."

"I missed you, too."

We talk and talk—so much to catch up on. I learn that Grace is an editor for a publisher and Katie is a personal trainer. I tell her about Zack and my business. "I came to Seattle a few times for work. I can't believe you were there. Oh, and I'm now divorced. He walked out on me after having an affair for a few years."

"Shithead."

"I know. But I'm all right. We had the life I thought I wanted, one with stability, but I see now that I don't need him for that. And I'm thankful that our relationship gave me Zack, the greatest gift of all."

"Yeah, my nephew is one cool kid," Grace says. "You know, I called the number you left when I got out of prison."

"Really?" I say. There's a tug in my chest. She did call.

"Your ex answered the phone. We even met up."

"What?" I whisper.

"Yeah, I insisted on speaking with you, even told him I'd knock on the door if he didn't let me. But John made it clear that you never wanted to see me again and that if I cared about you, I should stay away—for your happiness. He was so convincing." She swallows. "I didn't want to risk upsetting you."

Rage surges within me. "He never told me." It's all I can say. But I quickly let the anger go. He's not worth the energy.

"We're together now." Her eyes narrow, and she smirks. "By the way, that Lev is really into you."

A smile creeps onto my face, but I quickly erase it with a deep sigh. "We live on different continents. I just want to go home and help Zack through this mess, rebuild my life."

"He's too hot to let distance get in the way, hon," she says teasingly. "And think of the reunions." She sobers a little. "But right now, just get better. We'll talk about Mr. Hotness another time."

Just then, Lev knocks on the door. He's holding drinks

from the cafeteria. "Are you ready to leave?" he asks me, then looks at Grace, who's giggling like a teenager.

"What? Did I miss something?"

"Yes, I'm ready," I respond, giving Grace a playful scowl.

"I have a hotel suggestion," Lev says. "My colleagues sometimes stay there—it's safe and secure, in a quiet waterfront area. Or I could arrange a private house instead of a hotel?"

"Will some of your team members be staying at the hotel?" I ask. With Yuri still at large, I'll take all the security I can get.

"They might be."

"So we'll be in good hands then," Grace says. "Are your team members as charming as you?"

I glare at her.

Lev looks at me like a lost kitten.

I can't help but laugh.

Chapter 52

Lev

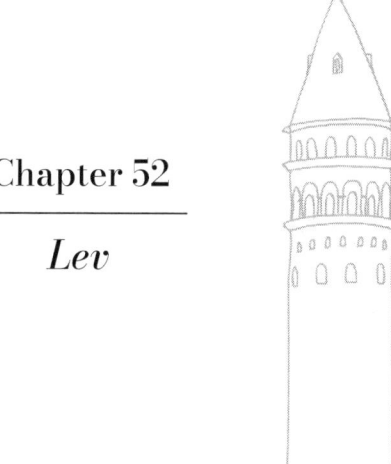

My father called yesterday. "Don't leave without seeing your old man," he said. So here I am, in a quiet café, my fingers nervously drumming on the table as I await his arrival.

I glimpse him through the glass, and moments later he enters and scans the room until our gazes lock. He strides confidently toward me. At seventy, he still moves with a youthful energy.

We hug briefly. The familiar scent of his aftershave brings back a flood of memories.

"Levent," he says, his voice gruff but affectionate.

"Hello, Dad," I reply, surprised at how easily the word has been slipping from my lips the last couple of days.

A silence stretches between us. I clear my throat, wrapping my hands around my coffee mug for comfort. "It's good to see you without being chased or chasing someone. Thank you for helping me."

His eyes soften. "Thank you for calling me, son. I always hoped you'd reach out one day."

I think of how many times I almost called, especially around Pera's birthday. I sip my coffee, and it suddenly tastes extra bitter.

"So, how are you, and how is my granddaughter?"

"She's good. Fourteen now. She's amazing." Pride seeps into my voice. "I'm busy. Life goes on, you know. And you?"

His weathered hands fidget with the water glass. "I've had my ups and downs," he says. "But ten years now, I've kept my promise. I've been working with authorities, no dodgy stuff." A moment passes. "Son," he says, his voice tinged with hope, "can I finally meet Pera?"

I nod. "I'll bring her sometime. There's a school break at the end of October, so we could visit. Grandma would be overjoyed to see her."

"I would love that," he says, a smile spreading across his face. "Thank you."

I take a deep breath, steeling myself. "So, what's your story with Yuri?"

My father's shoulders rise and fall, and he looks off into the distance as though peering into the past.

"I met Yuri not long after you and your mother left," he begins, his voice low. "He was already living in Istanbul. He ran away from his family—mainly his abusive father—when he was just fourteen." My father's hands clench. "I saw the deep scars on his back. Brutal reminders of years spent under his father's belt."

I'm suddenly chilly despite the café's warmth. "So you met him when he was a minor?" I blurt, then scold myself. *Listen without letting emotions get involved.*

"Yes, he was seventeen," my father says. "But he'd already been in the art-theft world for a couple of years. A friend recommended him, and after our first job, we continued together. I taught him everything I knew. He looked up to me."

"You said he was like a son to you," I say, my tone still as bitter as my coffee.

"I didn't mean it that way," my father retorts sharply, his eyes flashing. "I was trying to express how closely we'd worked together. I have only one son."

He dips his head. "Like I mentioned, when he learned I had a son, Yuri became obsessed with you. And he didn't take it well when I told him I was done after my last prison term."

I lean forward, curious despite myself. "How did he find out I was your son?"

My father shrugs, his brow furrowed. "Given his obsession, I'm sure he was digging. Maybe he finally connected the dots."

"Makes sense," I mutter, studying my father's face. "You still care for him, don't you?"

"Yes," my father admits, his gaze dropping to the table. He swallows hard before meeting my eyes again. "He was a broken young man, desperate for affection, a loving father. But if I knew where he was now, I swear I'd tell you and the authorities."

319

"How did you find the gift shop and all the other information about him?"

He lowers his voice. "I work with the National Crime Agency—but that's top secret. So I still know people who are connected to Yuri. I made a few calls."

Again, the silence stretches between us, filled with café noise. "I have a question," I say finally.

"Yes?" he replies, his tone cautious.

"Would you help me with something else?"

He chuckles. "Heavens, I hope it's got nothing to do with anything in the historic area."

"No, nothing like that," I assure him. "Can you find out if the Peacock edition of *Pride and Prejudice* is with Yuri or if he handed it over to someone else? It has *E* and *H* inscribed on the first page."

This time he leans in, a twinkle in his eye. "Is this for Ava?"

Sighing, I say, "Yes, I care very much about her."

"Uh-huh."

"What?" I ask, giving him a pointed look but unable to suppress a slight grin.

"It seems like it's moved beyond caring, son." Lines at the corners of his eyes crinkle. "Now, tell me more about this book."

The background noise of the café fades and it becomes just the two of us, father and son, once again connecting through a rare treasure.

Chapter 53

Ava

Grace and I chose to share a large room with two beds instead of getting separate rooms. It's just like when we lived together. Lev's company discount helped with the cost, which I'd been concerned about, but my hospital bill was substantial and my credit-card balance is reaching the sky. Still, there's nothing I can do about it right now. I'll deal with it when I return home.

I place the Rubik's Cube on the bedside table and join Grace on the balcony, which overlooks the Bosphorus. Ferries glide by. "I wish we were here under different circumstances," I say with a sigh. "It's quite a place, Istanbul."

"It brought us back together—it will always be a special place." Grace places her hand on my good shoulder. "Maybe we can return with Katie and Zack one day."

"I'd like that," I reply. "But seriously, we could've found a less dramatic way to reunite, right?"

Grace laughs then hurries to answer the knock at the door. Room service, delivering our early-evening meal— spaghetti Bolognese and green salad. I move to help, but Grace waves me off, insisting she's got it covered. "I was so proud of how smart you were," says Grace, as she serves us both. "I love that you have the Rubik's Cube with you."

"Thank you," I say. "You know, my right arm is pretty strong. You don't need to do everything for me."

"Shush, little sister, and eat your salad." She grins then looks at me seriously. "Ava, I'm so sorry I left you all alone, but I'm so proud of the incredible woman you've become."

"That's in the past now. I'm never letting you go. And thank you."

We settle in to eat.

"You know the drugs that got me locked up?" says Grace. "They weren't even mine. I took the fall for someone else. Someone I thought I was in love with."

"You did?"

She nods. "For Josie."

"I remember her. You hung out all the time."

"Yeah, she had a troubled home life. She told me lots of sad stuff about how she grew up, her family." She twirls some spaghetti around her fork. "Remember how we used to check if the spaghetti was ready by throwing strands at the ceiling?"

"Oh yeah," I say with a laugh. "If it stuck, it was done. Why didn't we just taste a piece or use a timer?" We crack up.

When our laughter dies down, Grace continues. "When the police stopped us that night, Josie told me she had crack in the vehicle and begged me to take the blame, saying I'd be fine but she'd go to jail for life. She had prior charges. It all happened so quickly that I didn't think it through—I just wanted to protect her. It was her car, and with California's three-strikes law, she'd be facing a life sentence. She was still a resident over there. I couldn't let that happen to her. But I didn't realize how much of the drug was actually in the car. That's why my jail term ended up being so long."

"Wow," I say with a frown. "So, to protect her, you left me all alone."

"No, no, Ava. I didn't think I'd be charged. She convinced me I wouldn't face jail time since I had no prior convictions. But the judge decided to make an example out of me."

I blink back tears. "When I saw footage of Zack leaving Elaine's house, it triggered memories of that time. I imagined him like you, walking off in handcuffs."

"I was naive and blindly in love," Grace says, her eyes fixed on her food. "It all became clear when I was sitting in that courtroom being sentenced and watching her walk free."

I reach for her hand, a pang in my chest. "It's gone

now," I say softly. "Adiós, goodbye. Just a thing of the past. Now it's time for us to heal."

She squeezes my hand.

As we wind down for the night, after calling Zack and Katie and watching a movie, Grace asks, "So, what happens with the book and Zack now?"

"I don't know. I'm not sure if Elaine's son reported to the police or not. Zack might have to face the consequences. I'm gutted that I couldn't find the book, but I have no regrets about rushing here to try to save him. I'd do it again in a heartbeat." I say.

"And no regrets about meeting Lev, either, right?" she says teasingly. "Another kind of heartbeat."

"Night night, sister," I say, flicking water at her from my glass.

Even though it's past midnight, I toss and turn and finally give up on sleeping.

"Are you awake?" I whisper.

"Yes," Grace says, turning on the bedside light. "I was thinking of reading my book, but I wasn't sure if the light would bother you."

I examine her for a moment.

"I can't believe you're an editor at a publishing company. I knew you loved reading, but I didn't know you wanted to work in the literary world."

"I did a lot of reading when I was inside," she admits. "It helped me cope. I even started a book club there. When I got out, I completed a degree in English. I have a master's in communications and journalism, too." She smiles sadly. "Mom passed us her love of reading."

"Yeah, she did."

"Do you read the last chapters of books now?" Grace asks quietly.

"Not really."

"Ava, my dear," Grace says, her voice filled with an ache.

"But I did actually read a few pages in Istanbul."

"You did?"

"Yeah, it was a Turkish translation of an Agatha Christie novel. I read a few pages from the last chapter. It felt good. I know it doesn't really count."

"According to who? I love that. You did it. I'm so proud of you."

"Maybe the key is to alter one small thing and see how it changes the whole," I say excitedly.

She shifts over in bed and pats the space beside her. I snuggle in, and we lie facing each other with our hands tucked under our heads.

"I miss Dad," she says, her lips morphing into a thin line, her face tightening. "Mom's dreams never included us, you know."

"Yeah," I say, gently wiping a tear away from her cheek.

Grace blinks slowly. "I once told her that I was gay, and she told me I was too pretty for that."

"Oh, Grace," I say. "I'm sorry."

"Mom was just bitter and unhappy," Grace continues.

"But Dad loved her so much. He loved all three of us." A small smile forms on her face.

"I know. I wish I could remember more about him. Sometimes I wonder about my biological father, too. Not because I want to get to know him or anything, but because I'm curious about what Mom went through, what happened."

Grace nods. "It's okay to be curious. It doesn't change the fact that you still love Dad."

We lie in silence for a while. "I don't think I asked you earlier—how did you meet Katie?"

Grace tells me that Katie was her personal trainer when they fell for each other. They've been married for over ten years now.

"She's my first love. My match and my pain."

"What about Russell?"

"Russell? The guy I dated in Phoenix?" She laughs. "That was just a cover-up. For appearances. Silly teenagers, but it worked. It took a while for me to come out."

"Russell was your fake boyfriend?" I exclaim, with a small burst of laughter. "You were the golden couple."

"I know. He sends his regards. He and his husband are close friends of mine."

"That's so great." I grin. "I had a bit of a crush on him."

"Yeah, we knew," Grace says with a laugh. "How about Mr. Hotness? How did you two meet? Have you kissed yet?'"

I think of all my encounters with Lev and a wave of heat rushes over me. Grace sits up. "Ohmigosh!"

"Stop, Grace," I say, shifting to my back and pulling the sheet over my face.

"Those crimson cheeks are glowing proof that there's much more to this story!"

"Yeah." My muffled confession surprises me. "He's intelligent, caring, cultured, worldly—and he's a great dad."

"And how about your heart and your body? What's their score on him?"

Sexy, sturdy, earthy, magnetic. During our night together, it felt as if my body knew how to be around him, as if it was finally finding its place. Despite my efforts to push Lev out of my mind and heart in the following days, my body refused to listen to reason. I haven't been able to shake the goosebumps, racing pulse, and tingling skin.

I pull the covers down a little and peek out. Grace is lying on her side, her head resting on her palm, watching me intently. A grin spreads across her face. "Your eyes say it all."

"But I need to get back to Zack and Elaine and sort out my life," I blurt. "I've spent so much of my savings here, I'm behind on my work, and my plants are probably dead. I live in LA, he lives in London, his business is his life, and we have teenage kids. And did I mention I know only three words in Turkish?"

Grace strokes my hair. "That's a long list. But it's there because you created it, right? Try changing your perspective. Imagine placing everything in the center of a circle instead. Suddenly, it's not such an intimidating list anymore."

I like that idea. Would Lev join my circle?

"This is precious, Ava. You're falling hard for him."

"I'm not," I whisper. "I don't do lovestruck. That's not me."

"Love changes you. Think about it: our hearts start beating for another person in addition to ourselves. It's a different rhythm, and it resets our entire being. It's scary but also incredible. I think it's one of the greatest gifts we humans have been given. Follow love. Everything else will fall in. And really," she says with a wink, "what's stopping you from doing your long list of things and also doing Lev?"

"Grace!" I shriek, pulling the sheet over my face again.

"No, I don't mean it like that . . . Well, actually, I do. But seriously."

We both burst into another fit of laughter.

Chapter 54

Ava

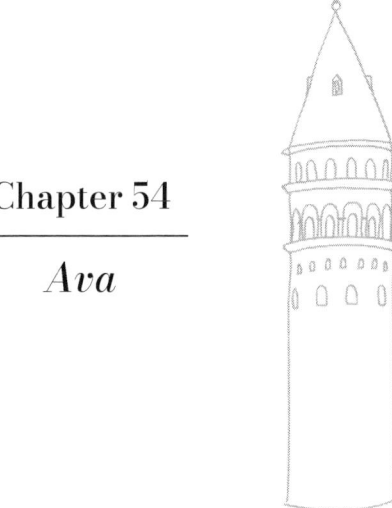

I snap open my eyes as my phone rings, its vibrating buzz cutting through the quiet of the hotel room. I quickly grab it trying not to wake Grace. Sitting up, I see Zack's name on the screen.

His face appears on the screen as I answer the call.

"Hi, darling. Are you okay?" I whisper, glancing over at Grace.

"I'm fine, Mom," Zack says. "I know it's only 7:00 a.m. over there, but something strange happened yesterday, and I can't wait any longer."

I hear Grace stir, and before I can reply to Zack, she sits up, stretching. She rubs her eyes and gives me a smile.

I say, "Can we please have just one day—one day— where nothing strange happens?"

Grace lets out a long yawn, "What's up, kiddo?" she asks loudly.

"Hey, Aunt Grace," Zack says.

Grace moves to sit next to me, leaning in so we can both see Zack on the phone.

Zack's eyes appear magnified. "You know how I've been helping Elaine with her photos? I've digitized hundreds of them. Now I'm working on Harold's photos— and in them was a photo of Grandma."

I perk up, exchanging a glance with Grace. "Grandma?"

"Yes," Zack gushes. "I'm sure it's her. You have that photo of the three of you on your office desk: Grandma, Aunt Grace, and you."

"Do you think it could be someone who looks like her?" Grace asks.

"I'm sure it was her. I checked the photo when I got home. She's standing next to this guy who has his arm around her waist. Harold and Elaine are in the photo too."

My heart jumps into my mouth.

"What a coincidence," Grace says. "Mom with your neighbors?"

"I think this is more than a coincidence," I say. "Harold was a movie producer with many movies under his belt."

"Goodness gracious. They worked together."

Zack scratches his forehead. "Elaine said the man was a friend of Harold, an actor. It's uncanny, Mom, but he looks eerily similar to you. Especially his eyes and his nose."

I fell numb as Zack continues. "Elaine remembers them as a couple, but she only met them a few times at some parties. They were in Harold's social circle. She said that the woman was gorgeous."

"Did you take a photo of the photo, Zack?" Grace asks. "Can we see it?"

"I wanted to tell you guys first. And I wouldn't do it without asking Elaine," he says sheepishly. "I can ask her next time I see her, but there's a date on the back—and it's from a year before your birthday, Mom."

Uneasiness envelops me. "No, darling, don't ask her. I'm coming home soon anyway. I think we all need time to digest this before asking Elaine. Let's not stir the pot just yet. We don't even know what this means." Despite my words, emotions threaten to overwhelm me, to dismantle the calm facade I'm trying to maintain.

After Zack hangs up, Grace says, "Talk about timing. You just told me that you wonder about your biological father sometimes. This might be a clue."

"An actor," I murmur. "They were a couple. But Mom was married to Dad . . ." My heart hurts. I know how betrayal feels. "Dad must have been very upset. And he loved me as his own daughter."

Grace places her hand on mine. "Because you were his daughter. Don't ever doubt that."

"Yeah, I know. Anyway, that photo means nothing. I'm not sure if I want to find out more." I shrug. "I'm gonna take a shower."

Later that morning, as we sip coffee in the hotel room, Grace flashes a playful smile in my direction. "I couldn't help but notice how quickly you jumped to get ready after that message from Lev arrived."

"Come on," I say, rolling my eyes. "I was just getting ready for the day.

"You're so cute when you're flustered. And that lipstick suits you."

A knock on the door interrupts our banter. "Looks like the source of your flusteredness has arrived," Grace announces.

I glance at myself in the full-length mirror before Grace walks past me to answer the door.

Lev walks in with a playful bow. His ruggedly handsome face catches the morning light. "Good morning, beautiful ladies."

"Good morning, Mr. Darcy," Grace says.

Lev looks bewildered and I roll my eyes again.

We all make ourselves comfortable on the balcony. Grace pours hot water into a cup, the steam rising as she carefully adds a tea bag for Lev.

"So, it looks like I'll be returning home without Harold and Elaine's book," I say, staring down at my empty hands. "I still can't believe Harold got the book here in Istanbul in the first place."

"Maybe the book is chasing another story," Grace says. "Maybe it needed to return to Istanbul to come full circle."

"Funny you say that," I say. "Elaine said something similar."

Lev says softly, "I'm sure of that," then adds, "Before you guys leave, how about we spend some time and explore a bit of Istanbul?"

Grace shrieks with excitement, "Oh, I love that!"

"Umut will love it too," I chime in.

Lev grins mischievously, "Yes, of course, Umut joins us."

We sit in silence for a moment, each lost in our own thoughts. I'm not really in the mood for a touristy day in Istanbul, especially after my epic failure to find that book. To make matters worse, I now know exactly who has it. But spending the day with these three still makes my heart race.

"I have some exciting news to share," Lev blurts. "Frederica is taking over my company."

"What?" Grace and I say in unison.

"She practically runs the operations anyway. It will be a gradual process, and I'll help her settle in as long as necessary. I'm excited for both of us."

"What happened? Why?" I ask, suddenly worried. I know his dedication to his business.

"It's time. Lately, I've started to question my priorities. Frederica will run the company better than I do. I know that. She'll look after the team, clients know and trust her, and, most importantly, Pera will see so much more of her father." He sips his tea. "Though I'm sure she'll complain about that too." We laugh. "And I'm no longer going to hide who my father is or what he was. I enjoy what I do, but starting the business was my attempt to prove to myself that I'm not defined by who he was."

"After all these years apart, you called your father to help you find Ava," Grace says. "That's a heck of a thing to do."

"I'd stop at nothing to find Ava," he says, stealing a glance at me.

This man makes my heart sing.

Chapter 55

Lev

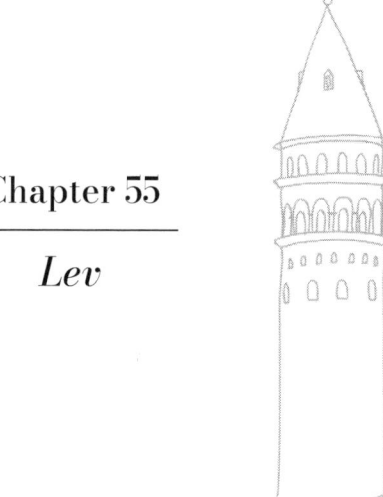

On Tuesday morning, Ava, Grace, Umut, and I sit on the balcony of the sisters' hotel room reviewing our itinerary for the grand tour of Istanbul.

I still can't believe that just last Thursday, I was frantically searching for Ava, racing through the streets of Istanbul with my heart pounding in desperation to find her. And now, here I am, planning a guided tour with her through the same places. It feels surreal. My heart races again, but for an entirely different reason—being so close to her, breathing in her scent, watching her every expression. I have this overwhelming urge to pull her close, to keep her near. I wonder what our story will become. Do I even stand a chance? For now, all I can do is savor every single moment with her.

It's been two days since Ava worked with a police sketch artist. Tomorrow, she and Grace plan to book their flights back to the States, following Ava's doctor's appointment to make sure she's cleared for travel. But today, Umut and I are taking them on a grand tour of Istanbul.

We'll start with the historic area. All of the sites on our itinerary are within walking distance of each other.

- Basilica Cistern
- Hagia Sophia
- Blue Mosque
- Topkapı Palace
- Grand Bazaar

Our first destination is the Basilica Cistern, per Ava's wishes. I didn't think I'd return this soon, but hey, anything that my Ava Jane wants. "My Jane"—it's ingrained in my mind like a private joke. I dream of a day when she falls for me as deeply as I've fallen for her. I would wait an eternity. Even that sliver of possibility makes my daft heart beat faster.

"You jumped into the water here?" Ava says teasingly.

"Yes, and I'd jump again if I needed to save any of you," I say with a grin.

Umut gives me a high five.

After exploring all the other places on our list, we head to the Grand Bazaar, the world's oldest mall. Umut informs the group that it has over three thousand shops and that a James Bond movie was filmed on the rooftop. We stroll through the maze of small shops surrounded by arches, domes, and vaults.

"I think Istanbul is the definition of cool," Grace says.

"How so?" I ask.

"It's so diverse, a metropolis that's over eight thousand years old and has hosted the greatest civilizations. Then there's the food. Plus, Umut lives here." She wraps her arm around Umut's shoulder. He beams and continues leading the way through the narrow streets.

A few hours later, the three of us finally team up to drag Grace out of the bazaar. She's determined to visit every single store and chat with every single vendor.

We hop aboard a two-story ferry for a tour of Istanbul on the Bosphorus Strait. It's like having front-row seats to the ultimate Istanbul show. As the engine hums to life, we glide along the waterway that separates Europe and Asia. The skyline puts on a spectacular performance just for us. We sail past waterfront palaces, towering mosques, grand churches, and ancient walls—we even duck under a couple of stunning bridges.

Grace and Umut walk along the deck while Ava and I sit quietly, soaking in the beauty.

"You ever feel like some cities have a soul?" Ava says. "They can be emotional, loud, quiet, confused, serene, wise, old, young, happy, or troubled. Istanbul is all of that and more."

"For sure," I reply.

Laughter floats to us as Grace and Umut toss bread to

the seagulls. "I think Grace is Umut's new best friend," Ava jokes with a pout.

My gaze lingers on her lips. How is she breathtaking even when she's pouting? I love her smile the most, but every expression she wears captivates me.

My phone rings, breaking the moment. "I need to take this," I tell Ava, before answering. "Hello, peanut," I say.

"Hey, Dad," she says. I smile as Pera's face appears on the screen, but it quickly falters as she launches into the reason for her call—she's once again asking for permission to go to the Taylor Swift concert.

I take a deep breath, trying to keep my composure. "Pera," I say firmly. "We've already discussed this."

"My friend is going, and so is her brother. A bunch of my friends are going, actually."

I feel a knot tighten in my chest. "Okay, sounds like a lot of them are going," I say. "But you're not."

"This is so unfair, Dad!"

"I'm sorry. I'll make it up to you."

"Whatever. Have a great day," she says and hangs up.

I tighten my grip on the phone. I'm just a father who's concerned about the safety of his daughter.

"It's not the end of the world, you know," Ava says, pulling me out of my thoughts.

"Sorry about that," I say as the entire conversation happened right next to Ava. "And, Pera thinks that not getting to see her idol—Taylor Swift—is the end of the world."

Ava's brows shoot up. "Ouch."

338

"Yeah, it's painful," I say, appreciating the support.

"I was saying ouch for Pera. You're telling me that Taylor Swift is in London and she can't go? That's pretty tough. It's an end-of-a-teen-world type of tough."

"You think so?"

"Yeah. Why won't you let her go to the concert?"

"She's only fourteen, and there'll be thousands of people," I say, and sigh. "I always check out the places she's going beforehand, and this is a huge venue. It was easier when she was younger and I could go places with her. Now that she's older and wants to do things without me, it's tough." I inhale deeply. "I'm at a loss."

"Well, going to concerts with friends is what teenagers do. She's growing. She's not only your little girl but also her own person. She'll never forget this."

"She won't?" I ask, suddenly feeling desperate.

"Nope. Could you maybe explore ways to make it as safe as possible? Perhaps you could ask a favor of a colleague—have them keep a discreet eye on her group. This way, you still let her fly on her own a little."

"I suppose I could do that," I say. "Thank you."

Ava smiles. It looks as though the sun has risen on her face.

Chapter 56

Ava

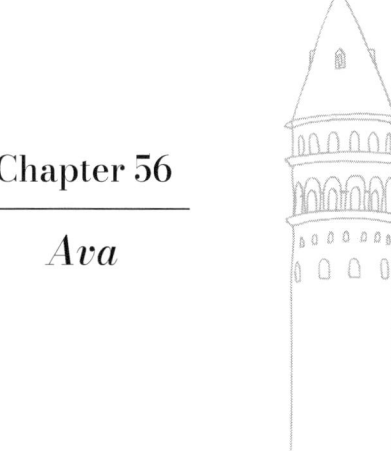

As our boat tour concludes, Lev's eyes glint with mischief. "I've still got some time before I'm due to visit my grandmother. If you all aren't too tired, we could try our luck at Galata Tower. Maybe go to the top."

I let out a shriek of delight. "I have loads of energy to spare for that tower!" Since it's a ticketed museum, there were some lines, and I didn't get a chance to go up.

Umut, however, looks at the time on his phone. "I have to meet my friends," he says, then pulls me into a tight hug before departing. Lev and Umut exchange a few words out of earshot.

"I've actually got to head back to the hotel for an online meeting with my team," Grace says apologetically. Lev calls her a car.

I catch Lev's eye and grin knowingly. "Umut wouldn't let you call a car for him, would he?"

"He's stubborn," Lev replies, with a mix of affection and exasperation.

Passing cafés and shops along the cobblestone path, we make our way toward Galata Tower. It feels like my heart is trying to burst out of my ribcage and race all the way up to the tower! Our hands brush and then our fingers lace themselves together, finding their places and saying what words cannot.

When we get to the tower, I caress the uneven surface of the rough bricks and let my eyes wander up the structure, which disappears in the clouds. "I'll miss this tower."

"Let's get tickets and join the queue," says Lev.

Thankfully, there are only a few people.

When we enter, I request that we take the elevator up. "But let's take the stairs down. I want to touch each level of this tower."

"As you wish," Lev responds.

As we rise into the enchanted tower, the gentle hum of the elevator fills my ears. It feels as though we're ascending to another world. Maybe even to the moon itself. I'm overwhelmed by his scent. My skin tingles.

We step out, and as Lev takes my hand again, his as sturdy as this tower, all the butterflies inside of me flutter their wings.

He points to the stairs. "Two more flights to the top."

Each stone of the narrow, spiraling steps is carved into a unique shape and feels rough under my fingers as I run them along the wall. We reach a small window with a curved top and a rectangular ledge set within a slight arch that juts out from the main wall.

"This is breathtaking." I peer out at the city below before we ascend to the top floor. Larger versions of those windows are lined up across the round wall of the tower.

Each frames a unique view of the city; they're like paintings. I pivot slowly, taking in the different scenes: the Bosphorus, the historic area with its intricate domes and minarets, and the modern cityscape with its towering skyscrapers.

"Oh, look, that's Galata Bridge," I say excitedly, then look at Lev. "Thank you for taking me here. What a treat just before departing."

"Ready for the best?" he asks, beckoning me to the final flight of stairs.

I burst outside onto the top and inhale deeply. My eyes widen as I take in the panoramic views around me. Unable to contain my excitement, I move around the tower several times, soaking in every detail from every angle. Lev stands by the entrance waiting for me.

"Do you ever imagine what it would be like to see your life from a 360-degree viewpoint?" I ask, approaching him.

"I'm happy with one angle," he says, his gaze on me. My cheeks flush, and heat spreads to my chest. His magnetic pull draws me in slowly. Our hands interlock, his grasp firm. We stand together, our backs pressed against the cool brick wall. My hair flies in front of his face, and he closes his eyes as he breathes in. "I love your hair."

The city twinkles as the sun gets ready to set. I take a moment to enjoy the warmth in my chest that comes only from being near him.

"Would you like me to take a photo of you?" asks Lev, noticing others taking pictures.

"Yes, please," I say, "but I'd like a selfie. Together."

He shifts to stand close behind me, one arm extended to capture the moment, the other enveloping my waist, thrilling me. On the screen, our eyes are bright with joy and our smiles beam. I pull my hair over my left shoulder. He lowers his head toward my right shoulder and the camera clicks.

"How does this look?" he asks, continuing to hold me close as he shows me the photo with the Istanbul sunset backdrop.

I examine it. It's been years since I've seen myself this happy. "It's perfect," I say, despite all the imperfect parts —my aching shoulder, his stitched face.

Our lips meet tenderly. Time stops as we stand at the top of Galata Tower, lost in each other.

As our lips part just an inch, his gentle hand caresses my face. "Just remember this," he whispers.

Chapter 57

Ava

Round and round I go down the stairs of the tower, Lev on my heels. I feel dizzy when we step out at the bottom, but I know it's a good kind of dizzy. Our hands meet again and my heart skips a few more beats.

"Shall we head to our table?" Lev points to the café where we met.

"Sure," I say, and soon we're seated. "I'd never in my wildest dreams have thought that this would become *our* table."

Lev smiles. "Nothing is a coincidence in Istanbul." He leans closer. "Or in life." His Adam's apple bobs. "Believe me, I'm a pragmatic guy, but for the past few weeks, I've officially become a believer in cosmic powers, destiny, and meant to be. Because when we kiss, everything in the universe seems to align."

I swear I can feel my pulse pounding in my chest as I look at him.

He gently reaches across the small table and takes my hand. "I'm not asking for anything right now," he says softly, "and you don't need to make any decisions. Go home, do what you need to do. The only thing I'm asking is that you remember us. Just remember. I have no doubt about what I want. I'll wait as long as it takes to take you out for a date, if you allow me to."

A warmth spreads across my face, quickly radiating through my entire body. "Thank you," I say softly, without taking my eyes off his.

Our hands laced, we order our coffees.

I notice someone approaching our table just as Lev pulls up a third chair. "I'd like you to meet someone. This is my father, Rasim."

I rise. "We've already met, but it was a tad chaotic then," I say with a smile.

"It's lovely to see you again," he responds. We shake hands, and Rasim takes a seat.

After some lively conversation about our day in Istanbul, Rasim passes a bag to Lev—a canvas messenger bag with an earthy tone and leather trims—who then hands it to me. "This is for you," he says.

I take it with a confused frown.

"Unzip it," Lev says with a big smile. "But please be careful with your coffee. No splashing business here."

I do as requested, and the scent of old paper fills the

air. My pulse races and my knees weaken as I see a white protective sleeve inside.

"Is this? Oh my— Is this Elaine's book?"

"Yes," says Lev. "There's a cotton glove in the bag, for handling it."

I place the book back inside the bag and hold it tightly against my chest. I want Elaine to see it first. Leaning back in my chair, I close my eyes for a moment. Tears threaten to spill over. "But how?" I whisper. "Did you buy it? I'll pay."

"Nothing to pay, and this gentleman made it possible." Lev points at his dad.

"Well, teamwork," Rasim says. "Everyone contributed, including you, Ava."

I blink. "Me? How?"

"Yuri's accomplice was captured yesterday in part thanks to your help with the shoes. I followed some leads and worked with the police, who found him. He made a full confession, which included details about where Yuri was hiding the book."

Rasim clears his throat. "You're finally returning this book to its rightful owner. I cleared it with the authorities. It's yours to return to your friend."

"Thank you both so much," I say, my heart feeling as if it could explode.

"My pleasure, young lady." A big grin spreads across Rasim's face. It looks like Lev's. His gaze flickers between Lev and me. "I think the book is ready to leave Istanbul now."

I smile as well. Elaine and Harold's love story wins once again.

Chapter 58

Lev

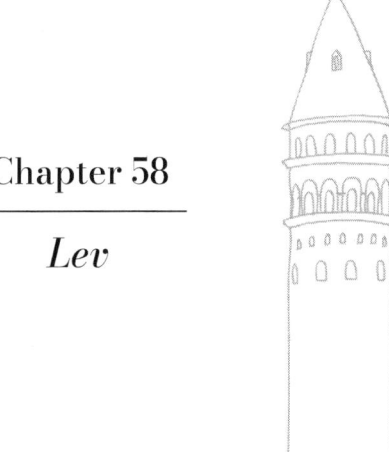

The cries of the seagulls mingle with the lapping of the waves. Dad and I take our seats on the upper deck of the ferry. We're on our way to visit my grandma, who wept with joy when I called to tell her I was on my way—with my father. We're in for a good meal. My grandmother is convinced that anyone who steps into her home must be absolutely famished. Feeding people is her sacred duty, and she ensures no one ever leaves her table without a full belly and a warm heart.

My phone buzzes. I read the text from my colleague in London confirming the concert arrangements. "I need to make a quick call to Pera," I tell Dad.

"I can't wait to meet her," he says, his eyes bright.

I dial my daughter, two hours behind us in London.

"Hi," she answers.

"Peanut, I have some news for you."

"Yeah?" Her curiosity is palpable.

"Because you're such a responsible and hardworking daughter, I've decided to let you go to the concert." Her excited squeals nearly drown out my voice as I continue. "With a few conditions."

"Okay," she says eagerly. "Okay. What are they?"

"One of my colleagues will accompany you, but he'll keep his distance. You won't even know he's there."

"But I don't think there are any tickets left for him!" she says anxiously.

"Don't worry, I've already arranged it," I say, omitting that I sourced the ticket from the resale market. Ava would be smirking.

"Dad, I can't believe this!"

"One more condition," I add playfully. "No dating until you're twenty-five. No, no, let's make it thirty."

"Okay," Pera says without hesitation, giggling. "You're the best!"

I can't help but smile as I end the call. My daughter thinks I'm the best. I cherish the moment.

Chapter 59

Ava

race jumps up and down when I tell her the news back in our hotel room. The bag hasn't left my chest. I have a good cry in her embrace.

It's just after 6:00 a.m. in LA, but I call Elaine anyway. When she doesn't answer, I video-call Zack. He answers sleepily.

"Zack! Zack, guess what I have in my hand." I hold up the bag.

He gasps, his hands fly to his mouth, and he stares for a beat. "Is that . . . Really?"

"Yes. Although I haven't actually seen it yet. Can you go to Elaine's in an hour and call me from there? She should be up then."

"Yes!" Zack pumps his fists in the air. "You're the best mom!"

Grace and I break into a little dance, making Zack laugh.

For the next hour, I stare at the bag and check the clock.

"Good morning, Elaine," I say joyfully, when the video-call from Zack finally comes in. "I have a surprise for you." I show her the bag.

Elaine gasps. "Is that it?" she says, her voice trembling. "Oh my goodness, you did it! I knew you could!" Tears spill down her cheeks.

"I'm really sorry, Elaine," Zack says, tears in his eyes. "And Mom. I'm sorry."

Elaine extends her arm, and Zack leans into her as they sit side by side. A big smile spreads across my face, and my heart leaps as tears begin to flow. After all, Zack is a good kid, and I'm not a bad mother.

Grace holds the phone as I unzip the bag and carefully retrieve the book in its white protective sleeve. Revealing the book within feels like opening a treasure chest.

"Hold on, let me put on the glove," I say.

I slowly take out the book. It has a dark-green cover with a peacock. Zack gasps again, and Elaine blinks. Grace watches intently, her eyes glistening and wide with curiosity.

As I lift the front cover, I see the letters:

H & E

"It's incredible," Grace says softly.

Grace keeps a gentle hand on my good shoulder, wiping away tears.

It's Tuesday afternoon. I stepped into this city exactly two weeks ago. After the darkness comes the dawn. With a happy sob, I say, "Love wins, friendship wins, family wins."

Chapter 60

Lev

Three Days Later

A va sinks into her seat, her beautiful eyes locking on mine. I'm chuffed to be taking her out on a date. She's wearing the little pendant I got her, which has to be a good sign, right? And she agreed to this date, so things are looking up.

"May I offer you a preflight beverage?" asks the flight attendant.

It's Friday afternoon, Grace left this morning, Elaine's book is on its way home with a special courier, Zack is back in San Jose, and Pera is a happy Swifty.

As for Ava and me?

"I still can't believe we're on our way to Tuscany," Ava says, her eyes wide with wonder.

I grin. She agreed to dinner, but I hadn't specified where. "Well, it happens to be on the way home for both of us."

She shakes her head, a stunning smile playing on her lips. "You're absolutely mad, you know that?"

I watch, mesmerized, as she takes a sip of her drink. A glistening trace remains on her lower lip.

Her gaze meets mine, curiosity sparkling in her eyes. "Do you always whisk your dates away to Italy in first class?"

I shake my head. "First time," I say. "I've never flown with a date, actually."

Ava leans in. "So, where exactly are we going?"

I take a sip of my own drink, savoring the moment. "San Gimignano. It's this charming medieval town with many towers that look like they're straight out of a fairy tale."

Her eyes light up. "Oh, I love towers."

"I know," I say with a smirk. "But that's not our only stop."

She raises an eyebrow. "Oh? What else do you have up your sleeve?"

I lower my voice. "Remember when we were sipping wine in my room, and you mentioned you'd hop over to Tuscany just for a taste?"

A soft blush colors her cheeks.

I ask, "How about we visit a few other towns in Tuscany and stroll through the vineyards together?"

"In three days? Sure, I'd love to," she says, and we both fall into a quiet moment, our fingers laced together.

She gazes down at our hands, her voice soft, "Just remember."

I nod.

"I don't need to remember," she says, almost to herself. "Those moments are impossible to forget."

I lift her hand and press a kiss to it.

After a pause, her voice turns playful, "So, Lev," she says, "are you secretly a very rich guy or something?"

"I am now," I reply, placing a kiss on her cheek. "And I've recently discovered my all-time favorite wine." My eyes linger on her lips.

We still have so much to learn about each other. Yes, I come from wealth on my mother's side, and I've built my own thriving business. But sitting here next to Ava, I understand that my wealth is truly in my relationships.

The reality of a long-distance relationship looms in the back of my mind—the challenges it will bring, the time zones we'll have to navigate. But looking at her now, I know I'll do anything to shorten those distances, if she'll let me.

"What are you thinking about?" Ava asks, seemingly catching my expression.

I take another sip of wine, giving myself a moment to think. "I've been thinking about Istanbul, about us, how we met. And about how incredible it would be to keep having these dates all over the world. Maybe next time in Paris. Then we could take the Eurostar to London. Or New York. Anywhere you want." I pause to gauge her reaction. "That is, if you'll still have me after Tuscany." I tuck her hair behind her ear.

"Well, you've set the bar pretty high." She chuckles and raises her glass. "To Istanbul, where it all started."

The plane banks gently. Life has no guarantees, but I will work tirelessly for us. I have plenty of hope for a future full of adventures with the woman I love. Yes, I know one thing with certainty—she's the woman I love.

Our glasses meet with a soft chime. "And to our story," she says.

Chapter 61

Ava

Four Weeks Later

What felt like the end of the road has turned out to be just the beginning. It's been over a month since I was in Istanbul.

Lev and I left dreamy Tuscany as an official couple, both of us misty-eyed at the airport. Despite my initial protests about his paying for my flight home, I enjoyed the luxury of lying flat on the airplane and texting him from thousands of feet in the air.

I feel as if I'm experiencing the giddy excitement of first love, something I never truly felt before, even in my youth. I have permanent butterflies in my tummy. We speak daily, like lovestruck teenagers—"You hang up!"

"No, you hang up!"

He's claimed my heart, mind, and body in a way I never thought possible. Our calls often take on a flirtatious tone, especially during our early-morning chats when I'm still in bed, next to our framed selfie on Galata Tower. We crave each other.

I'm still not sure how we'll handle this long-distance thing, but I'll see him in four weeks, over Thanksgiving. Not that I'm counting the days or anything, but I could tell the hours and minutes.

We're heading to Grace and Katie's place in Seattle, and after that, Lev and I will go on a road trip through Washington and Oregon.

He wants to tell Pera about us, but I've asked him to wait. I'm worried that she might not accept me, especially since I'll be the first girlfriend of her dad's that she'll meet.

Today, Grace is arriving for a visit. At LAX, as I wait for Grace to land, I examine the photo of my mom, Harold, Elaine, and a tall man whose arms are around my mom's waist. I have a copy of it on my phone. His name was Antonio Rizzi, and he was my biological father.

He played a significant supporting role in a movie in which my mother had a minor part. I had unknowingly watched my father on screen many times when I was young. How strange is that?

At first, it was hard for Grace and me not to feel upset with our mom and sad for our dad, who loved her so much. But we spent many nights talking it through and concluded that since none of them were alive anymore, there was nothing to do but let it rest and move on. This peace gave me clarity—I want to meet my biological family, if they're open to it.

Grace emerges from the crowd, and I wave

enthusiastically. She runs toward me, and we embrace tightly. Since Istanbul, we've spoken on the phone almost every day. It's strange—it feels like we never parted.

"What a lovely place you have," she says, as we pull up to my house.

"It's on the market," I say, my chin high. "I'm not only embracing change—I'm initiating it."

"You look like a proud peacock," she says with a chuckle. "Good job, sister."

I usher her inside. "I don't like this thing hanging here anyway," she says, pointing at the bare metal centerpiece in the hallway. "Is this modern art of some sort?"

"It was a chandelier once. And yeah, I'm letting go of anything that doesn't serve me anymore."

"So where are you moving to? Come to Seattle, pleeease?" She frowns adorably.

"Believe it or not, I don't know yet," I say. "I'm working on un-becoming first, starting with the house. It was my shell and I don't need it anymore. Maybe I'll get a small condo in a coastal town, so Zack always has a home."

"You always have a room in our home," Grace says with a smile. "What about your work?"

"I'm thinking about taking on more jobs that involve travel and working on-site. My big client has asked me before, but I've always said no. Now they're excited— they've even mentioned a year-long contract in Europe."

"Europe? Isn't that near London?" Grace teases.

"Yes, but I'm doing this for myself. I wish I had

361

traveled more. That trip also made me realize how tiny a space I occupy in the world."

She nods, a playful grin on her face. "And on that trip, you found looovee."

"I did," I reply.

That evening, we call Umut, and he answers with a beaming smile. He's been spending a lot of time with Lev's grandmother, helping her with chores like carrying groceries and accompanying her to the local market for the weekly shopping. We're also talking about him going back to school. He's a proud young man, determined to keep working and supporting his siblings. Grace and Umut talk regularly, and she's developing a plan to help his younger stepsister and stepbrother with their education.

I think about the moment I met Umut. I was holding the keys to a bookstore in Istanbul. What a wild turn of events. Mr. Babayan hadn't even given me a chance to explain. Before I knew it, I was covering for him and his wife so they could celebrate their wedding anniversary. I'm so glad I did.

Then we call Zack, who's in his dorm room in San Jose catching up on his studies. We call each other more often than we used to.

After the call, I clear my throat. "There's one more thing that no longer serves me." I retrieve the wooden box that's been living in a drawer. Grace's eyes follow me as I carry it to her. "It's time to let go of Mom's book."

"I'll take it." Her expression softens. "This is our mother's tale, not yours or mine." She lightly touches the box and sets it on the couch beside her. "Are you ready for tomorrow?"

"As ready as a cat for a bath. But thank you for flying down to support me."

"Of course. I couldn't let you meet your uncle alone."

My uncle. Once we discovered that Antonio Rizzi had a brother named Roberto, I was surprised by how eager I was to call him when Zack found his contact information. I reached out to him a week ago.

"Is this Roberto Rizzi?" I said.

"Yes, it is."

"Hello, my name is Ava, and my mother's name is Corinne Jenkins. You may have known her?"

"Ava? You're Corinne's Ava? My niece?"

"Uh . . . Am I your niece?" I whispered, barely audible.

"Yes, you are!" he practically shouted, his voice ringing in my ear.

And just like that, we ended up talking for almost an hour. We were both stunned to realize that we live only a few miles apart. We quickly arranged a time to meet.

And so, tomorrow, I'll be meeting my uncle, Roberto, a third-generation Italian American, which might explain why Mom dreamed of visiting Italy.

As Grace parks in Roberto's driveway—I was too nervous to drive—uncertainty engulfs me. My heart feels as if it's about to rip itself right out of my chest, and my stomach sounds like a tumble dryer.

Grace takes my hand. "I'll reverse right now and take us home if you want me to."

But then, a man with silver strands in his thick, wavy hair emerges from the house. His strong jawline is similar to my father's.

"That's one excited uncle," Grace says. "Look at him —he's sprinting."

"Ava!" he calls.

I get out, and he envelops me in a firm hug. My arms hang awkwardly at my sides, but I slowly lift them and wrap them around his back.

Moments later he steps back, holding me at arm's length, and studies my face. Shaking his head in disbelief, he murmurs, "I can't believe this. Antonio's daughter. Your eyes are just like his, and your nose—it's the spitting image of his."

I gently brush the top of my nose. *I love it.*

"Have I been here before?" I ask, as we walk inside his house.

"Yes, many times," Roberto says. He beckons us into a living room with high ceilings. Large windows offer a view of the manicured gardens. I halt when I see two crystal chandeliers casting a warm glow.

"You're the man in my memories! The one who made me fly in the air."

"You remember?" He beams. "Yes, that was me. You loved that."

A heat radiates through my chest as I take a deep breath.

He offers us drinks and I drain a whole glass of water in one go, my chest heaving as I take deep, refreshing breaths.

He sits across us. "Your mother meant everything to Antonio," he explains. "We were all left heartbroken when he passed away. There was a big mistake on the set. After his death, my mama was never the same."

My ears start buzzing, "Mistake?" I manage to mutter.

"Yes, it was a serious mistake that the set assistant handed another actor a loaded gun instead of the empty one. Corinne was also on set and witnessed everything."

Grace gasps softly, her hands covering her face. We share a glance, and I can feel my face going pale. She tilts her head slightly, and tears begin to well up in both our eyes.

With her head dipped, she almost whispers, "That explains her unhappiness and bitterness toward life itself."

My palms grow clammy. I wipe away the tears from my face. "Mum told me once, 'He's gone, it was a mistake.' I always assumed she was talking about me or her own mistake. But she was really talking about the mistake on the set."

"I'm so sorry," Roberto says.

"No, please, go on," I urge.

"Okay. One day, Corinne arrived with a tiny infant, my brother's daughter. You. I instantly fell in love with you. I didn't know that Corinne was already married. She was aloof, always keeping her distance. I pleaded with her to let me see you more often, but she only brought you every few months. It broke my heart when she suddenly disappeared without a trace. I searched for her, and that's when I discovered she was married and had moved from her last address. Just like that, she was gone. I didn't know what to do."

I nod with a small smile, blinking more often.

"I'm sorry that we lost so much time, Ava," Roberto says, as he pulls a crumpled tissue from his pocket and blows his nose. "But I'd love to stay in touch and introduce you to more of your family, including my wife and my kids, your cousins. In your own time, of course."

"I'd really like that," I say. "Let's not waste any more time."

Chapter 62

Ava

As I prepare breakfast the following day, I reflect on meeting my uncle yesterday and how wonderful it is to have my sister around. My *family*! A knock at the door interrupts the moment. "Could you get that, please?" I holler.

Grace responds from somewhere in the house, her voice distant. "Sorry, I can't."

Wearing oven mitts and an apron, I open the door. And my heart just about leaps out of my chest. Lev stands in front of me. I throw myself into his arms, my feet lifting off the ground.

"Am I dreaming?" I sing.

He chuckles, spinning me around. "I heard about some stellar breakfast, so I just had to stop by."

"Oh my, are you really here?"

He smiles. "Let's see." Our lips meet, and his kiss

ignites my core, a warmth that's been there since I
met him.

He explains that he has a few free days and couldn't
wait another month to see me. It's Thursday and he'll have
to leave on Sunday evening, but I quickly push that
thought aside. Right now, I'm in his arms, and that's all
that matters.

As we enter the house, Grace watches us with a doe-
eyed look.

"Did you know?" I ask.

"Yep, everyone knew," she replies. "Zack, Elaine,
Katie, Umut—even the mayor."

"You little minx," I say, shaking my head with a
smile.

After breakfast, Lev approaches me with a small
package in his hands. "I have something for you."

I open it to find a London-themed porcelain coffee cup.
Inside is a small card. I remove it and shoot a look at Lev.
"From Pera?"

He nods.

Hi Ava,

*I'm really looking forward to meeting you. I'd
love to join you at the family Thanksgiving dinner
in Seattle. I've heard a lot about you and can't
wait to share some funny stories about Dad.
Trust me, I've got the inside scoop!*

Pera

PS - Thank you for watching my dance show and persuading Dad to let me go to the concert.

"Aw," I coo, pressing her card against my chest. "Thanks to that concert, I'm in her good book, for sure," I say with a chuckle. "When and how did you tell her about us?"

"A few days ago. She's more observant than I give her credit for. She figured out I was dating someone. Apparently I have 'starry eyes.' She wouldn't leave me alone until I told her who this person was. When I told her, she said she'd been hoping it was you."

"This is so sweet. Zack and Pera will get to meet." I can feel my heart literally expand with joy.

"And my mother can't wait to meet you," says Lev.

"I wish Denise could join us for Thanksgiving," I reply. A few weeks ago, I called to invite her, and we ended up chatting for a long time. Unfortunately, she already has other plans, but we'll meet another time.

Later that day, we drop Grace off at the airport. She has a deadline and can't stay longer, though she wishes she could.

"Any news on Yuri?" I ask, on our drive back to my place. I know Lev has been restless about it.

He inhales sharply. "Not yet. But Frederica will take over completely in a few months, and I'm considering joining the Art and Antiques Unit of the Metropolitan Police as a consultant."

I know without a doubt that he won't stop until Yuri is

found. His pursuit fills me with unease, but I trust his judgment and will stand by him. He wouldn't do anything foolish—unless he's at the Basilica Cistern.

"That sounds great," I reply.

He goes on to explain how it might work and the case-by-case approach that would give him the flexibility to travel when he wants.

"Oh, I love that part, the flexibility to travel," I say, with a grin.

We make a quick stop at Elaine's place, so I can introduce her to Lev. Her face lights up as she looks at him. "Ava never mentioned how handsome you are," she says with a grin.

As soon as we step into the hallway at home, Lev's strong arms scoop me up, lifting me high into the air. He spins me around effortlessly, and I laugh in surprise, feeling the world whirl around us. His warm breath tickles my ear as he whispers, "You are simply dazzling."

I smile. My source of light was always within me. I'll keep shining.

Thank you and a Bonus Chapter!

Dear reader, I'm so grateful that you've taken the time to read this book.

I'd be incredibly grateful if you could leave a review on Amazon or Goodreads—it would mean a lot.

Would you like to know what the characters are up to next? Here's a bonus chapter to give you a sneak peek.

https://gtlondonauthor.com/AvaLevBonus

More from G.T. London

See all my books on Amazon.com at:

https://geni.us/GTLondonAuthor

What's Next?

Nalu Town in Hawai'i is making a comeback in a heart-
pounding, three-book collection.

Let's Stay Connected

Here are some great ways to stay connected and be the first to know about all things related to my books.

1 - The Newsletter: Join my newsletter family for updates on upcoming books, special deals, and events. Visit my website to join at GTLondonAuthor.com

2 - Author Page: Follow my Amazon author page for the new release updates.

3 - Facebook Reader Group:
facebook.com/groups/GTLondonReaders

4 - Email: gtlondonauthor@gmail.com

5 - Social Media: Check the "About the Author" section for social media details.

6 - Events: I love meeting the readers. Tell me about any literary events near you, maybe your book club. I might be able to attend—in person or virtually.

A Note From the Author

Writing Ava and Lev's story was an absolute joy. This novel actually began as a novella in Istanbul, but the story grew, taking me on a journey that expanded it into a full-length novel.

Life's twists and turns often shape our paths, and perhaps that's why I connect so deeply with these characters. They certainly had their share of unexpected turns along the way.

My journey has taken quite a few unexpected turns—from a career in healthcare and business, with degrees in statistics and an MBA, to discovering my true calling as a full-time novelist in my 50s. Looking back, I can see how everything led me here, even if it wasn't clear at the time. After years of living in London, I never imagined I'd one day call Hawai'i home. In my 40s, as a divorced woman, I certainly didn't expect to find love beyond my dreams. Yet, it found me.

Ava and Lev's story is about bold choices, taking chances, and the lengths parents will go to for their children. A central theme across all my novels is how life becomes richer and more exciting when love leads the way—whether through friendship, family, siblings, or romance—regardless of background, origins, education, gender, or even the narrow streets of Istanbul.

Jason, now my husband, was an American from the West Coast who was in London for a few months when we met and had our first date. It was lovely, but he later confessed that he could barely understand my accent—a blend of languages from growing up in one country and moving to another. It made for a fun start, with him nodding a lot.

Many moons later, after years of a long-distance relationship, we're married and have made several moves: Jason moved to London, then we relocated to Scottsdale, and then to Hawai'i. Our professional paths have also shifted along the way.

Now, with two authors under one roof, our household is constantly buzzing with activity—publishing dates, first or tenth drafts, editing, formatting, revising, and plotting fill our days. Beyond that, we share a love for travel, and writing has taken us to some incredible places; each book begins in one part of the world and is developed or finished in another.

Here's to the twists and turns—and to many more books to come!

Special Thanks

THANK YOU, Reader: Thank you for picking up my book and joining me on this journey!

I'm now a three-time author, with this novel joining my two earlier works. London, Hawai'i, and Istanbul—the settings of my three books—have all been homes to me at various points in my life, and some still are today.

I'm thankful for all the people who work with me and help me grow as a writer.

A special acknowledgment goes to Camille Pagán. Not only do I adore her books—she's an incredible author—but she has also been an invaluable coach. Attending her programs was one of the best decisions I've made. Her no-nonsense approach, always backed by data and research, has been a tremendous help. With her input, my book descriptions have become stellar.

I also want to thank my wonderful editors. Ema Barnes, played a crucial role in transforming this from a novella into a full-length novel. Rachel Small, my copy editor, this is the third book that we have worked on together, and I'm a fortunate author to benefit from your insights.

As always, my heartfelt thanks go to my family, near

and far, for their unwavering support—especially to my husband, Jason, my partner in adventure, my writing buddy, and always my first reader.

Thank you to my amazing friends who cheer me on, offer their support, and read my books.

A special shoutout to my dedicated early readers.

And to Asya Blue, my cover designer—thank you for your amazing creativity! I absolutely love the cover, and I'm so grateful you went beyond my specifications to bring it to life.

Thank you, everyone, for your continued support and inspiration!

And my eternal appreciation goes to **YOU**, the fabulous reader. Thank you!

About the Author

G.T. London is the Amazon chart #1 best-selling author for Eight Weeks Later, both in USA and Canada. She writes contemporary romance blended with mystery and suspense. Her novels are rich with secrets, unexpected twists, and family saga.

For most of her adult life, she lived in the bustling city of London, where she worked as a healthcare executive, as well as a business and leadership coach and trainer, in both the UK and Canada.

G.T. London holds an MBA from Warwick Business School in the UK and has served as a guest lecturer for MBA students. She mentors at business schools internationally and leads writing workshops.

Now a full-time novelist, she has published articles for Entrepreneur and Training magazines and currently lives in Hawai'i with her author husband, Jason.

She loves crafting life-affirming stories that sweep readers away to far-off lands, where dramas, twists, and unexpected turns unfold, just like life itself.

Currently, she is writing her next book while also outlining the one that follows and plotting the one after that.

facebook.com/gtlondon.author

instagram.com/gt.london.author

goodreads.com/gtlondon

amazon.com/author/gt.london

bookbub.com/authors/g-t-london

tiktok.com/@gt.london.author

Printed in Great Britain
by Amazon

53364211R00218